Even More Suspect Speaking

**Even more
of the frustrations
and blessings
of life with aphasia**

James Stephens

Published by DMS Publishing, 2024

Even More Suspect Speaking

This is a work of fiction.
Similarities to real people, places, or events are entirely coincidental.
Mostly.

First edition: June 2024
Copyright © 2024
James Stephens and DMS Publishing.

Epub ISBN: 978-0-473-71238-9
Kindle ISBN: 978-0-473-71239-6
Paperback ISBN: 978-0-473-71237-2
Draft2Digital Paperback ISBN: 979-8-224-09106-5

Written by James Stephens
email: james.stephens.dms@gmail.com
facebook: https://bit.ly/3bH6kZr

Even More Suspect Speaking

Aphasia is the loss of a previously held ability to speak or understand spoken or written language, due to disease or brain injury. *Even More Suspect Speaking* features stories and poems about people who have difficulty in verbal communication.

People with aphasia.

People with aphasia have individual communication difficulties:

- some can't read very well, or their attention span runs out;
- some have lost some of their vision so it makes it hard to read text;
- some can't find the sense in the syntax;
- some lack contextual understanding, or comprehension of ideas;
- some understand the words, but they can't pronounce them;
- some insert other words or phrases instead of the ones they actually mean.

The vocabulary of these stories is deliberately adult because aphasia doesn't diminish intellect.

These stories and poems give a taste of what aphasiacs go through.

More of the frustrations and blessings of life with aphasia.
Every day.
Every conversation.

The Suspect Speaker series (*The Suspect Speaker, More Suspect Speaking* and *Even More Suspect Speaking* and another, fourth book in the pipeline)* is aimed at four different groups:
- People with aphasia
- The carers, families and supporters of people with aphasia
- People who had no idea about aphasia but wanted to know more about the condition and, coincidentally…
- People whose main language was not English. The progressive versions are useful for English vocabulary.

Even More Suspect Speaking is a bit different from the previous two.

This book comprises:
- seven short stories (not **short** short, but short)
- poems (with particular styles) about aphasia and its consequences
- a set of five interrelated short stories called "The Kumanu Group".

Just like the two previous books, the seven short stories and the interrelated 'The Kumanu Group' have shorter and longer versions – but just two versions rather the three versions that first two books had.
The poems are, well, poems – and they are short, so no shorter versions are required.

Often people with aphasia have "stamina issues" when reading. It can be exhausting.

The stories are in short sections or "chapters" indicated by an interrupted line:

— — — —- ~~~ — — — —

These breaks in the stories could help to pace the tales, so it is not tiring for people with aphasia.

The "A" versions have a bigger font, shorter sentences with more gaps.

The "B" versions have more descriptive prose.
The "chapters" are still there for people with aphasia who can read well but, of course, people with**out** aphasia can pace themselves!

Enjoy.

James Stephens

Acknowledgements

AphasiaNZ (http://www.aphasia.org.nz/) and their amazing CAA's (especially Kate, Crista and Jenny)

Wellington, Hutt and Kāpiti Aphasia Community

Naomi Bondi: *Speech Language Therapist and an amazing rock climber*

Cecilia McNeil: *editor*

And my whānau:
- my wife, a saint in every way
- my children (six of them) who were magnificently supportive
- and grandchildren (now SEVEN of them!) who kept me grounded – sometimes literally.

Common conventions and terms used in the book:

Talking: 'single quotes'.
References or titles: "double quotes"
Thinking: *italics*.
Emphasis: **bold**
Ellipsis: eg … Usually I use it as an indication that time has passed between one word or phrase and another. Sometimes, a **long** time [aphasia!].

Things to know about Aotearoa New Zealand

Aotearoa New Zealand has three official languages:
- **English** (British) – so conventions are British: eg. 'colour' rather than 'color'.
- **Te reo Māori** – the language of the people in Aotearoa before colonisation by Britain in the 1800s
- New Zealand Sign Language

The first two are used extensively in the stories.
[The latter is not appropriate for books!]

Te reo Māori can have a macron over certain vowels eg: the letter 'ā' in Māori. It signifies a long vowel sound.

I have defined some 'local' or uncommon terms as footnotes in the stories.

Aotearoa New Zealand = New Zealand = NZ.
"Aotearoa" is the Māori name for New Zealand. New Zealand the colonial name for this country.
I used **Aotearoa New Zealand** for our country, acknowledging the different strands of our cultural heritage. Often the colonial terms are lacklustre, especially the main islands of

the country: the **South Island**, and the **North Island**. The Māori names are, respectively, **Te Waipounamu** (jade, greenstone), and **Te Ika-a-Māui** ("The fish of Māui", a well known legend.) Much better!

Kiwis = people from Aotearoa New Zealand [as opposed to 'kiwi', a native, nocturnal, flightless bird.] By the way, the fruit called 'kiwi' is a major export crop from Aotearoa New Zealand and it references the brown feathers of the kiwi bird.

whānau = Māori term for 'family', mostly 'extended' family rather than 'nuclear' family.

kia ora = a Māori greeting common in Aotearoa New Zealand. Literally it means "have life" or "be healthy".

taonga = a treasured possession in Māori culture, especially items of historical cultural significance.

pounamu is a hard, highly valued jade. It is also called greenstone. Māori regard pounamu as a taonga (treasure) by Māori, as do most Kiwis, many of whom have a strong spiritual connection to the stone.

whare = house (Māori).

marae = meeting place (Māori), usually including the wharenui (big house) and the area and buildings around it.

taniwha = in Māori mythology, they are large supernatural beings that live in deep pools in rivers, lakes, dark caves, or in the sea.

Aotearoa New Zealand native birds often referenced in my books include:
kiwi, tūī (parson bird), pīwakawaka (fantail), kererū (wood pigeon), kōtare (kingfisher), korimako (bellbird), ruru (morepork owl), pukeko (swamp hen) and the extinct huia, and moa.

Even More Suspect Speaking

==================================

Poems

==================================

The Kumanu Group

==================================

1A: Yeti

It wasn't fair.

In Alex's mind there were a lot more expletives.

Alex was an 'outdoor bloke'. His physical aptitude was exemplary.
Hunting, fishing, tramping, running, swimming, skiing…
He was physically apt.

Alex was lean but muscled in the right places.
He was good looking in an outdoorsy-way.
Confident but studiously casual, he had a ready grin for any occasion.

That was before the accident.

He was competing in an Ironman Triathlon in Taupō[1]: swim, bike riding and running.
He never made it to the run.

---

[1] Taupō is a town and a lake in the centre of Te-Ika-a-Māui (the North Island) of Aotearoa New Zealand. It is famed for trout fishing, geothermal pools, mountain biking, rock climbing, and nearby skiing on Mount Ruapehu.

He was hurtling down the road when a panicked tabby cat raced across the road in front of him.
He avoided the cat, but not the Rottweiler dog that was chasing the cat.
He collided with the dog, tearing off his helmet and smashing into a concrete wall.

He was immediately whisked to the hospital.
Apart from bruises, scrapes and grazes, he got off lightly.

His head – not so much.
TBI. Traumatic Brain Injury.
And the complications that go with this.

He had no family close to him.
His father departed when he was four years old.
His mother left him when he turned twenty-one, saying: 'You're an adult now. Deal with it!'

So, he dealt with it. After a fashion.

Over six months he rehabilitated. His intelligence, his body's movements were fine.
But his speaking?
The words were almost there, on the tip of his tongue, but they refused to emerge.

He stuttered, and when he got the words out, they were often mispronounced, mistaken or misordered.

He had aphasia.

— — — — —. ~~~ — — — — —

Before the accident he was a salesman at Urban Bro Hunting Emporium in New Plymouth: an outdoor activities supermarket.
But after…

'I like you Alex. You were the best!' his manager reasoned, 'but I can't have a salesman that can't sell. But you can be in the stockroom. Okay?'

It was not okay. The job was boring, boring, boring.
His 'colleagues' – his supposed 'mates' – were unsupportive. They had no experience with a person that could not communicate. After a fortnight they ignored Alex completely.

When a new member of the sales team said to one of Alex's 'mates': 'Who's the retard?'

That got Alex's goat[1].

He leapt up and decked him, out cold.

Then he went to the managers office, flung his keys down and stated: 'Done! Done! Done!'

His actual mates, his friends, were the same: ignored him, spoke over him, got on with their lives without him.

Purposeless, inconsequential, futile, Alex thought morosely. *I am a BBQ without a gas bottle, a boat without a bung, a burst balloon. I am irrelevant.*

Apparently he was irrelevant to his girlfriend of five years. She announced, bluntly, that she was going to university in Auckland, and: 'a long-distance relationship never works, so we should break up now.'

With aphasia he couldn't voice his opinion clearly anyway.

It wasn't fair. He felt useless. Diminished. With a lot more expletives involved.

So he moved to Queenstown[2], the adventure capital of Aotearoa New Zealand.

— — — —-- ~~~ — — — —

---

[1] 'get someone's goat' = 'To make someone annoyed or angry'

[2] Queenstown is in the south central end of Te Waipounamu (South Island) and famed for its outdoor adventure activities.

Queenstown!

Bungee jumping, mountain biking, rock climbing, tramping, jet boating – and in the winter: skiing and snowboarding.

And it was winter.

Alex knew someone in Queenstown.

Jiāo Wen was the owner and manager of SkiRescue: a rental shop in the village.

Jiāo was a great customer of Urban Bro Hunting Emporium. And he knew Alex.

Alex went to see his potential boss.

The interview went like this:

Alex: 'Kia aura…aum…member…re-mont-mem-ber me…. um… Alex.'

Jiāo: 'Sure! Sure! Alex – from Urban Bros. Not seen a'lot from awhile. How y'boss?'

Alex: 'Um, sure, sure…um…still that….'

Jiāo: 'Wha' yo' want? In Queens-Town? Hol'day? Escape?'

Alex: 'Nah…nah… Um…um…Job? Anything for a … job?'

Jiāo: 'Ah…ah…wot can y'do? Sales man? I need a new one. But why yo' talk funny?'

Alex: 'Um…brain…um…brain 'jury…words…um… stuff…stud…stuck…'

Jiāo: 'Ah…no'good, no'good. Sales man shoul'be good with words. But jiùjiu[1] … Yes, my jiùjiu, my uncle. He has a ski school down th'mountain. Yo' fit? Ski?'
Alex: 'Sure, sure…ski is good…yes…yes…can told…tell him?'

Painful. But, that is the nature of aphasia. It is like a new language that you can barely understand – for the speaker **and** the listener.

Alex went up the mountain to the Ski School. The uncle was also named Jiāo – a little confusing.

SkiRescue Jiāo was short and stout with black hair. Jiùjiu Jiāo was tall and lean and has a bald head.

Alex strutted his skiing and snowboarding expertise and ten minutes later he was hired.

Jiùjiu Jiāo was not fussed about Alex's lack of words.
'You – demonstrator,' he said 'She – instructor,' as he pointed across the room.

The 'she' in question was a slim woman, conventionally good-looking with an assured,

---

[1] jiùjiu = Mandarin (informal) for his mother's brother = uncle.

haughty, demeanour. Her name tag proclaimed her 'Lucy'.

Lucy assembled the students and told them what they had to do.
Alex's role was to demonstrate, and correct, their efforts to ski well.

The "team" worked well – for the customers.
Personally, Alex was lonely. Lucy was not a 'colleague' as such.
Jiùjiu Jiāo was absent most of the time.

The "students" were aged six to eighteen. Because of his aphasia he barely spoke to them, so their descriptions of Alex ranged from "pretty-aggro" to "abominable snowman" to "drongo-rongo".

Alex went to the pubs, sometimes picked up girls for a one-night-stand, but they were not interested in a relationship. They were seeking "a winter holiday good time!".

— — — —- ~~~ — — — —

About five weeks after his move to Queenstown, he was on the slopes.

He had finished 'school' for the day so he went up the mountain to the more difficult runs.
It was about four o'clock in the afternoon and most of the tourists had descended so he was basically alone.

The chilly air revitalised him.
He had his orange puffer jacket, olive green over-trousers and black and green fleece-lined gloves.
His face was protected with a red-coloured balaclava and snow-goggles.
On his head he had a lime-green beanie with a whimsical pink pom-pom.
He placed his goggles up on his forehead and looked out to the magnificent vista before him.
This is the best view in the world, he thought. *Perfection.*

Suddenly, he saw a woman down the slope before him.
Her posture told Alex she was not a skilled skier – an aura of anxiety clouded her body.
Alex was alarmed because he knew there was a forty-metre cliff about four metres on.
I have to warm her...

He started down the slope hollering 'Stop! Stop!'
The woman took no notice.
Typical! Alex assumed.
Likely she is wearing ear-pods! She doesn't know...

He closed on her, all the while shouting 'Stop! Cliff! Stop!!'
But the woman didn't turn around or halt.
'Stop! Stop!' yelled Alex and he grabbed her shoulders and hauled her away from the cliff edge.

Somehow, it didn't go the way Alex expected.

The woman jumped and was panicked.
She pushed him back forcefully and frantically signalled at him.
She wanted to scrabble away, but Alex caught her firmly.
He pulled her close. 'Stop! Stop!' he shouted forcefully. 'Cliff! Cliff!'

Eventually the woman lost her terrified look.
She visibly relaxed in Alex's arms.
He said, much more gently, 'Cliff. Cliff.'
He wanted to make it clear to her what danger she was in.
'Here...there...cliff...' he began.

He indicated a horizontal plane with his hand, level with his eyebrow.
Then he dropped it down to his navel.
He did it again, and again, annotating the process.
'Live' at the upper point, and 'Not live' for the lower.

She eventually comprehended his live meme.

She looked at Alex closely and waved with her hands and arms. Alex was completely puzzled.
Alex interrupted her. 'Why not halt!' he said exasperatedly.
'Not stop! Danez…danber…um… dan-ger. Much. Why no listen-ing?'

She looked him in his eye and shrilly announced: 'Dead! Dead!'
She nodded and said again: 'Dead! Dead!'
Oh no! Alex thought with alarm. *She wants to end her own life by jumping over the cliff!*

He instantly replaced his hand on her shoulder and again moved her away.
Well, that was the intention.
His ski and the ski poles tangled up with hers and they overbalanced.
He found himself on the icy ground and the woman embracing him in a compromising position.

Well – "embracing" could be a moot point.
And certainly the "compromising position" was not romantic.

In fact, the woman was extremely annoyed.
She glared at him.
Again, she gestured at him and she shouted, 'Deaf! Deaf! Deaf! Deeaaffffffff!.'
With the last word, she drummed her fists on his chest.
Surprised, he released her.

She sat down beside him on the ground.
Alex sat himself up beside her.
'Sori! Sori!' he apologised. 'Did-n't un-der-stood… um…un-der-stand.'
The woman looked at him intently, focusing on his lips.
Oh! She is lip reading. Oh dear!
My speech is – suspect.

Alex spoke, relatively, clearly.
'I had…have from Apha-ziah. Brain inju-rent -ce. I have….um… Sori…sori!'

She was suspiciously puzzled. She wondering if his apology was sincere.
After a moment she gave him the benefit of the doubt.

She mimed a cup of tea or coffee.
Alex was keen to make sure he understood. 'Coff-fee? Yo want…?'

— — — —- ~~~ — — — —

Alex rose and helped her get herself up.
The two of them went to the chairlift.
They took it down to the village and walked to the café.

With a notepad and pen, and a mixture of stuttered words they communicated.
Her name was Maren.
She had been deaf her whole life.
She was proficient in New Zealand Sign Language.
She knew about aphasia and understood that Alex's intelligence was not affected.

Maren thought: *Alex is a good person: kind, considerate, brave.*
She offered to teach him sign language.
Alex accepted graciously.
Actually, his thoughts were: *Maren. She hot. Learning sign language would be a good ice-breaker and a chance to…?*

That's it. The story of how they met.

Alex was a quick learner.
By the time their winter jobs were over he said to her
– in sign language – 'Can you be my partner?'
Maren's answer – not in sign language – was a
passionate compromising embrace.
Intended this time.

Alex was fond of saying: 'Make do hea-ven.'
He means: 'I can't talk properly. Maren can't hear
properly. But we make it work. Together.'

For Alex, one question remained.
In a mixture of faultless sign language, notepad and
iPad writing and drawings, Alex "said":
'What did you say when I first met you?
You were in a panic. What did you sign?'

Maren grinned and replied with a pen on paper –
one word and a shaggy drawing:

Yeti!

1B: Yeti

It wasn't fair.

This is the assessment from many impartial observers about Alex's situation. In Alex's mind there were a lot more expletives involved in this description. But, still, it wasn't fair.

Alex was an 'outdoor bloke'. His academic record was only average, but his physical aptitude was exemplary. Hunting, fishing, tramping, running, swimming, surfing, windsurfing, mountain-bike riding, skiing, snowboarding, rock climbing, caving… Briefly put, he was physically apt.
Alex was just under two metres tall, lean but muscled in the right places. At twenty-four years he was good looking in an outdoorsy-way with loose ink-black hair, intense green eyes, a patrician nose and generous lips. Confident but studiously casual, he had a ready grin for any occasion.

That was before the accident.

He was competing in an Ironman Triathlon in Taupō[1]: 1.9km swim in the clear, fresh waters of Lake Taupō, 90km return bike course heading into the undulating farmland surrounding the town and a three-lap run on a course which followed the shores of the lake.
He never made it to the run.

---

[1] Taupō is a town and a lake in the centre of Te-Ika-a-Māui (the North Island) of Aotearoa New Zealand. It is famed for trout fishing, geothermal pools, mountain biking, rock climbing, and nearby skiing on Mount Ruapehu.

On the return bike leg, he was hurtling down the road passing hapless and helpless competitors when a panicked tabby cat raced across the road in front of him. He avoided the cat, but not the Rottweiler dog that was chasing the cat. He collided with the animal, careering over the road, tearing off his helmet and smashing into a concrete wall – a crumpled ball of twisted metal and body.

The officials and the first aid responders were quickly on to the mess and he was immediately whisked to the hospital. Apart from bruises, scrapes and grazes on his body from the impact of the road, he got off lightly. His head – not so much. A rebar, a reinforcing steel bar in the concrete, penetrated his skull. Only slightly. Not 'life-threatening'. But that was enough.
TBI. Traumatic Brain Injury. And the complications that go with this.

He had no family close to him. No siblings. His father departed, incommunicado, when he was four years old. He was somewhere on the globe. His mother left him when he turned twenty-one, saying: 'You're an adult now. Deal with it!' She was somewhere in Australia. She phoned him twice after the accident – once to see if he was dead, and the other to say: 'I can't afford to come back. You're okay now. Deal with it.'

So, he dealt with it. After a fashion.

Over six months he rehabilitated with physio-, cardio-, osteo-, chiro-, occupational and speech therapists. His intelligence, his body's responsiveness and movements were fine. His comprehension – was okay. Well, not worse than before. But his speaking? The words were almost there, on the tip of his tongue, but they refused to emerge. He stuttered, and when he got the words out, they were often mispronounced, mistaken or misordered – his syntax was all over the place.

He had aphasia.

————-- ~~~ ————

When the ACC[1] ran out after six months, he returned to work and his life. The worst month he had ever experienced!

Before the accident he was a salesman at Urban Bro Hunting Emporium in New Plymouth: a hunting, fishing, tramping, hiking, camping, rock climbing, mountain biking supermarket.
But after…

'I like you Alex. You were the best!' his manager reasoned, 'but I can't have a salesman that can't sell. You can't talk the customers around. I got a place for you though. You can be in the stockroom. Sorting it out. Okay?'

It was not okay. With no commissions his pay plummeted. And the job was boring, boring, boring. His 'colleagues' – his supposed 'mates' – were unsupportive. Admittedly they were raw teenagers and twenty-somethings who had no experience with a person that could not communicate, who stuttered or answered incoherently with every question. After a fortnight, when they were talking in the lunchroom, they ignored Alex completely. Or talked over him as if he were not there. But when a new member of the sales team was introduced, and he said to one of Alex's 'mates': 'Who's the

---

[1] ACC = Accident Compensation Corporation. Everyone in Aotearoa New Zealand is covered by ACC's no-fault scheme if they're injured in an accident.

retard?' That got Alex's goat[1]. He leapt up and decked him, out cold. Then he went to the managers office, flung his keys down on the desk and stated, succinctly and unequivocally: 'Done! Done! Done!'

His actual mates, his friends, were marginally supportive, but gradually they went the same way as his work colleagues: ignored him, spoke over him, got on with their lives without him. *Purposeless, inconsequential, futile,* Alex thought morosely. *I am a BBQ without a gas bottle, a boat without a bung, a burst balloon. I am irrelevant.*

Apparently he was irrelevant to his girlfriend of five years. She had stood by him over the six months of his rehabilitation, but she announced, bluntly, that she was going to university in Auckland, and: 'a long-distance relationship never works, so we should break up now.' Shocked, he didn't say anything about the conversation. With aphasia he couldn't voice his opinion clearly anyway, so actually it was a soliloquy.

So – it wasn't fair. He felt useless. Diminished. With a lot more expletives involved, in Alex's mind.

Nothing and nobody meant anything to him in New Plymouth, so he moved to Queenstown[2], the adventure capital of Aotearoa New Zealand.

— — — —· ~~~ — — — —

---

[1] 'get someone's goat' = 'To make someone annoyed or angry'

[2] New Plymouth is on the central west coast of Te Ika-a-Māui (North Island). Queenstown is in the south central end of Te Waipounamu (South Island) and famed for its outdoor adventure activities.

Queenstown! Bungee jumping, helicopter rides, parasailing, mountain biking, rock climbing, tramping, jet boating, kayaking – and in the winter: skiing and snowboarding.

And it was winter. Alex knew someone in Queenstown.

Sort of.

Jiāo Wen was the owner and manager of SkiRescue: a ski, snowboard and tramping rental shop in the village. Jiāo was a great customer of Urban Bro Hunting Emporium.

And he knew Alex.

Maybe he can get me a job? Alex optimistically thought. So, he went to see his potential boss.

The interview went like this:

Alex: 'Kia aura…aum…member…re-mont-mem-ber me…. um… Alex.'

Jiāo: 'Sure! Sure! Alex – from Urban Bros. Not seen a'lot from awhile. How y'boss? Still drivin' th'Ford ute?'

Alex: 'Um, sure, sure…um…still that….'

Jiāo: 'Wha' yo' want? In Queens-Town? Hol'day? Escape? Yo' got that girl preg'nt?'

Alex: 'Nah…nah…not like it. Um…um…Job? Anything for a …job?'

Jiāo: 'Ah…ah…wot can y'do? Sales man? I need a new one. The other guy … Use. Less. But why yo' talk funny?'

Alex: 'Um…brain…um…brain 'jury…words…um…stuff… stud…stuck…'

Jiāo: 'Ah…no'good, no'good. Sales man shoul'be good with words. Hav't'be. Um … nah, nah…um…

But jiùjiu[1] … Yes, my jiùjiu, my uncle. He has a ski school down th'mountain. He need a new one. Instructor. Yo' fit? Ski?'

Alex: 'Sure, sure…ski is good…yes…yes…can told…tell him?'

---

[1] jiùjiu = Mandarin (informal) for his mother's brother = uncle.

Painful. But, that is the nature of aphasia. It is like a new language that you can barely understand or comprehend. For the speaker **and** the listener.

So, Jiāo rang his jiùjiu, and Alex went up the mountain to the Ski School. The uncle was also named Jiāo – a little confusing but you would not confuse the two if you met them. SkiRescue Jiāo was short and stout with a black thatch of hair. Jiùjiu Jiāo was tall and lean and his bald head shone in the pallid winter sun.
The 'interview' was on the slopes. Alex strutted his skiing and snowboarding expertise and ten minutes later he was hired. Jiùjiu Jiāo was not fussed about Alex's lack of words. 'You – demonstrator,' he said, leading Alex into the Ski School building. 'She – instructor,' as he pointed across the room.

The 'she' in question was a slim woman, about 160 cm tall, conventionally good-looking with red hair and an assured, haughty, demeanour. Her name tag proclaimed her 'Lucy'.

Lucy assembled the students and told them what they had to do. Alex's role was to demonstrate, and correct, their efforts to ski well: basics like pizza slicing or snowplough[1]; avoiding face-plants[2]; french fries[3]; negotiating the camber;

---

[1] Officially called snowplough, a technique used when first learning to ski where your skis tilt together in the shape of a pizza slice. A way of controlling speed before learning to turn

[2] Falling straight onto your face - self-explanatory really

[3] Largely used when first learning to ski parallel. Basically having your skis next to (parallel) to each other like French fries lined up

carving; avoiding catching an edge[1]; jump turn; on-piste and off-piste issues; negotiating the moguls[2].

The "team" worked well – for the customers. Personally, Alex was lonely. Lucy was not a 'colleague' as such. She used him as a tool, an automaton that she could programme to do her will, despite the fact that **she** could not do any of the things she was talking about. Jiùjiu Jiāo was absent most of the time, and when he was present, he was **not** present.

The "students" were aged six to eighteen. The older ones were narcissistic and the younger ones, oblivious about social niceties. Because of his aphasia he barely spoke to them, so their descriptions of Alex ranged from "pretty-aggro" to "scowly-monster" to "abominable snowman" to "drongo-rongo".

Alex sort of "socialised". He went to the pubs, sometimes picked up girls for a one-night-stand, but they were not interested in a relationship, especially when they discovered his communicative disability. They were seeking "a winter holiday good time!" – not a therapy session.

— — — — —· ~~~ — — — —

About five weeks after his move to Queenstown, he was on the slopes. He had finished his 'demonstration stint' for the day so he went up the mountain to the more difficult runs. It was about four o'clock in the afternoon and most of the tourists had descended the ski-runs and made it back to

---

[1] On a snowboard, when the edge of your board accidentally catches on the snow, it tends to pull you abruptly towards that edge and, in general, has you falling flat on the ground.

[2] Bumps that are either carved or naturally formed by skiers and boarders turning around them. Often occur towards the end of the ski day

their utes and four-wheel off-road trucks, driven to their hotels, pubs or hot pools, so he was basically alone. The chilly air revitalised him. He had his fluorescent orange puffer jacket and olive green over-trousers with the extra insulation and black and green fleece-lined gloves. His face was protected with a red-coloured balaclava and snow-goggles, topped with a lime-green beanie with a whimsical pink pom-pom, a favourite with the kids in his class.

He placed his goggles up on his forehead and looked out to the magnificent vista before him: the snow covered peaks and the valleys, rocks peeking out like frozen taniwha[1], the azure blue sky above and the deep royal blue of the lake below. *This is the best view in the world,* he thought. *Perfection.*

Suddenly, he saw a woman down the slope before him. Her posture told Alex she was not a skilled skier – her back was hunched over, her legs and skis were pigeon-toed, and an aura of anxiety clouded her body. She shuffled a metre or two to the right. Alex was alarmed that the woman didn't know where she was going.
He knew there was a forty-metre cliff about four metres on.
I have to warm her…

He started down the slope, his skis biting the fresh snow, hollering 'Stop! Stop!' The woman took no notice. *Typical!* Alex assumed. *Likely she is wearing ear-pods, listening to some rap-crap! She doesn't know…*

He closed on her – forty metres, thirty metres, twenty metres – all the while shouting 'Stop! Cliff! Stop!!' but the woman

---

[1] taniwha = in Māori mythology, they are large supernatural beings that live in deep pools in rivers, lakes, dark caves, or in the sea.

didn't turn around or halt. Instead she was approaching the lip of the cliff oblivious to the danger she was in. 'Stop! Stop!' yelled Alex and he angled his skis sideways, grabbed her shoulders, and hauled her away from the cliff edge.

Somehow, it didn't go the way Alex expected.
His heroism fell flat.

The woman jumped and was clearly shocked and panicked. Her face was a parody of Edvard Munch's *The Scream*: her eyes were opened wide, her mouth was a rictus of dismay, her legs were collapsing. She pushed him back forcefully and frantically signalled at him – certain vigorous terrified gestures with her whole shoulders, arms and hands. She wanted to scrabble away, but Alex caught her firmly, pulling her close and shuffling them away from the cliff face. 'Stop! Stop!' he shouted forcefully. 'Cliff! Cliff!'

Eventually the adrenaline dissipated and the woman relinquished her terrified wide-eyed look. She visibly relaxed in Alex's arms. He said, much more gently, 'Cliff. Cliff.'
He released his hold on her left shoulder and indicated the cliff face. He wanted to make it clear to her what danger she was in.
A newbie, thought Alex. *I guess she didn't know about the cliff and it's hard to see the contours on the snow with so much glistening and reflective ice among the rocks.*

'Here…there…cliff…' he began. He indicated a horizontal plane with his hand, level with his eyebrow. Then he dropped it down to his navel. He did it again, and again, annotating the process with a spoken 'Live' at the upper point, and 'Not live' for the lower. She eventually comprehended his live meme and looked around at the threatening landscape.

Alex led her over to the edge of the cliff and she cautiously looked down on the tumbling rocks and boulders below.

She looked at Alex closely and waved with her hands and arms in a specific way: waving, shaking, finger spread out or closed. Alex was completely puzzled. She did it again, a repetition – the same gestures as before, but Alex interrupted her. 'Why not halt!' he said exasperatedly. 'Not stop! Danez…danber…um… dan-ger. Much. Me…shout-tink. Why no listen-ing?'

She looked him in his eye and shrilly announced: 'Dead! Dead!' She nodded, encouraging Alex to understand and said again: 'Dead! Dead!'
Oh no! Alex thought with alarm and trepidation. *She wants to end her own life by jumping over the cliff!*

He instantly replaced his hand on her shoulder and again moved her away from the cliff edge. Well, that was the intention. Unfortunately his ski and the ski poles tangled up with hers and they overbalanced, crashing down on the packed snow. Poles, gloves, hats, backpacks went every which way. Alex made sure that they were away from the drop by rolling but that made the tangled mess messier. In the aftermath of their collision, he found himself on the icy ground and the woman was above him, embracing him in a compromising position.

Well – "embracing" could be a moot point. And certainly the "compromising position" was not romantic. Not sexy. At all.

In fact, the woman was extremely annoyed, extremely aggravated, and extremely bruised. She glared at him. Again, she gestured at him but this time focusing on her head and ears. At last he was provided a soundtrack that made sense

to him as she shouted, 'Deaf! Deaf! Deaf! Deeaaffffff!.' With
the last word, she drummed her fists on his chest. Surprised,
he released her. She sat down beside him on the ground and
grimaced as she rubbed her shins and knees. She
unshackled her boots from the skis and cast around for her
gloves. His gloves were closer and she appropriated them to
warm her freezing hands.

Alex sat himself up beside her. He unshackled his boots from
the skis and buried them upright in the snow. He did the
same with hers, so they would not run over the cliff. 'Sori!
Sori!' he apologised. 'Did-n't un-der-stood...um...un-der-
stand.'
The woman looked at him intently, focusing on his lips.
Oh! She is lip reading. Oh dear! My speech is – suspect.
Alex concentrated and spoke clearly.
Well, as much as he could.
'I had...have from Apha-ziah. Brain inju-rent -ce. I
have....um... Sori...sori!'

Her eyes squinted. She was suspiciously puzzled and clearly
was wondering if his apology was sincere. After a moment
she gave him the benefit of the doubt. Her eyes gentled and
her mouth was not so fierce. She rubbed her gloved hands
then, with her right wrist and hand, she mimed a cup of tea
or coffee. The clear charade was invitation enough but, given
the past few minutes, Alex was keen to make sure he
understood. 'Coff-fee? Yo want...?'

— — — —- ~~~ — — — —

A blissful smile was confirmation. Alex rose and helped her
get herself up, sorted out the skis, poles, hats, gloves and
backpacks and the two of them went to the chairlift. They
took it down to the village and walked to the café across the

carpark. They were lucky enough to find an isolated booth so their disjointed conversation would not be noticed or interrupted by other patrons.

With a notepad and pen, and a mixture of stuttered words and silences they established a friendly rapport. Alex learnt that her name was Maren and she was a maid at the big hotel in the village. She had been deaf her whole life because she had cCMV – Congenital cytomegalovirus. She had overcome every obstacle and she was proficient in New Zealand Sign Language. She knew about aphasia and understood that Alex was 'conversationally impaired' but his intelligence was not affected.

Maren thought: *Alex is a good person: kind, considerate, brave, thoughtful and with a good sense of humour.*
She offered to teach him sign language.
Alex accepted graciously.
Actually, his thoughts were more like: *Maren. She hot. And cool. Huh – oxymoron. Maybe I could have a chance with her. Learning sign language would be a good ice-breaker and a chance to…?*

That's it. The story of how they met.

Alex and Maren spent every non-working moment together over that winter season. Alex was a quick learner. By the time their winter jobs were over he said to her – in sign language – 'Can you be my partner?'
Maren's answer – not in sign language – was a passionate compromising embrace. Intended this time.

They moved to Wellington. Maren was a sign language teacher in the Deaf Studies Department at the university and Alex was a disability consultant for the Ministry of Work and

Income. Alex was fond of saying: 'Make do hea-ven', by which he means: 'I can't talk properly. Maren can't hear properly. But we make it work. Together.'

For Alex, one question remained.
In a mixture of faultless sign language, notepad and iPad writing and drawings, and the unspoken telepathic relationship-language connecting them as a couple, Alex "said": 'What did you say when I first met you? When I tackled you before the cliff. You were in a panic and you signed at me. What did you sign?'

Maren grinned and replied with a pen on paper – one word and a shaggy drawing:

Yeti!

2A: Unwelt[1]
and a personal communication issue

I went to the Govett-Brewster Museum in New Plymouth to see works from Len Lye[2].
He is, arguably, the most gifted creative artist that this country has known.

Len Lye grew up in Aotearoa New Zealand, moving to London in 1926.
In 1944 he moved to New York and lived for the rest of his life in its art world.

Len was a kinetic artist, direct film maker, painter, writer, theorist, philosopher, lecturer, and poet.
He was something of an "artist's artist", and his innovations have had an international influence.

Len was also an important kinetic sculptor – what he referred to as "Tangibles".
He said: "All of a sudden it hit me - if there was such a thing as composing music, there could be such a thing as composing motion."

---

[1] Umwelt - the specific way each particular organism experiences the world.

[2] Many references for Len Lye are on the internet, including videos (YouTube) of his kinetic sculptures. The Len Lye Foundation has much more information and videos of his works: https://www.lenlyefoundation.com/

His kinetic sculptural designs were often not possible in his day because the technology and the material were not invented yet.

Versions of them have been included on the New Plymouth walkway (Wind Wand) and the Wellington Harbour (Water Whirler) and in the Govett-Brewster Museum in New Plymouth.

So, I went to the Govett-Brewster Museum, principally to see his kinetic sculptures.
His "Tangibles".

— — — —· ~~~ — — — —

Snakes:
From the foyer, a well lit hallway led to a darkened room.There are spotlights above, affixed to the ceiling.
Then I see them – seven slender steel chains, ten metres long.
Each has a steel ball affixed at the lower end.
The steel ball was almost immobile and the chains moved and circled around.

If you jerk a rope up and down, the rope replicates the pattern of a wave.

It was like this.
The 'jerking' was caused by a mechanism in the roof.

The installation was named 'Snakes', but it was an inadequate description.
It was more industrial – alien almost.
But I guess "Snakes" is barely passable as a description. Certainly they were sinuous, fluid.

The seven "snakes" were not at the same part in their 'programme'.
No 'synchronised swimming' here!
It seemed to be random, but I suspect not.

I looked at the floor. The shadow from the spotlights made a two-dimensional shadow play on the floor.
It was like a monotone moving mandala. Fascinating.

— — — —- ~~~ — — — —

Fire Bush:
The bunch of noodles, in a pot of boiling water – they fan out.
Both the Fire Bush and the Fountains have the same idea.
A bunch of steel wires, gathered together, fan out in hyperbolic curves.

.

The Fire Bush has a thinner gauge wire.
Its mechanical motive mechanism was more vigorous.
The spotlight above them was ruby red.
It turned the wires luminescent red, yellow, orange, gold.
A wayward strand was escaping the frenzy.
Out on is own, shining meteorically, a random spark.

Eventually, the motion slowed down, exhausted.
In the hiatus I glimpsed something there.
A phantom phoenix, wings gathered, ready to launch in the air.
Then it disappeared as the Fire Bush revved up its furious, frenetic dance once more.

Fountain (two of them):
Unlike the Fire Bush, the mechanism of the motive force for the Fountains was even, steady.
Each move was seamless. Choreographed.
The two Fountains had a larger gauge wire, so their motion was more graceful.
Shimmering, fluid, slow-motion geysers.

The spot-lights above were unfiltered so a silvery, liquid quality was projected.
It seemed that the metal was transmuted into water.
But this is an illusion.
The water moves. The metal doesn't.

That was the illusion.
A "moving" fountain but frozen at the same time.
Paradoxical.

Grass:
This 'tangible' is so, so simple but so elegant.
Unassuming but ingenuous.
Unpretentious but charming.

A wooden board has about forty steel wires poking up.
Like an elongated and spaced-out toothbrush.
The board has no adornment.
The board is mounted on a black plinth.
The motor tilts the board this way and that.
The rocking motion inspired the wires to move to and fro.
Like a zephyr moving reeds of grass in a pasture.

The wires were individual so their movement is haphazard.
But not random. Not chaotic.
It is like life.
Human activities, human development, human relationships.
Consequence. Not random. Not chaotic.
Maybe destined. Mesmerising.

— — — —- ~~~ — — — —

Universe:

The other exhibits have certain sounds.
The muted argument of wires clashing together in the Fountain and Grass.
The more vigorous confrontation in the Fire Bush.
But this was different.
It was a definite 'dong'.

I turned into the room.
A curved loop of steel is fixed on a wooden bench.
Above there was a small ball suspended from the ceiling.
The steel loop flexed, changing its shape to all sorts of elliptical orbits.
Sometimes the steel hits a ball and the rude bell sounds: "dong".
Sometimes it is "Dong".
Sometimes it's "DONG".
Sometimes it misses the ball completely.
Mysterious, and unearthly.

Other people were coming in from the other room.
The audience waits in anticipation.
When will it strikes the ball? This time? Next time?
How hard will it strike it – dong, Dong or DONG?

I wonder about his names though.

The only one that is creatively named is "Universe" .
Apparently, that was a name that was chosen for him.
Lye renamed it Universe after a young boy said the
sound it made reminded him of "the universe".

Maybe that boy could name the rest of them too!
Fire Bush, Fountain, Grass are basically descriptive
enough but not very creative.

And, as I said, Snakes is a very inadequate name for
that installation.

Maybe Ahi[1], Mexican Wave, Zephyr, and Boa
Constrictor would be more creative?
So, why the mundane names?
But, maybe, Len Lye wants the tangibles to speak for
themselves, rather than be fancifully labelled.

— — — —- ~~~ — — — —

These are my thoughts about Len Lye's work, in
particular his kinetic sculptures.
These are my thoughts.

Speech? I can't make a speech about this subject.
I can't make a speech at all.
I have global aphasia.

---

[1] Ahi = the Māori for 'fire' in a sacred sense.

The words are still there, but I am stuck, choked.
I can't pronounce them.
Or mispronounced. Or mistaken.

Writing?
I tire easily and the words mix up in my brain.
I can't read or write coherently.[1]
So, I can't write about it.

Drawing?
I could attempt to draw it.
My artistic skill is at the level of a four year old.

Sign language?
I can't convey the subtlety, the depth of my thoughts.
No-one can understand the profound effect of Lye's
work in my soul.

I need someone to telepathically translate my
thoughts into writing or speech or …
Huh! That's sci-fi!
Speech, writing, drawing, sign language…
Basically I can't communicate.

---

[1] Please "suspend your disbelief!" The author is pleading to encourage the reader's willingness to suspend doubt and believe what is patently impossible, for the sake of enlightenment. Despite that you have **read** this account, the author is seeking to understand that these are actually his thoughts, not his prose.

I went to visit the Govett-Brewster Gallery and these are my thoughts.

So?

So what?

What sort of use are my thoughts if I can't share them with anyone?

Isolating. Disconnecting. Alienating.

It is frustrating. In the extreme.

That's my aphasia.

2B: Unwelt[1]
and a personal communication issue

I went to the Govett-Brewster Museum in New Plymouth to see works from Len Lye[2] arguably the most gifted creative artist that this country has known.

Len Lye was one of the most colourful and important artists to have emerged from Aotearoa New Zealand. He was born in 1901 in Christchurch but his father died when Len was only two. His most vivid childhood memories came from the time he lived in the lighthouse at Cape Campbell at the top of the South Island. This gave him a lifetime interest in the patterns of waves and the forms of nature and marine life.

Len Lye grew up in Aotearoa New Zealand, moving to London in 1926 to embrace the excitement of modernism and the Jazz Age. In 1944 he moved to New York and lived for the rest of his life in its bohemian art world.

Len was a maverick, never fitting any of the usual artistic labels. He was a kinetic artist, direct film maker, painter, writer, theorist, philosopher, lecturer, and poet. Although he did not become a household name, his work was familiar to many film-makers and kinetic sculptors – he was something

---

[1] Umwelt - the specific way each particular organism experiences the world.

2 Many references for Len Lye are on the internet, including videos (YouTube) of his kinetic sculptures. The Len Lye Foundation has much more information and videos of his works: https://www.lenlyefoundation.com/

of an "artist's artist", and his innovations have had an international influence.

Len was one of the first Pākehā artists to appreciate the art of Māori, Australian Aboriginal, Pacific Island and African cultures, and this had great influence on his work.

He reinvented the technique of drawing directly on film. In various films he used a range of dyes, stencils, air-brushes, felt tip pens, stamps, combs and surgical instruments, to create images and textures on celluloid. His animation for the 1935 film "A Colour Box" was made by painting vibrant abstract patterns on the film itself, synchronising them to a popular dance tune. It used no camera work for anything except the title cards at the beginning of the film and it was the first "direct film" screened to a general audience.

A panel of animation experts convened in 2005 by the Annecy Film Festival put this film among the top ten most significant works in the history of animation. His later film "Free Radicals", not completed until 1979, was also in the top 50. Free Radicals used black film stock and he scratched designs into the emulsion. The result was a dancing pattern of flashing lines and marks, as dramatic as cadenza.

Len was also an important kinetic sculptor – what he referred to as "Tangibles". He saw film and kinetic sculpture as aspects of the same "art of motion".
He said: "All of a sudden it hit me - if there was such a thing as composing music, there could be such a thing as composing motion. After all, there are melodic figures, why can't there be figures of motion?"

His kinetic sculptural designs were often not possible in his day because the technology and the material were not invented yet. He had massive design plans for them in a temple of kinetic sculptures reaching 200 metres in the air. Reduced versions of them have been included on the New Plymouth walkway (Wind Wand) and the Wellington Harbour (Water Whirler) and in the Govett-Brewster Museum in New Plymouth.

So, I went to the Govett-Brewster Museum, principally to see his kinetic sculptures. His "Tangibles".

————-· ~~~ ————

Snakes:

From the foyer, a well lit hallway led to a darkened room. The floor space was at least twenty metres square.There are spotlights twenty, twenty-five metres above, affixed to the ceiling. They spotlighted the floor like virtual cropping circles, the space darkening between. Then I see them – seven slender steel chains or cables ten metres long. Each has a steel ball affixed at the lower end and each had two spotlights above. The spotlights picked them out like giant sparkling necklaces with glorious silvery highlights. The steel ball was almost immobile and the chains or cables moved and circled around in complex patterns.

If you jerk a garden hose or a rope up and down, the hose or rope replicates the pattern of a wave travelling along its length. It was like this but transposed – from horizontal to vertical. The 'jerking' was caused by an obscured mechanism in the roof.

The installation was named 'Snakes', but it didn't exactly describe the art works – an inadequate description. It was more industrial, technological, sci-fi – alien almost. "Snakes" as a title was like a person who had never seen a walrus describing it as a dog. But I guess "Snakes" is barely passable as a description – certainly they were sinuous, serpentine, fluid.

The motive mechanism was not uniform. It was complex leading to linear, semi-circular, and helix patterns – sometimes slow and elegant, sometimes frenetic and vigorous. The resultant 'waves' were multifarious: some crescent-like, some S-shaped, some multi-shaped like a string that had been plucked and some Pythagorean had touched them in their integer partitions resulting in harmonic wave motion.
[I play the cello, so I know how harmonics work!]

The seven "snakes" were not at the same part in their 'programme' [if there was a 'programme']. No 'synchronised swimming' or a 'Busby Berkeley chorus line' here! It seemed to be random, but I suspect not.

Mesmerised by the myriad activity above me, at last I looked at the floor. The shadow from the spotlights, two for each snake, made a two-dimensional shadow play on the floor, like a monotone moving mandala. Fascinating.

I could have stayed there for hours, but in the next room there were three installations: Fire Bush, two Fountains, and Grass.

————– ~~~ ————

Fire Bush:

If you have a bunch of noodles, and you place them in a pot of boiling water they fan out. Both the Fire Bush and the Fountains have the same idea – a bunch of steel wires, gathered together at the lower end of a plinth, that fan out in hyperbolic curves, dictated by gravity.

The Fire Bush has a thinner gauge wire and its mechanical motive mechanism was more vigorous. The spotlight above them was ruby red and it turned the wires luminescent red, yellow, orange, gold. The wire strands danced this way and that, the extremities were sparking and frazzled with the red light above them. A wayward strand was escaping the frenzy – out on is own, shining meteorically, a random spark.

Alchemists favour "fire" as another element and this sculpture has a combustible, alchemical energy about it. It was a whirling, swirling dervish dance, abrupt and exhilarating. Eventually, the motion slowed down, exhausted. In the hiatus I glimpsed something there, in the ruby redness, the shining gold glinttendness of the steel foliage – a phantom phoenix, wings gathered, ready to launch in the air. Then it disappeared, or maybe reappeared again, as the Fire Bush revved up its furious, frenetic dance once more.

Fountain (two of them):

Unlike the Fire Bush, the mechanism of the motive force for the Fountains was even, steady, each move was seamless. Choreographed. In musical terms: slurred, legato. Not staccato and accented like the Fire Bush. The two Fountains had a larger gauge wire than the Fire Bush, so their motion was more graceful, more balletic and more coherent.

Shimmering, fluid, slow-motion geysers. One of them was taller and upright. The shorter one was more splayed and it had a circular base as it was catching falling autumnal leaves. The spot-lights above were unfiltered so a silvery, shining, liquid quality was projected onto the strands of wire. It seemed that the metal was transmuted into water, fluid and glistening. But this is an illusion.

An idea came to me. It was like electrical AC – alternating current. In AC, the charge follows a wave along the wire so each individual element excites the next one but each element stays in its own space. It is like a Mexican wave: the wave happens, but each person is still in their seat [or above it!]. In an actual water fountain, the drops of water move from the outlet, cascading with the gravitational trajectory to their destination.

The water moves. The metal doesn't. That was the illusion. A "moving" fountain but frozen at the same time. Paradoxical.

Grass:

This 'tangible' is so, so simple but so elegant, unassuming but ingenuous, unpretentious but aesthetically charming.

A wooden board, one metre long and twenty centimetres wide, has about forty steel wires poking up in a rectangular array – each two centimetres apart from the next one, like an elongated and spaced-out broom or a toothbrush. The wires are fifty centimetres long. The board has no adornment – no carving, sanding, turning or painting. In fact, it seemed to be a left-over off-cut from a construction site!

The board is mounted on a black plinth. And the motive force? Simply, the motor tilts the board this way and that on a fulcrum in the centre. The rocking motion inspired the wires to move to and fro, like a zephyr moving reeds of grass in a pasture [hence the name!] The wires were individual so their movement is haphazard – but not random. It is the consequence of the other wires and the tilt of the board and gravity. Not chaotic.

It is like life. Human activities, human development, human relationships. Consequence. Not random. Not chaotic. Maybe destined.
Mesmerising.

—————· ~~~ ————

Universe:
Before I went to the next room, I was aware of a sound. The other exhibits have certain sounds – the muted argument of wires clashing together in the Fountain and Grass and the more vigorous confrontation in the Fire Bush. But this was different. It was a definite 'dong', like a clapper striking a rude bell, and it was not rhythmic. It seemed to be random but, given the genius of Len Lye, the randomness was more likely to be variables that I didn't appreciate or understand.

I turned into the room.
A curved loop of steel, about two metres in diameter, is fixed on a wooden bench, about forty centimetres above the floor. Above there was a small ball suspended from the ceiling. The steel loop flexed, changing its shape to all sorts of elliptical orbits, like a giant two-dimensional soap bubble. Sometimes

the steel hits a ball and the rude bell sounds: "dong". Sometimes it is "Dong". Sometimes it's "DONG". Sometimes it misses the ball completely. Mysterious, and unearthly.

Then, I saw the trick.
Other people were coming in from the other room. The gallery attendant was unobtrusively there and I saw him operate a remote control, like a garage remote. The loop moved, slightly, then more vigorously, and the loop deformed. Aha! I had rumbled the secret. Inside the wooden bench electromagnets were switched on and off by this remote. The magnets attract the steel loop this way or that. The movement, side to side, deforms the elliptical shape in the steel band and sometimes, occasionally, the ball strikes.

The audience waits in anticipation. When will it strikes the ball? This time? Next time?
How hard will it strike it – dong, Dong or DONG?

This one is about two metres in diameter (the loop), but Len Lye wanted it bigger! The written description said:"Lye wanted this loop to be enlarged to about ten times and serve as a kind of gateway to some temple."
Wow - that was something!

Another sign contained a quote from one commentator: "Informed by the artist's audacious experimentations with movement, Universe remains one of Lye's most beautifully resolved sculptural works. ... We are captivated by its fluid movements and quirky self-generating soundscape."
I agree completely.

I wonder about his names though.

The only one that is creatively named is "Universe" and apparently, that was a name that was chosen for him.
Originally titled Loop, Lye renamed it Universe after a young boy said the sound it made reminded him of "the universe". Maybe that boy could name the rest of them too! Fire Bush, Fountain, Grass are basically descriptive enough but not very creative. And, as I said, Snakes is a very inadequate name for that installation. Maybe Ahi[1], Mexican Wave, Zephyr, and Boa Constrictor would be a creative way to describe the installations?

It is interesting because Len Lye loved jazz, and jazz composers tend to be very creative in the naming of their pieces – often punning or make colloquial references to their nicknames, associates or circumstances.
Miles Davis – "Milestones", "Miles Ahead"; Charles Mingus – "Mingus Dynasty"; Dizzy Gillespie – "Gettin' Dizzy"; Herbie Mann – "Super Mann"; …
So, why the mundane names?
But, maybe, Len Lye wants the tangibles to speak for themselves, rather than be fancifully labelled.

— — — —- ~~~ — — — —

These are my thoughts about Len Lye's work, in particular his 'tangibles', his kinetic sculptures.
These are my thoughts.

---

[1] Ahi = the Māori for 'fire' in a sacred sense.

Speech? I can't make a speech about this subject. I can't make a speech at all.

I have global aphasia, and dyspraxia – my tongue and lips can't form the words that I mean to make.

The words are still there, but I am stuck, choked. I can't pronounce them.

I have about thirty words that I can manage to stutter out, but even then they are likely to be in the wrong order.

Or mispronounced. Or mistaken.

Writing? I tire easily and the words mix up in my brain so I can't read or write coherently.[1]

So, I can't write about it.

Drawing? I could attempt to draw it. They say that a drawing can convey a thousand words, but my artistic skill is at the level of a four year old: stick figures, no perspective, no shading.

Sign language? Sure, I can convey 'amazement', 'magnificence', 'awe' – but that can't convey the subtlety, the depth of my thoughts. No-one can understand the profound effect of Lye's work in my soul.

I need someone to telepathically translate my thoughts into writing or speech or …

Huh! That's sci-fi!

---

[1] Please "suspend your disbelief!" The author is pleading to encourage the reader's willingness to suspend doubt and believe what is patently impossible, for the sake of enlightenment. Despite that you have **read** this account, the author is seeking to understand that these are actually his thoughts, not his prose.

Speech, writing, drawing, sign language...
Basically I can't communicate.

I went to visit the Govett-Brewster Gallery and these are my thoughts.
So?
So what?

What sort of use are my thoughts if I can't share them with anyone?

Isolating. Disconnecting. Alienating.

It is frustrating. In the extreme.

That's my aphasia.

3A: Eight Problems with Aphasia (4+4)

Glenn and Arihia have been married for
twenty-two years.
Glenn used to be a bank manager.
Six years ago, he had a stroke.
He has non-fluent aphasia and dyspraxia.

His speaking is suspect.
Many times he can't get the right words out
of his mouth, or he mispronounces them.
Usually his sentences are hesitant, hyphenated or
drawn out.
His writing takes him four times longer than it used to.

After six years, Glenn couldn't talk coherently
to his family and they seemed to ignore his aphasia.
Sometimes he was very grumpy or irritated
by the kids or Arihia.

Glenn made a deal with Arihia.
He would write everything down.
She could respond the next day – but by writing,
not talking.

Talking is too ephemeral, Glenn thought.

But writing is considered, certain, concrete.

To write my concerns is best, even if it takes me longer…

Glenn began, typing his reply on his laptop.

It took him almost four hours, but he was pleased with the result.

He emailed it to Arihia.

— — — — —- ~~~ — — — —

Glenn #1: Interruptus maximus

My speech language therapist told you about all sorts of things you could do.
For my aphasia.

One of the things was not interrupting me.
And you were very good. At the beginning.
But in the last year you have been interrupting me more and more often.

For example, last week I was attempting to talk to you about our neighbour.
I can't recall everything that happened, but it was something like this:

Me: To-day, this…our…the nay…nay…the nay…

You: The newspaper?

Me: No…no… Our… we… the nay… the nay-toor…

You: The National Party? Huh…I can't believe what that National government is doing! And what about climate change, and education and…

Me: No! … No… Our… we… the nay… the nay-iss… um…isss…um the…

You: The Nissan across the road? What about the car? I think it is stolen.

Me: Yes! Yes! No… Our…the nay-boor…
nay-boor… Nay-boor! Pers-son. Nay. Boor!

You: Our neighbour? The neighbour at the back of our place? Hmm. They are very dodgy.

Me: No…no…um…the…the…our…nay-boor. They…they…was look-ing…for the…the…um…

You: Their mail? Their letterbox is falling down so no wonder if their mail is kua ngaro[1].

Me: No…no…nah…it's…it's …their house…um… the thing…the thing …the house….no…

You: Their house? Something wrong about their house? The roof needs to be repainted…

Me: No…no…the water thing…the water… the hou-se…

You: Water? Something wrong with the swimming pool?

---

[1] kura ngaro = disappeared, lost (Māori)

Me: Nah…nah…hou-se…the hou-se…sprink-le water…the hou-se…

[In my arms I gestured a long hose and waved one hand around like a sprayer/sprinkler.]

You: Ah –- you mean the hose. Not house. Did you give our hose to them?

Me: No…nah…not the hou-se…hose…Just like… the…the…um…the…

You: Not the hose. Did you give our sprinkler to them? I am not sure if they will give it back to us? Last month they borrowed our ladder and they have not given it back to us. You have to tell them. Kia kaha![1] We need the ladder back.

Me: Um…um…lad-der… it…it….isn't…um…not hou-se… the… um…the ..the…

You: What have you given them now? What?

Me: Um…um…the…the…the atta…atta…um…the atta…

You: Attack? What do you mean 'Attack'? We'll never get our the ladder back!

Me: No…no…the attach…the ments…the attach-ments…just attach-ments…

You: Ah! Just the attachments for the hose. Why didn't you say so? We have several of them. Not a problem.

---

[1] Kia kaha! = be strong! (Māori)

Basically, that is the conversation we had
last week.
It was impossible to talk to you because you
interrupted me so many times.
And that is typical now.
Can you stop interrupting me when I attempt to speak?

Arihia #1: Waiting…waiting……waiting………..
Kia ora Glenn for your very forthright account.
I agree that I interrupt you – sometimes.
I'm sorry about that and I will try to be better.

In my defence, there is an issue.
I applaud your use of an ellipsis[1] as an indication
that time has passed.
But **that** is the issue.

Sometimes, they should be more than doubled
or tripled to convey the amount of time that
your hesitations takes up.
I apologise.
But your hesitancy can be L…O…N…G… … …

And sometimes, you don't **finish** the sentence
anyway.

---

[1] ellipsis = a set of three dots […] that can indicate an unfinished thought,
a leading statement, a slight pause, an echoing voice, or a nervous or
awkward silence. Mostly, in this book, it indicates a pause in the speech.

It can be very difficult holding the aural space for the rest of your sentence when you don't finish it!

Maybe, you can indicate when you need a hand. Or write it down. Or draw it?

But please, please finish your sentences.

————- ~~~ ————

Glenn #2: Too Hard
I concede that my sentences are unwieldy.
Sometimes what I want to say makes sense,
but when I try to say it – it is too hard.
Aphasia muddles my words up.
Sometimes what I say is not what I want to say at all.
Mistooken words. [Is that a real word?]
Sometimes, it is too hard to get it right and I have to abandon my sentence.
Sorry! I will do better.

The aphasia website coined a phrase: Brain Blink! Maybe I can say to you: 'Brain blink'.
And you will understand when I can't finish the sentence?

I should do more with physical and body language. Write, draw or do charades.

Arihia #2: It all about context
Ngā mihi[1]. I think 'Brain Blink' is a good idea.
But six years ago you had no words at all.
You have come so far!
Don't use 'Brain Blink' as a crutch.

I have a disgruntlement myself.
Context.
Sometimes it is difficult to understand your
sentences if I don't know the context.
Without context, I have nothing to hang my hat on.
It doesn't need to be a spoken word.
Again, a gesture, writing or drawing would do.

For example:
You and I were biking along the Waikato River Bike
Trails last month.
You often point out things that caught your fancy.
If you are facing away from me it makes it hard to
hear what you are saying.
Admittedly, your aphasia doesn't help!

This time, on the trail, you were twenty metres
ahead beside a pine tree.
'Svig. It's svig!' you yelled, as you half turned.
By the time I got to the place, I was puzzling what
"svig" is.

---

[1] Ngā mihi = thank you, acknowledgements (Māori)

Then I heard a sound – a horrible grunting noise.
You mean 'Pig', I thought, fearfully looking around
at an enraged boar.
Then I realised the sound was two branches rubbing
together in the wind.
I looked at the pine tree, and I understood.
*It is **big**.*
I rode on – but my lizard brain was still looking for
the pig.

If you indicated the size of the pine, it would make
it easier to understand what you were saying.

— — — — — · ~~~ — — — —

Glenn #3: Aural pollution

Ah! I see. Context.
I like your allusion –
"Without context, I have nothing to hang my hat on."
I will see if I can get your hook for your hat!

Sometimes the aural environment is too confusing.
I can't sort all the sound information out.
Especially with the children.
And the TV or radio confuses me when people
are talking.
Or your whānau[1].

---

[1] whānau = family (extended)

Your sisters and mother talk so loud!
And they talk over each other.
I love our kids and your whānau, but it's too much.

Arihia #3: Solutions abound

Oh darling! I hear you!
My mother and sisters are too much for me too.

Well, what we can do is…

- We can make sure that the TV or the radio is turned off.
- or that the conversations are not in the lounge.
- Our kids: When the kids have a fight we could have a tokotoko.[1] So only the person who has it can speak.
- We can the conversation in a formal setting – for example our office?

The other whānau?
We could move your La-Z-Boy[2] to the back wall.
It is confined, so only one person can speak to you.

That could take care of the "talking over" conversations. Okay?

---

[1] A tokotoko is a traditional Māori carved ceremonial walking stick. On a marae it is a symbol of authority and status for the speaker holding it.

[2] La-Z-Boy = furniture chain known for its signature chair recliners.

But I can tell them again about you aphasia.
They will understand.
Or I will **make** them! Grrrrrr!!!!

————- ~~~ ————

Glenn #4: Wary weary
Thanks darling! That's my girl!
I appreciate that.

The other thing is tiredness.
Later in the day my brain gets tired.
My talking deteriorates.
Sometime I think that I have a quota of words for each day.
When the quota is done, my words disappear.

Arihia #4: Weary wary
You could nap in the day when I and the kids are not here?
It's okay to have a nap – your brain is still "rewiring".
You can say that they are RPNs –
"Restorative Power Naps".
It's therapy!

Actually, it's true for all of us.
It's not only you. It's **us**.

I have a quote from R W Emerson:
"Finish each day and be done with it.
You have done what you could.
Some blunders and absurdities no doubt crept in; forget them as soon as you can.
Tomorrow is a new day.
You shall begin it serenely and with too high a spirit to be encumbered with your old nonsense."

Actually, you – we – could rework your routine.
I am always up before six a.m.
We could walk around the streets and the lake before the kids are awake.
We could discuss anything that takes your fancy.
Take a note from Emerson: "A new day".
Not the "old nonsense".
It could be fun!

This is not a 'disgruntlement'. It what it is,

I miss, **absolutely miss**, the way you read to me when I was going to sleep.
Before your stroke.

It was so perfect – the sound of your voice, lulling me to sleep.
I know it was a trial for you!

I know you had to read the same page over again three or four times. But was bliss for me. Heavenly.
I miss that.
A lot.

— — — —- ~~~ — — — —

When Glenn read the last paragraph of Arihia's letter he responded by walking over to Arihia as she was reading a magazine at the kitchen table.
He hugged her, tenderly.

He said, with a heart-felt achiness:

'Sleep…read. Me too. Miss … that. Maybe I can… better. Read … again. For sleep.'

He kissed her forehead.
Then, excitedly, he leapt up and raised his hands in a "ta-dah!" gesture.

'A-ha! Repet-it-tion! Maybe I can rad… read…the some…same page…over and over and over and over…and get better at it! Woohoo!'

3B: Eight Problems with Aphasia (4+4)

Glenn and Arihia have been married for twenty-two years.
They have four children.
Arihia is a high school Geography teacher.

Glenn used to be a bank manager but, six years ago, he had a stroke and, as a result, he has non-fluent aphasia and a mild form of dyspraxia.

His speaking is suspect – many times he can't get the right words out of his mouth, or he mispronounce them. Usually his sentences are hesitant, hyphenated or drawn out. Extremely drawn out!

After his stroke, he worked with a speech therapist and practised his writing and reading to recover these skills sufficiently. His writing takes him four times longer than it used to.

After six years, Glenn was a little disgruntled about the way conversations were happening. He couldn't talk coherently to his family and they seemed to ignore his aphasia. Sometimes he was very grumpy or irritated by the kids or Arihia because he could not voice his indignation.
It caused some ructions in their usually placid home environment. Glenn realised that door slamming or banging his fist on the table in frustration was not a viable option in the long term!

Because Glenn realised that he couldn't argue his position to Arihia verbally, he made a deal with her. He would write everything down. She could respond the next day – but by writing, not talking.

Talking is too ephemeral, Glenn thought, wishy-washy. Too insubstantial. But writing is considered, certain, concrete. You can edit or rewrite it to better explain your thoughts. To write my concerns is best, even if it takes me longer…

Glenn began, typing his reply on his laptop, with a digital dictionary, thesaurus and cut and paste features – an absolute necessity for him. It took him almost four hours, but he was pleased with the result. He emailed it to Arihia.

— — — —· ~~~ — — — —

Glenn #1: Interruptus maximus
Six years ago, my speech language therapist told you about all sorts of things you could do that would make it easier to communicate with me. For my aphasia.

One of the things was not interrupting me when I was trying to talk to you.

And you were very good. At the beginning.
But in the last year you have been interrupting me more and more often.

For example, last week I was attempting to talk to you about our neighbour.
I can't recall everything that happened, but it was something like this:

Me: To-day, this…our…the nay…nay…the nay…

You: The newspaper?

Me: No…no… Our… we… the nay… the nay-toor…

You: The National Party? Huh…I can't believe what that National government is doing! Ngā karetao o te kāwana kakī-whero![1] Don't start me! We are going back twenty years to have a fair and just society And what about climate change, and education and…

Me: No! … No… Our… we… the nay… the nay-iss… um… isss…um the…

You: The Nissan across the road? What about the car? I think it is stolen. It seems to be there all the time. No-one is using it and I don't believe it belongs to any of our neighbours.

Me: Yes! Yes! No… Our…the nay-boor…nay-boor… Nay-boor! Pers-son. Nay. Boor!

You: Our neighbour? The neighbour at the back of our place? Hmm. They are very dodgy. Kia tūpato ki tērā momo![2]. I think they are growing weed in their backyard. Certainly it stinks of dope coming over the fence…

Me: No…no…um…the…the…our…nay-boor …at… at… left…for us… Left. They…they…was look-ing… for the… the…um…the…

You: Their mail? Their letterbox is falling down so no wonder if their mail is kua ngaro[3]. Especially when the wind. It was a gale last week!

Me: No…no…nah…it's…it's …their house…um…the thing… the thing …the house….no…

You: Their house? Something wrong about their house? The roof needs to be repainted. Or replaced. It is very rusty…

---

[1] They are red-necked government puppets.

[2] Kia tūpato ki tērā momo! = Beware of that type! (Māori)

[3] kura ngaro = disappeared, lost (Māori)

Me: No...no...the water thing...the water...the hou-se...

You: Water? Their swimming pool? Something wrong with the swimming pool?

Me: Nah...nah...hou-se...the hou-se...sprink-le water...the hou-se...

[In my arms I gestured a long hose and waved one hand around like a sprayer/sprinkler.]

You: Ah –– you mean the hose. Not house. Did you give our hose to them?

Me: No...nah...not the hou-se...hose...Just like...the...the... um...the...

You: Not the hose. Did you give our sprinkler to them? I am not sure if they will give it back to us? They have a very laissez-faire attitude to giving things back to us. Last month they borrowed our ladder and they have not given it back to us. You have to tell them. Kia kaha![1] We need the ladder back. Can you make sure that they return it.

Me: Um...um...lad-der... it...it....isn't...um...not hou-se ... or sprink...just ...just... the the... um...the ..the...

You: What have you given them now? What?

Me: Um...um...the...the...the atta...atta...um...the atta...

You: Attack? What do you mean 'Attack'? You have not antagonised them now? We'll never get our the ladder back!

Me: No...no...the attach...the ments...the attach-ments... just attach-ments...

You: Ah! Just the attachments for the hose. Why didn't you say so? We have several of them. Not a problem.

Basically, that is the conversation we had last week.

Writing, I can say: "The neighbour at the back of our property didn't have the attachments for their sprinkler. We have

---

[1] Kia kaha! = be strong! (Māori)

several, so I gave one to the neighbour so they can water their garden."
But it was impossible to talk to you because you interrupted me so many times.

And that is typical now. Can you stop interrupting me when I attempt to speak?

Arihia #1: Waiting...waiting......waiting...........
Kia ora Glenn for your very forthright account of your pouritanga[1].
I agree that I interrupt you – sometimes. And I can concur that it seems to be more often in the last year. I'm sorry about that and I will try to be better.

In my defence, there is an issue.
I applaud your use, in your writing, of an ellipsis[2] as an indication that time has passed between one word or phrase and another. But **that** is the issue.
Sometimes, your ellipsisis, ellipsised, ellipsisii...should be more than doubled or tripled in an effort to convey the amount of time that your hesitations takes up.
I apologise that I interpret what I think you are going to say and get it wrong – your example demonstrated that succinctly. But your hesitancy – your aphasiac hesitancy – can be long.
L. o. n. g.
L...o...n...g... ... ...
And sometimes, you don't **finish** the sentence anyway.

---

[1] pouritanga = melancholy, gloominess. (Māori)

[2] ellipsis = a set of three dots [...] that can indicate an unfinished thought, a leading statement, a slight pause, an echoing voice, or a nervous or awkward silence. Mostly, in this book, it indicates a pause in the speech.

It can be very difficult holding the aural space for the rest of your sentence when you don't finish it!

So – I will try to not interrupt you. Ka pai[1]. Just like before. Maybe, you can indicate when you need a hand to express your thoughts. Just a gesture? Or write it down. Or draw it?

But please, please finish your sentences.

— — — — — ⋅ ~~~ — — — —

Glenn #2: Too Hard
I concede that my sentences are unwieldy.

Sometimes, in my head, what I want to say makes sense, but when I try to say it – it is too hard.
Aphasia muddles my words up and sometimes what I say is not what I want to say at all. Mistooken words. [Is that a real word?]
And you know, apart from my aphasia I have a mild form of dyspraxia too. Mispronounced with mistooken words!
Sometimes, it is too hard to get it right and I have to abandon my sentence. Sorry! I will do better.

One commentator in our aphasia website coined a phrase: Brain Blink! That's apt, I think.

Maybe I can say to you: 'Brain blink', and you will understand when I can't finish the sentence?

But I concede that I should do more with physical and body language: write, draw or do charades.

---

[1] Ka pai = That's fine, okay. (Māori)

Arihia #2: It all about context

Ngā mihi[1]. I think 'Brain Blink' is a good idea.
But I think you should not use 'Brain Blink' as a concession.
A surrender! Six years ago you had no words at all. You have come so far! Don't use 'Brain Blink' as a crutch.

And it is important that we can communicate. Even if it takes a long time. I **know** that.
And it could be fun. Not a chore.

You remember "the psychic log"? It took a while to sort out that you were indicating "an excited dog!' That was fun!

Well – I have a pouritanga, a disgruntlement myself.
Context.
Sometimes it is difficult to understand your sentences if I don't know the context.
And it would help with my "interrupting behaviour" as per your initial disgruntlement – Glenn #1: Interruptus maximus !

When you are speaking, can you give me a clue about the context. What are you talking about.
Without context, I have nothing to hang my hat on.
It doesn't need to be a spoken word. Again, a gesture, writing or drawing would do.

One time, when we were watching a TV show, and I thought you said: "The stepping stones dumped the dark." It took a while to get your meaning because it was not a thing I have ever heard of. You explained that when a TV show had run out of ideas, the reviewer's critical expression is: "The show

---

[1] Ngā mihi = thank you, acknowledgements (Māori)

has jumped the shark!"[1]. I value that cultural information, but it took a long time to explain to me. The context would be helpful, like "a saying" or a drawing of the TV and question mark? Then I would have more idea of what you are saying.

Another example.
You and I were biking along the Waikato River Bike Trails last month. You remember that?
You are a good biker, much faster than me, but you wait for me to catch up every two or three minutes. And I appreciate that so much. Ngā mihi.
You often point out things that caught your fancy, but if you are facing away from me or the wind is blowing the other way – it makes it hard to hear what you are saying.
Admittedly, your aphasia doesn't help!

This time, on the trail, you were twenty metres ahead and you gestured to something on the side of the path. 'Svig. It's svig!' you yelled, as you half turned. Then you adjusted your gears for a downhill ride and as you disappeared you again yelled: 'Svig!'
By the time I got to the place, I was puzzling what "svig" is. A plant? A fungus? A bird? A table?
Then I heard a sound – a horrible grunting noise. *You mean 'Pig'*, I thought, fearfully looking around at an enraged boar with razor-sharp tusks.

---

[1] The idiom "jumping the shark" or "jump the shark" is a pejorative that is used to argue that a creative work or entity has reached a point in which it has exhausted its core intent and is introducing new ideas that are discordant with, or an extreme exaggeration of, its original purpose. The phrase was coined in 1985 by radio personality Jon Hein in response to a 1977 episode from the fifth season of the American sitcom Happy Days, in which the character of Fonzie (Henry Winkler) jumps over a live shark while on water-skis.

Then I realised the sound was two branches of a pine tree rubbing together in the wind. I looked at the pine tree, and I understood. *It is **big.***

And it was – a massive, gnarled tree like a gigantic multi-fingered hand. It was very impressive. I rode on – but my lizard brain was still looking for the pig. But if you indicated the size of the pine with your free hand, it would make it easier to understand what you were saying.

— — — —· ~~~ — — — —

Glenn #3: Aural pollution

Ah! I see. Context. I will see what I can do about that.
I like your allusion – "Without context, I have nothing to hang my hat on."
I will see if I can get your hook for your hat!
Especially with the important conversations.

I have to say, sometimes the aural environment is too confusing. I can't sort all the sound information out. Too many conversations, or noise – I can't cope with that and I shut down. Especially with the children. And the TV or radio confuses me when people are talking. All the aural stimuli.

Or your whānau[1]. Your sisters and mother talk so loud!
And they talk over each other – I can't handle that.
But what can I do? I can't avoid them – I love our kids and your whānau, but it's too much.

Arihia #3: Solutions abound

Oh darling! I hear you! My mother and sisters are too much for me too – but whānau! What can we do?

---

[1] whānau = family (extended)

Well, what we can do is…
- When we have a lot to discuss, we can make sure that the TV or the radio is turned off, or that the conversations are not in the lounge.
- Our kids: When the kids have a fight -- "an altercation" I should say, they **never** fight – rather than talk over each other as they usually do, we could have a tokotoko[1] so only the person who has it can speak. **And** it is culturally appropriate! This is something that the kids should learn.
- Otherwise, we can the conversation in a formal setting – for example our office? Very "old school" but, again, good for the kids!

The other whānau – especially my mother and sisters: they will respect the tokotoko. But the protocol for the tokotoko is for public speeches, so most of our conversations would not be – um – valid? Inconsequential.
What about this. Usually you are sitting in the middle of the lounge, but we could move your La-Z-Boy[2] to the back wall. Or outside, get yourself in the sheltered corner of the BBQ. Both of them are confined, so only one person can speak to you. That could take care of the cross-purposes or "talking over" conversations. Okay?

But they know – all our whānau – know that you have aphasia. I can tell them again, and you can say "Too much!" and they will understand. Really! They will **understand.**
Or I will **make** them! Grrrrrr!!!!

————-·~~~ ————

---

[1] A tokotoko is a traditional Māori carved ceremonial walking stick. On a marae it is a symbol of authority and status for the speaker holding it.

[2] La-Z-Boy = furniture chain known for its signature chair recliners.

Glenn #4: Wary weary

Thanks darling! That's my girl! I appreciate that.
Your suggestions are very apt.

The other thing is tiredness.
Usually when people are over, or the kids are ratty, it is later in the day. My brain gets tired. My talking deteriorates.
You know The Far Side cartoon? The one in the classroom and one kid raises his hand to the teacher and said: "Mr Osborne, may I be excused. My brain is full!"

That's what it's like.
Sometime I think that I have a quota of words for each day, and when the quota is done, my words disappear. Or become hard to find. What can we do about that?

Arihia #4: Weary wary

Well – **I** think you know about **that**! Too much red wine at dinner? Not enough hydration in the day? Playing on your computer – okay! – **working** on your computer at all hours of the night.

Maybe, you need to get some sleep. Or some naps in the day when I and the kids are not here? It's okay to have a nap – your brain is still "rewiring".
It is not like a "old-person's nap". You can say that they are RPNs – "Restorative Power Naps". It's therapy!

Actually, it's true for all of us. After my day at teaching geographical concepts for the masses, and the kid's days at their respective schools, we are all tired. And at the end of the day the comments can be – well, fractious. It's not only you. It's **us**.

I have a quote from R W Emerson:
> "Finish each day and be done with it. You have done what you could. Some blunders and absurdities no doubt crept in; forget them as soon as you can. Tomorrow is a new day. You shall begin it serenely and with too high a spirit to be encumbered with your old nonsense."

Actually, you – we – could rework your routine.

You admit that your talking is much better in the morning than the evening. Maybe, you should come to bed earlier so wake up earlier. I am always up before six a.m. We could walk around the streets and the lake before the kids are awake and we could discuss anything that takes your fancy. Constructive talking. Take a note from Emerson: "A new day". Not the "old nonsense". It could be fun!

I have to say that – and this is not a 'disgruntlement', it what it is – I miss, **absolutely miss**, the way you read to me when I was going to sleep. Before your stroke. It was so perfect – the sound of your voice, lulling me to sleep. I know it was a trial for you! I know you had to read the same page over again three or four times, but was bliss for me. Heavenly.
I miss that. A lot.

— — — —· ~~~ — — — —

When Glenn read the last paragraph of Arihia's letter he responded, not with another letter, but by walking over to Arihia as she was reading a magazine at the kitchen table.
He hugged her, tenderly.

He said, with a heart-felt achiness:

'Sleep…read. Me too. Miss … that. Maybe I can…better. Read … again. For sleep.'

He kissed her forehead. Then, excitedly, he leapt up and raised his hands in a "ta-dah!"gesture.

'A-ha! Repet-it-tion! Maybe I can rad… read…the some… same page…over and over and over and over…and get better at it! Woohoo!'

4A: FensterIn [1]

When she got home from the hospital, she was different.

She had been there for ten days.
I heard some cars pull up in the driveway.
I caught the scent of her perfume wafting in the air.

There she was.
Her eyes had black rings around them.
Her brow was furrowed.
She walked with an uncertain step.
Clearly she had had an ordeal.

I desperately wanted to hold her, kiss her, but…her husband was there too.
He was 'helping her'.
I expect he was too busy – as usual.
This arrogant, sorry excuse for a husband.

I know! I know! She was married.
She was not free. Blah-de-blah …
But I loved her. I adored her. And she loved me too!

---

[1] FensterIn is a German word (from "das Fenster," which literally means "window"). The term is useful if you have to sneak into your lover's bedroom by climbing through the window so that you can sleep with them in secret. In this story, the 'window' is replaced by a 'back door'.

The husband got in the car and drove away.
Work, I suppose. It was always 'work'.
I suspect the secretary.

I crept into the house by the back door. There were many other people in the kitchen.
One person, built like a rugby prop forward, was holding forth.
Something about 'stroke' and 'aphasia'.
These weren't terms I recognised.
*I walked down the hallway to **her** bedroom.*

She was huddled in bed, teary eyes closed.
I was just about to go to her but the others came in from the kitchen.
They were cheering her up with trivialities and gossip.
She roused herself and faced them with a ghastly grin that didn't meet her eyes.
The prop-forward brute muscled in and shooed everyone out of the bedroom.
So everyone left including, regretfully, me.

— — — —- ~~~ — — — —

It's complicated.

The husband – he didn't like me at all.
He always turned his back on me.
And he had threatened me three or four times – his chin jutting out, the whites of his eyes flashing and snarling at me: 'Get out! Get out!'

So, I got out. Let live and fight again? Maybe? Maybe I was a coward.

Before the hospital visit I was often in the garden, digging up weeds and watering the plants.
Often I met my nemesis – the next-door cat.
I don't like felines.
They are a law unto themselves.
I gladly chased her off.

I used to sneak in the back door. She was often in the kitchen, always welcoming and loving.
She made a fuss of me, kissed me and hugged me.

We often had lunch together in the garden when it was sunny.
She always murmured a few endearing words.
Absolute bliss...

*But somehow – some**why** – she doesn't want to divorce her husband.*
I tolerate her decision. I want her to be happy.
As the saying goes: 'Better to have a half-love than never to have loved at all.'

But, something has changed. She is different.

— — — —- ~~~ — — — —

She lies in bed often, catching her sleep.
Unusually her words are now stuttering and strange.
But it doesn't matter. Her words are only a soundtrack of her love for me.
It doesn't matter that they are hesitant and mismangled.
The notes are strange but the melody still sings to me.

It is a fortnight since she returned from the hospital.
*A visiting Speech Therapist comes on Thursday afternoon for her 'aphasia' issue [whatever **that** means].*
Her useless husband is 'working' for long hours.
[Again, I suspect the secretary.]

The back door is just ajar so I stealthily tiptoe in. I open her bedroom door.
She is dozing. I gently go the bed and gaze at her.

She stirs and sleepily opens her eyes.
Her delight is enormously encouraging.
She reaches for me, says broken words but all I hear is her intentions.
I get up beside her on the bed.
She welcomes me in her arms, kissing and cuddling me.

After our initial emotional flurry we rest and relax together.
The mingling of our breaths is a balm.
Ecstatic exhalation.

I almost fall asleep…but…wait?
A sound. Footsteps.
Her husband is at the door!
I spring to my feet and …

'Bruno! Bad dog. Get off the bed. Get off!
Sophie – I told you, the dog shouldn't be on the bed. It's so unhygienic.
Bruno! Go outside. Get! Get!'

4B: Fensterln [1]

When she got home from the hospital, she was different.

She had been there for ten days. As usual I was hanging around the garden, disconsolate, when I heard some cars pull up in the driveway. I caught the scent of her special perfume wafting in the air. I peeked around the corner of the house and saw a bustle of people on the path to the front door. They parted and there she was. Her eyes had black rings around them, her brow was furrowed and she walked with an uncertain step, as if she didn't know how her foot was meeting the ground. Clearly she had had an ordeal.

I desperately wanted to hold her, kiss her, but...her husband was there too. He was 'helping her' but I know he was annoyed that she was taking so long to get into the house. I expect he was too busy – as usual. This arrogant, sorry excuse for a husband.

I know! I know! She was married. She was not free. Blah-de-blah ... but I loved her. I adored her. I revered, idolised, worshipped her. And she loved me too!

I loitered around the garden and sure enough, after a few minutes, the husband made his escape, got in the car and drove away. Work, I suppose. It was always 'work'.

---

[1] Fensterln is a German word (from "das Fenster," which literally means "window"). The term is useful if you have to sneak into your lover's bedroom by climbing through the window so that you can sleep with them in secret. In this story, the 'window' is replaced by a 'back door'.

I suspect the secretary.

*I crept into the house by the back door, but there were many other people in the kitchen. I knew some of them – the next door neighbours and her sister from Whanganui[1] way, but some I have never seen before. One person, a big, strapping girl like a rugby prop forward, was holding forth, spouting technical information to the kitchen audience. Something about 'stroke' and 'aphasia' and 'speech therapy'. These weren't terms I recognised, so I left the room and quietly walked down the hallway to **her** bedroom.*

I could smell the depression. She was huddled in bed, head sunken on her breast, teary eyes closed. Her hands gripped the quilt as if it were a lifeline. I was just about to go to her, to comfort her, because I'm sure my presence would soothe and reassure her. But the others came in from the kitchen and they waylaid me.

They were talking ninety-to-the-dozen as if they wanted to cheer her up with trivialities and gossip. She roused herself and faced them with a ghastly grin that didn't meet her eyes. Fake jollity! I was going to step in but then the prop-forward brute muscled in and shooed everyone out of the bedroom.

I wasn't keen to tackle her – obviously, 'tackle' was the appropriate word – so everyone left including, regretfully, me.

— — — —· ~~~ — — — —

---

[1] Whanganui: a town on the west coast of Te-Ika-a-Māui, the North Island of Aotearoa New Zealand.

Maybe I should have stood my ground. Forced the issue.
I loved her. Totally. Desperately. Intensely.
But it's complicated.

The husband – he didn't like me at all. Of course.
When I was around, he was always 'hinting' (read: forcefully insinuating) that I should be elsewhere. He always turned his back on me. And, when she was not there, he had threatened me three or four times – his chin jutting out, the whites of his eyes flashing, his body like an athlete waiting for the staring gun, clenching a fist and snarling at me: 'Get out! Get out!'

So, I got out. Let live and fight again? Maybe?
Maybe I was a coward.
As I said, it is complicated.

Before the hospital visit, I used to bide my time, avoiding the husband. I was often in the garden, digging up weeds and watering the plants. Her "constant gardener"! Often I met my nemesis – the next-door cat. She was arrogantly strutting along the wall as if the entire world was her personal domain. I don't like felines. They are so detached and aristocratically indifferent. They are a law unto themselves – pontificating and pompous. I gladly chased her off.

When the husband left for 'work', I used to sneak in the back door. She was often in the kitchen, cooking cakes or preserving the fruit from the backyard orchard. And she was always welcoming and loving. She made a fuss of me, kissed me and hugged me. Heavenly.

We often had lunch together in the garden when it was sunny, idling around, lying on the lawn beneath the fruit trees, smelling the delicious aromas and glorying in the sunlight. She always murmured a few endearing words. She stroked my hair, toyed with my ears, my nose, my lips – all the funny things that lovers do. I placed my head on her lap forming a perfect 'T' shape – I imagined it stood for 'Tranquility'. We looked up in the azure sky, sparsely painted with fluffy clouds... Bliss. Absolute bliss...

But somehow – some**why** – she doesn't want to divorce her husband. I can't see it.
He is impatient, egocentric, conceited, narcissistic, selfish...
He barely speaks to her. She is basically a domestic servant. A maid. And she doesn't know he threatened me several times. Maybe she should know? Maybe that would make the difference? But I can see that it could be construed as 'sour grapes' on my part.

I tolerate her decision. I want her to be happy. And I just want to be with her.
As the saying goes: 'Better to have a half-love than never to have loved at all.'

But, after her stay in hospital, something has changed.
She is different.

— —— —— - ~~~ —— — —

She lies in bed often, catching her sleep. I don't mind that she has to rest – she clearly needs it. And I don't mind that she has barely spoken to me. Unusually her words are now *stuttering and strange, as if she has a gag in her mouth. But it doesn't matter. Her words are only a soundtrack of her love for me. It doesn't matter that they are hesitant and mismangled. The notes are strange, faintly discordant, but the melody still sings to me.*

But I do mind that the prop-forward wench is still here while the husband is working. She is always chasing me out of the room, or getting me out of the house entirely. Maybe the husband has put her up to it. I loathe her. I hate him.

I miss the lawn lunches. I miss the perfume of the delicious smells of the garden in the sunshine. I miss the murmuring, endearing, nonsensical things she would whisper in my ears. I miss the 'T'.

But, lately things are changing. It is a fortnight since she returned from the hospital and I detect a new routine.

*A visiting Speech Therapist comes on Thursday afternoon for her 'aphasia' issue [whatever **that** means]. Her useless husband is 'working' the long hours that he used to work before her hospital visit. [Again, I suspect the secretary.]*
And each day the prop-forward troll is there, but only for two hours in the morning.

I stay in the garden, behind the rose trellis, and wait for my chance. The prop-forward ogre leaves the house by the main door, goes to her car and drives away. The husband was already 'working'. It wasn't a Thursday. So no-one is in the house. Except her. My beloved.

The back door is just ajar so I stealthily tiptoe in, across the kitchen, up the hallway and open her bedroom door. She is dozing. A closed book is in her lap. Her glasses are discarded on the bedspread. I gently go the bed and gaze at her. She stirs and sleepily opens her eyes. Her delight is enormously encouraging. She reaches for me, says broken words but all I hear is her intentions. I get up beside her on the bed and she welcomes me in her arms, kissing and cuddling me.

After our initial emotional flurry we rest and relax together. The mingling of our breaths is a balm. Ecstatic exhalation. The moments seem like hours, the hours like moments. Her eyes are closed and she smiles. Her despondent, melancholic mood has almost dissipated, like a mist that melts in the sun of my passionate ardor and my constancy. [She always brings out the poet in me!]

I almost fall asleep…but…wait?
A sound. Footsteps.
A cough and a scent of familiar body odour.
Her husband is at the door! I spring to my feet and …

'Bruno! Bad dog. Get off the bed. Get off!
Sophie – I told you, the dog shouldn't be on the bed.
It's so unhygienic.
Bruno! Go outside. Get! Get!'

5A: Kathryn, Kate, Katie

My wife is so annoying.
Kathryn. Kate. Katie.
Sooooo annoying!

— — — —- ~~~ — — — —

Conviction
Certainty is a human fallacy.
[Unless you are the pope.]

Certainty is for angels and devils.
Conviction and certitude is Katie's default position.
Katie is **certain**.

And she is right, invariably -- as far as I know.
Maybe it is her angelic nature.
Or the other one.

Even the mundane topics.
For example, when we are walking on the beach, she turns to me and asks, faux-innocently: 'How many boats can you see?'

It's no use. I can change the topic, or bend over to examine a fake-stubbed toe, or stage a fit of coughing.
But the unanswered question remains: 'How many boats can you see?'
I am doomed. Always doomed.

'One, two, three…four….um…five?' I attempt.
With a guttural chuckle, she triumphantly points out nine boats.
Sometimes I accuse her of SESS.
Superior Eye Sensory Superpower.

And it's always the same.
'How many [shags], [rabbits], [horses], [chickens], [cars], [people],… can you see?'
She sees double my score, almost!
Every time.
SESS.
Soooo annoying!

— — — —- ~~~ — — — —

Humour
And her sense of humour?
Ah! She is a treasure. Annoyingly so.

She is a pun-queen.

When I text her about something that I need her to do, she always replies: Shirley.
[The punning subtext: Surely.]

Our granddaughter, two years old, came to visit.
Katie lifted her t-shirt and blew "raspberries"[1] across her skin, like a trumpet player.
Kate looked at us and commented: 'It should be blueberries.' Get it? 'Blewberries'!

[Actually, she continued, opining that they should be called "spittleberries."]

Or with our son-in-law.
At dinner, he wore a very classy suit and tie with waistcoat.
Kate declared he was "suit-a-ble".
She looked at his luxurious hair and beard and pronounced he was "hir-suit".
Then proceeded to announce that he was "Suit-a-Man". [Superman.]

Every so often, Kathryn treats herself to a lavish bath.
She gets everything ready:

---

[1] In the terminology of phonetics, the 'raspberry' [razzing or making a Bronx cheer] has been described as a voiceless linguolabial trill, transcribed [r̼] in the International Phonetic Alphabet, and as a buccal interdental trill, transcribed [ʘ͡r] in the Extensions to the International Phonetic Alphabet.

- sets her phone to silent and tucks it into the bedroom dresser;
- a portable stereo with her favourite Michael Bublé CD;
- hot water, a scented bath bomb and luxurious bath bubbles;
- a bottle of Hawkes Bay merlot;
- no electric lights but oodles of candles;
- and plush and comfy towels on the towel heater.

She calls it her 'Bublé bath'!

— — — —· ~~~ — — — —

Last winter, our grandson had the 'flu.
He was coughing all the time and his nose was filled with mucus.
So Katie cheerfully called the condition 'snot soup'.

One day while walking beside a local lake, we noticed many black swans on the water.
She pronounced that the waterway should be named "Swan Lake".
As an aside, she commented: 'Their ballet shoes are under the water.'

Later on, along the dunes at the Waikanae Estuary, we saw some little birds and some even smaller birds.

Kate confidently [with certitude!] named them dotterels.

'What about the mini ones?' I said, foolishly.

'They are dots,' Kate said, mischievously.

By the way, about the birds. As a hobby, Kathryn collects collective nouns for birds. Personalised, of course.

- A cutlery of spoonbills.
- A nunnery of tōrea (oyster catchers with their black plumage and orange legs).
- An abbey of pūtangitangi (paradise ducks with their feathers like monks' or nuns' habits).
- An iridescence of tūī.
- A dogfight of pīwakawaka.
- A plumpness of kererū.

— — — — —- ~~~ — — — —

Similitude

She and I have a 'shorthand' – common with people who have been together for a long, long time.

A gesture, a word or a phrase can catch a multitude of memories that are special to us.

When we are holding hands, for example, we have a secret handhold.
One time I commented about this to her.
Apparently her diamond ring catches on things.
Her little finger is bent outwards – an old netball injury.

In our home, we have a faceted glass crystal on a string. A prism.
She always moves the prism where the sun is shining through.
The sun's rays refract its light through the prism.
It is like a rainbow – shimmering, dancing, spinning.
Real but insubstantial.

When she moves the prism most people think is quaint.
But I know – I **know** – it is a memorial for her mother.
Katie always associates rainbows with her mother's spirit rising above our mortal plane.
An angelic presence.

Katie's attitudes can be harsh though.
She decries the poaching of 'rainbows' for the LGBTQIA-community.
Rainbows are a natural phenomenon.
She doesn't like it that a group of people has taken the concept over.

Actually, I get her point.

Stubborn too.

Sometimes Kathryn uses things that are not supposed to be used for that purpose.

For example, using a rock to bang screws into a piece of wood.

I say: 'You should have a drill and screwdriver or it will….'

She says: 'Moo! Moo!'

My attempted remonstration collapses in a chuckle.

It is an old 'knock-knock' joke that we enjoyed many years back.

    Knock-knock.
        Who's there.
    Interrupting cow.
        Interruptin…
    Moo! Moo!

— — — —- ~~~ — — — —

Curiosity

Kathryn is a scientist.

But it didn't stop her idly dreaming about fanciful imaginings.

Walking in the bush, we see tūī and pīwakawaka flying with their usual kamikaze speed around the tangled trees.
Musing, she said: 'What do birds see? Maybe they see air currents or paths.
Maybe they see these golden pathways.
Maybe it is the same for butterflies?
A streaming golden path…
A golden brick road that leads to butterfly heaven…'
Ah Katie! Fanciful and fantastic.

Choices
But I am all over her in the geo-terrestrial stakes.
If I turn her around two or three times, she can't find where to go.
I am always orientated.

When we are passing a river, she is puzzled. '
The river is flowing this way? Why?' my wife asks.
I am incredulous.
'How can you function?' I say to her.

We pause at the beach front.
'Which way should we go – north or south?' I graciously question her.
'We should go north, I think,' she says decisively.

We go down the beach – southwards.
The illusion of choice.

— — — —. ~~~ — — — —

So.
My annoying but beautiful, intelligent, angelic wife.
My wife with aphasia.

Yep.
She has aphasia. PPA.
Primary Progressive Aphasia.
The one there is no recovering from.
A form of dementia.

About four years ago, her words 'slipped'.
She couldn't remember the names of the places we went to last week.
She thought it was a 'senior-moment'.
By the end of the year, she was fanciful about naming things in the kitchen.
She called the toaster an oven.
The dish-washer a sprinkler.
The coffee machine a "drinking thing".
I thought she was joking .
But when she couldn't remember the names of her grandchildren we made an appointment.

The result – PPA.

'Primary progressive aphasia – PPA – is a type of frontotemporal dementia,' the doctor tells us. 'Degeneration of the frontal or temporal lobes of the brain. These areas include brain tissue involved in speech and language. It is quite rapid, quite anomic…'

Blah, blah, blah!
The scientific rhetoric doesn't help.
My loved one is losing her words, her conversational faculties, her memories.
It comes and goes, but mostly it goes.
It is a tragedy.

Kathryn and I – we have taken steps. Together.
We have our wills and bequests in order and we have our Powers of Attorney sorted.
I have a Remembrance Album of all sorts of things that have special meaning for us:
  • photographs of her mother and father and siblings;
  • our travels, vacations, and expeditions;
  • our children and grandchildren at various ages;
  • our pets – cats and dogs and birds;
  • the waterfalls, lakes and beaches we have walked around;

- concert and play programmes.

It jogs her memory – for a little while.

I have a dedicated playlist on her phone that she can listen to, any time.
Music seems to revive her memories of certain events or people.
I treasure that reprieve.

It is hard for all of us.
Her words are vanishing.
Her sense of logical sentence structure is disappearing.
Her puns are history. Her SESS is forgotten.
Her spoken recall is disorganised.
And the memories are fading.

But we have a secret handshake.

And, occasionally, there is a surprising interruption of: 'Moo! Moo!'

5B: Kathryn, Kate, Katie

My wife is so annoying.
Kathryn. Kate. Katie.
Sooooo annoying!

———–· ~~~ ————

Conviction

Certainty is a human fallacy. Unless you are the pope, I guess.

Certainty is for angels and devils. I'm never sure about anything, but conviction and certitude is Katie's default position. The tweet of an unknown bird, the age of that woman going past, the breed of that dog, the relationship between two men sitting on a bench, the careers of people across from us on the bus, the hidden issues that cloak our daughter's pondering... Katie is **certain**.

And she is right, invariably -- as far as I know.
Maybe it is her angelic nature.
Or the other one.

Even the mundane, inconsequential topics. For example, when we are walking on the beach, enjoying the setting sun, the blue sky turning to baby pink and clouds spotlighted with an escalating fiery glow, she turns to me and asks, faux-innocently: 'How many boats can you see?'

It's no use. I can change the topic, or bend over to examine a fake-stubbed toe, or stage a fit of coughing. But despite my scintillatingly subject-change-choice, pseudo-anguish

about my metatarsals, or my near-fatal paroxysm of asthmatic wheezing, the unanswered question remains: 'How many boats can you see?'
I am doomed. Always doomed.

'One, two, three…four….um…five?' I attempt.
With a guttural chuckle, she triumphantly points out nine boats. I dismally look at what she is pointing at – my five obvious boats **plus** another obscured by an island, two minuscule interruptions on the horizon, and a flashing sail that I took to be a seagull. Nine boats.

Sometimes I accuse her of SESS. Superior Eye Sensory Superpower.

And it's always the same. 'How many [shags], [rabbits], [horses], [chickens], [cars], [people],… can you see?' She sees double my score, almost! Every time. SESS.
Soooo annoying!

I look at the big picture. Often, when we are returning from a walk, Kathryn will say: 'Look at the birds we have seen! Sparrows, riroriro, miromiro, tauhou, waxeyes, goldfinch, tomtits, chaffinch, tūī, pīwakawaka, kererū, blackbirds, gulls, terns, korimako, kōtare, harrier hawk, godwits, dotterills…
Me. I see big birds or small birds.

[Okay, okay - I know the difference between a sparrow, tūī, pīwakawaka and kererū, but the rest are big birds or small birds!]

— — — —- ~~~ — — — —

Humour

And her sense of humour? Ah! She is a treasure – annoyingly so.

She is a pun-queen.
When I text her about something that I need her to do, she always replies: Shirley.
[The punning subtext: Surely.]

Our granddaughter, two years old, came to visit. Katie lifted her t-shirt and blew "raspberries"[1] across her skin, like a trumpet player. Our granddaughter chortled in protesting delight. Between the repetition of her flatulent racket Kate looked at us and commented: 'It should not be raspberries. It should be blueberries.' Get it? 'Blewberries'!
[Actually, she continued, opining that they should be called "spittleberries."]

Or with our son-in-law. Usually he arrives for dinner in his labouring or gym clothes, but this time he wore a very classy suit and tie with waistcoat. Almost without a breath Kate declared he was "suit-a-ble", looked at his luxurious hair and beard and pronounced he was "hir-suit", and then proceeded to announce – with a nod to our five-year grandson, who was just acquainted with the back story for Clark Kent – that he was "Suit-a-Man".
[Clark Kent aka Superman.]

The same five-year-old was bringing a bowl of peas from the kitchen to the outside table where we were expecting to

---

[1] In the terminology of phonetics, the 'raspberry' [razzing or making a Bronx cheer] has been described as a voiceless linguolabial trill, transcribed [r̼̊] in the International Phonetic Alphabet, and as a buccal interdental trill, transcribed [ↄ͡r] in the Extensions to the International Phonetic Alphabet.

have dinner on a summer evening. He tripped on the terrace above and showered the peas on us below. On that cue Kathryn declared, with an extravagant gesture, 'Let's peas rain!' [Let peace reign!]

When we were walking on a rural track I pointed to a strange group of cows in the field beside us. There were about twenty of them [Katie said thirty-six!] Usually the heifers would spread out over the field, contentedly chewing grass and cud. This time, they were bunched up in the middle of the paddock just looking at each other with an absent-minded and puzzling look on their bovine faces. 'What are they doing?' I said, baffled. Quick as a sniff, she replied, 'They are a cowmitee.'

Every so often, Kathryn treats herself to a lavish bath.
Of course I indulge her. She gets everything ready:
• sets her phone to silent and tucks it into the bedroom dresser;
• a portable stereo with her favourite Michael Bublé CD [she **loves** Michael Bublé];
• hot water, a scented bath bomb and luxurious bath bubbles;
• a bottle of Hawkes Bay merlot – Te Mata Estate or Black Barn[1];
• no electric lights but oodles of candles;
• and plush and comfy towels on the towel heater.
She calls it her 'Bublé bath'!

— — — — —· ~~~ — — — —

---

[1] Hawkes Bay in the central east coast of Te-Ika-a-Māui, the North Island, has some of the premium winemakers in the country, including Te Mata Estate and Black Barn.

Sometimes her humour is … earthy. One time, when we are driving on the expressway, she went to exit the highway for our destination and she encountered a rumble strip. You know what I mean? The regular mini-bumps in a strip that alert the driver that she/he/they is entering the shoulder of the road. Kate whooped, swung her body side to side and chanted in a rap-style: 'Keep you judders away from my udders!'

Last winter, the other grandson had the 'flu. He was coughing all the time and his nose was filled with mucus, so Katie cheerfully called the condition 'snot soup'.

When the same child was "FaceTiming"[1] us, he delightedly used the avatar app that can change the image of your face to that of a cartoon character: a fox, a dinosaur, or a ghoul. He chose an octopus avatar, cheerfully waving his tentacles at us. Kate loudly announced, 'What the wheke[2]?' Our daughter was not amused, given that her son had learned some swear words at Kindy[3].

Our daughter, the octopus-wearing-grandson's mother, has the same shoe size as Kathryn. Kate's boots were leaking and she sent them to be repaired. She borrowed one of our daughter's pairs of boots for a week and after that she exclaimed: 'It was perfect. We should wheel-balance our boots!'
After a puzzled look between my daughter and me, Katie explained: 'You pronate and I supinate! When I get my boots

---

[1] FaceTime: a video chat between iPhone, iPad, and Mac users. Since the release of iOS 15, iPadOS 15, and macOS Monterey, anyone can join a FaceTime call from their web browser.

[2] Wheke = octopus (Māori)

[3] kindy = Kindergarten, an early-childhood preschool before Primary School.

back, we should swap the boots every week. The boots will get twice the wear … just like wheel balancing on the car! A win-win for us.'

One day while walking [yes, we walk a lot!] beside a local lake, we noticed many black swans regally swanning about on the water. About twenty of these majestic birds were serenely and elegantly dipping their long necks to reach the weeds on the bottom [Katie maintains the count was thirty-two.] She courteously referenced my musical persona, and pronounced that the waterway should be named "Swan Lake", facetiously commenting as an aside: 'Their ballet shoes are under the water.'

Later on, along the dunes at the Waikanae Estuary, we saw some little birds and some even smaller birds. They were sandy coloured with spotted freckles on their chests and relatively long legs. Their long beaks were digging down in the sand, searching for snails and sand hoppers. Kate confidently [with certitude!] named them dotterels.
'What about the mini ones?' I said, foolishly.
'They are dots,' Kate said, mischievously.

By the way, about the birds. As a hobby, Kathryn collects collective nouns for birds. Personalised, of course.
- A cutlery of spoonbills.
- A nunnery of tōrea (oyster catchers with their black plumage and orange legs).
- An abbey of pūtangitangi (paradise ducks with their feathers like monks' or nuns' habits).
- An iridescence of tūī.
- A dogfight of pīwakawaka.
- A plumpness of kererū.

— — — —· ~~~ — — — —

Similitude

She and I have a 'shorthand' – common with people who have been together for a long, long time. A gesture, a word or a phrase can catch a multitude of memories that are special to us.

When we are holding hands, for example, we have a secret handhold. We don't clasp interlocking fingers or one hand over the another. We have an odd clasp that leaves her ring finger out and her little finger exposed. One time I commented about this to her. Apparently her diamond ring catches on things and her little finger is bent outwards like a mis-pruned sapling – an old netball injury.

In our home, we have a faceted glass crystal on a string. A prism. She always moves the prism about the room, setting it in some window that the sun is shining through. The sun's rays refract its light through the prism onto the wall, like a rainbow – shimmering, dancing, spinning. Sometimes it rests on our clothes or hands or faces. A glimpse of something ephemeral. Real but insubstantial.

When she moves the prism to another site, following the sunlight, most people think is quaint, but I know – I **know** – it is a memorial for her mother. Kathryn's mother died twenty years ago. After her mother's funeral Kate noticed a rainbow in the sky. After that Katie always associates rainbows with her mother's spirit rising above our mortal plane. The prism is her reminder of the ever present intercession of the spiritual world in our physical realm. An angelic presence osmotically percolating into our reality.

Katie's attitudes can be harsh though. She decries the poaching of 'rainbows' for the LGBTQIA-community. Rainbows are a natural phenomenon and she doesn't like it that a group of people has taken the concept over. As if someone has the audacity to claim the sea as a spa bath for their own use. Or a waterfall as their personal water fountain. Actually, I get her point.

Stubborn too.
Sometimes – actually, often – Kathryn uses things that are not supposed to be used for that purpose. For example, using a rock to bang screws into a piece of wood. I have to comment on this – foolhardy, I know. I say: 'You should have a drill and screwdriver or it will not be good enough to hold whatever you are fixing.'

Actually, I get half the sentence out and she says: 'Moo! Moo!'
My attempted remonstration collapses in a chuckle. It would puzzle most people, but it is an old 'knock-knock' joke that we enjoyed many years back.

> Knock-knock.
> > Who's there.
> Interrupting cow.
> > Interruptin…
> Moo! Moo!

———–· ~~~ ————

Curiosity

As a child, she was always observant. Kathryn's brother recalls: 'Our older brother returned from a fishing expedition on the Petone pier. Katie was six years old. The vanquished snapper were lying like metallic models on the short grass in the backyard. They bore little resemblance to the iridescence and fluid flashes that we saw at the aquarium. Kate, with six-year old inquisitiveness and ingenuity, would prod the fish and, inserting a finger down its dangerous jaws, probe and pop the eyes out from within. But she didn't laugh with glee. She didn't react with horror. She was focused and curious. I had never understood why, but maybe it was an apprenticeship. Now, she is a marine biologist for NIWA[1].'

That's true. She is a scientist. But it didn't stop her idly dreaming about fanciful imaginings. When we were walking in the bush for example, with tūī and pīwakawaka flying with their usual kamikaze speed around the tangled trees, she stopped. Musing, she said: 'What do birds see? Maybe they see air currents or paths like an extra-sensory radar that make them avoid the branches in the bush. Maybe they see these golden pathways in the air like Dorothy and the yellow brick road. Maybe it is the same for butterflies? The seemingly haphazard journey of butterflies could be a streaming golden path… A golden brick road that leads to butterfly heaven…'

Or another example. At home Katie always raises the curtains well before dawn.
The dew on the outdoor furniture has been spotlighted, glistening by moon-glow and faint starlight. The patio, lawn and vege garden blend into an amorphous smudge. The two-dimensional silhouette of the fence, trees and the neighbouring houses are cardboard cutouts, all tones of blackness. The scene is like a school child's diorama, visible by the tiny eyehole.
In the half-light – or eighth-light actually – Katie explains: 'This makes me happy. I like to see the garden before the dawn because then you can be sure all the wrinkles of the day are rightly arranged for the full beatific effect of the

---

[1] NIWA = The **N**ational **I**nstitute of **W**ater and **A**tmospheric Research. [https://niwa.co.nz]

sunrise. Like maids-in-waiting arranging everything to perfection before the queen arises.'

Ah Katie! Fanciful and fantastic.

— — — — — · ~~~ — — — —

Choices

But I am all over her in the geo-terrestrial stakes. If I turn her around two or three times, she can't find where to go. She can't see landmarks, or the big picture, whereas I am always orientated.

When we are passing a river, ninety percent of the time she is puzzled. Disorientated.
'The river is flowing this way? Why?' my wife asks.
I am incredulous. I know that the sea is **this** way, the direction in which the river is returning to the ocean.
'How can you function?' I say to her.

We park the car and cross the path over the sand dunes to the sea shore. [Again, we walk a lot! Get over it!] We pause at the beach front.
'Which way should we go – north or south?' I graciously question her.
'We should go north, I think,' she says decisively.
I say to her: ' Where's north?'
She wave her arm through an arc of hundred degrees or more, and sometimes – only sometimes – she overlaps the true north in her gesture. I point out true north.
We go down the beach – southwards.
The illusion of choice.

— — — — — · ~~~ — — — —

So. My annoying but beautiful, intelligent, angelic wife.
My wife with aphasia.

Yep.
She has aphasia. PPA. Primary Progressive Aphasia.
The one there is no recovering from. A form of dementia.

About four years ago, her words 'slipped'. She couldn't remember the names of the places we went to last week and then, the name of the fish and sea creatures she was working on. She thought it was a 'senior-moment' – by the way, she loathes that description – so we didn't check with a doctor.

By the end of the year, she was fanciful about naming things in the kitchen. She called the toaster an oven, the dish-washer a sprinkler, and the coffee machine a "drinking thing". I thought she was joking but I saw from her earnestness and her undiscriminating judgement that she didn't understand her mistake in misnaming these kitchen gadgets. But when she couldn't remember the names of her grandchildren, or where the children were living, we made an appointment.

The result – PPA.

'Primary progressive aphasia – PPA – is a type of frontotemporal dementia,' the doctor tells us.
'Frontotemporal dementia is a cluster of disorders that results from the degeneration of the frontal or temporal lobes of the brain. These areas include brain tissue involved in speech and language. It seems you have non-fluent agrammatic PPA. It is quite rapid, quite anomic. Apraxia of speech may be demonstrated on single-word-level repetition tasks…'

Blah, blah, blah!

The scientific rhetoric doesn't help. My loved one is losing her words, her conversational faculties, her memories. It comes and goes, but mostly it goes. Like Kate's personality, it is a comfortable and familiar house that I and the children and grandchildren and friends all call "home"… but it is being dismantled brick by brick by an unseen but implacable, inexorable, dispassionate villain.

It is a tragedy.

Kathryn and I – we have taken steps. Together. We have our wills and bequests in order and we have our Powers of Attorney sorted. We see a speech-language pathologist every fortnight and she suggests other strategies to make communication easier. Something like use of "augmentative and alternative communication devices".

Kate has worked with computers, tablets, smart phones for many years but we have other "strategies". I have a Remembrance Album of all sorts of things that have special meaning for us:

- photographs of her mother and father and siblings;
- our travels, vacations, and expeditions;
- our children and grandchildren at various ages; our pets – cats and dogs and rabbits and birds and axolotls;
- our houses and cars;
- our favourite spots for camping expeditions;
- the waterfalls, lakes and beaches we have walked around;
- concert and play programmes;
- photo albums about her work with sea creatures;
- art prints of her favourite works…

It jogs her memory – for a little while.

And I have a dedicated playlist on her phone that she can listen to, any time. Music seems to revive her memories of certain events or people. I treasure that reprieve.

It is hard for all of us. Her words are vanishing and her sense of logical sentence structure is disappearing. Her puns are history. Her SESS is forgotten. Her spoken recall is disorganised. And the memories are fading.

But we have a secret handshake.

And, occasionally, when I least expect it, there is a surprising interruption of: 'Moo! Moo!'

6A:　　　Unspeakability

Talking is overrated.

— — — —· ~~~ — — — —

1:　　*A Place to Be*

I was obsessed by the shelves opposite the back door of our family home.
No. That is the wrong word.
Determined.

I crawled along the lino[1] from the kitchen and made for those shelves.
My brother picked me up by my jersey and returned me to the kitchen.

My brother, sister and Mum were discussing something.
They were distracted so I spun myself round and headed back. To the shelves.

I think there were four of them.
They were triangular and painted a pale yellow.

---

[1] 'lino' = linoleum, a floor covering which is made of cloth covered with a hard shiny substance.

I knew I could easily hoist myself in to the cupboard.

I wanted to hide in there. A wooden cave.
A shelter from family bustle.

I can't remember how long I was relaxing.
I suspect not long.
Maybe my brother craned me back.
Or Mum interposed.

That's my earliest memory.
I suspect it was before my first birthday.
I know I didn't argue my case with my brother.
Or my mother.
I have no words to argue with.
I didn't know "words".

Determination:

> *Desire is the key to motivation, but it's determination and commitment to an unrelenting pursuit of your goal, a commitment to excellence, that will enable you to attain the success you seek.*
> *– Mario Andretti*

————- ~~~ ————

2:   *Discovering*

When I was three and half, my sister and I ambled along the pavement, discovering.
She was five.

The gutter was always a treasure trove of strange and wonderful artefacts.
Time had no meaning as we sat down and surveyed the world beneath our feet.

Then, an amazing sight: a hedgehog!
It was quite tiny, about the size of an apple.
It crawled in slow motion along the gutter.
I reached to turn it over but my sister intercepted me.
'She has spines!' she warned. 'She will prick you!'
Good to know, I thought.

A car was backing out of the driveway beside us. I looked at my sister.
Any moment, she will alert the driver, I thought.
Any moment.

But she didn't. The car carefully reversed.
The car slowly reversed out of its driveway.
The rear tyre delicately clipped the nose of the hedgehog. A little bit of blood gushed out.
The hedgehog was motionless.

Then I realised. It was dead.
A slow motion execution.

I don't blame my sister, I really don't.
I thought my elders [my sister] would step up. But she was relying on the driver.
Since that time, I declared that I would not wait to speak out or act when I know something is not right.

Courage:
> *I learned that courage was not the absence of fear, but the triumph over it.*
> *The brave man is not he who does not feel afraid, but he who conquers that fear.*
> — Nelson Mandela.

— — — —· ~~~ — — —

3: The Fear of Cotton Wool

One day I was in the classroom in my primary school.
I was six.
A helicopter was passing over the school.
I climbed on the chair and then the desk for a better view.
I danced along the desktop and missed my footing.

I fell and whacked the back of my skull on the neighbouring desk.
The panicked teacher took me to the nearby doctor's office.

The nurse was tending the gash on the back of my head. I could feel the blood oozing out.
She faced me and grabbed cotton wool balls from the bowl in front of me.
She tended the wound.
Then she got another cotton wool ball.
And another. And another.

I was terrified. I couldn't speak. Frozen.
I thought she was packing the cotton wool balls into my skull. That my brains were leaking out and she was replacing them with cotton wool!

Later, I realised that the nurse had to have a handy rubbish bin behind me.
I should have asked her, but fear made me silent.
I determined: never again.

Confront fear:

> *Inaction creates terror, but action cures fear.*
> — Douglas Horton

—— —— —— —· ~~~ —— —— —

4: *Cops and Robbers and Strawberry Punnets*

When I was eight, my mother decided that I could walk home from school by myself.
One day, my mates and I played a game of cops and robbers.

Across from the schoolyard there was a concrete bridge above a stream.
There was a drop of, maybe, three metres from the bridge to the stream.
Six of us were the robbers.

We took turns dropping from the bridge and racing off to the path that returned to the road.

After four or five goes, I was climbing on the concrete balustrade. I was quite out of breath.
One of the robbers behind me shouted 'Get over!' and pushed me over the railing.
I fell. Luckily my arm broke my fall.

The game summarily ended and I walked home, alone.
My older brother was working on his car in the garage.
When he looked at my arm he was unequivocal: 'Hospital!'

Apparently I had a dislocated elbow and surgery was arranged.

In the morning I woke up in a hospital bed and vomited all over the sheet and blankets.
I was confused and disorientated.

A nurse heard me and she got me out of the bed and changed all the bedding.
I had not said anything to the nurse – too bewildered – but I indicated to her that I could vomit again.

"Okay," she said, fetching something from the set of drawers, "here. A container. If you're are sick again."
And she officiously left the room.

I studied the container. It was a strawberry punnet.
Clear plastic.
And holes.
Holes in the sides and the bottom of the punnet.

Even as an eight-year old, I couldn't see how it could work.

Five minutes later… **Bleeerrrrgggghhhhh!!!**
The holes in the strawberry punnet made a lovely Rorschach pattern on the bedding.

The nurse – now, the grumpy nurse – had to change
the sheets and blankets again.

Mistakes *[especially when they are someone else's]:*
> *Pointing out the mistakes of others won't
> make you better. Strive to be a positive
> influence instead.*
>> – Anon

———— ~~~ ————

5:   Painter

When I was thirteen years old, I got a job painting
the Marshalls' fence over the Christmas holidays.
The Marshall's were an old couple.
My thirteen-year-old self thought they were both a
hundred years old.

They were generous to me: the summer was hot and
they let me use their swimming pool any time; gave
me cordial with ice for morning and afternoon tea;
and roast lamb sandwiches for lunch.
It took me three and half pampered weeks to
complete the task.

For me, the roast lamb sandwich was a contentious
subject.

After Mrs Marshall served me up my cordial for morning tea, she fussed and bustled to get inside to put the roast in the oven.

It was often 27 or 30 degrees and her kitchen was stifling.
I feared for her "centenarian" health.

I wanted to say to her: 'Salad and sandwiches, cheese and crackers and cucumber would be perfect?'

But, I didn't.

I didn't think it was my place to interfere.
They were not only adult, they were ancient.
I realised that my adolescent opinion would be irrelevant to their way of "doing things".
They were stuck in their routine.

But, for myself, I vowed to accept change.

Inflexibility.
> *The only difference between a rut and a grave are the dimensions.*
> – Ellen Glasgow

Change:

> *Progress is impossible without change, and those who cannot change their minds cannot change anything.*
>
> – George Bernard Shaw

— — — —· ~~~ — — — —

6:   OCD

I used to bike from my place to the Marshalls and back every Monday to Saturday.
Every time I saw a squashed critter on the road, I had to pick it up.

Okay – I know what you are going to say. OCD[1].
Well, maybe.
But my thinking was:
'The creature was squashed on the road. If I move the carcass onto the roadside grass verge its nutrients will go in to the earth.
The cycle of life will continue.'

I don't think it was OCD because I didn't think that something bad would occur to me.

———————————

[1] OCD = Obsessive-compulsive disorder is a long-lasting disorder in which a person experiences uncontrollable and recurring thoughts (obsessions), engages in repetitive behaviours (compulsions), or both.

But I didn't want to be a waste.
I just wanted to have that death **matter**.

Even now, fifty years later, I still want it to matter.

Avoiding OCD:
> *Whenever you see small problems starting to*
> *ruin a great day, say to yourself:*
> *This Too Shall Pass.*
> > – Jocelyn Soriano

— — — — —- ~~~ — — — —

7:   Sandwich Board Destiny

When I was fifteen, I was enamoured by a girl who crossed my path almost everyday.

She had long blonde hair, kissable lips, an athletic body, a confident, upright stance and a serene face that promised intelligence.
I couldn't speak to her, adoring her from afar.

In the 1970s there was an adolescent ritual:
Friday night in the city.
The shops were closed on the weekend so they stayed open until late on Friday night.

I was looking for That Girl – and suddenly, she was there, walking past with her girl friends.

And still, like a plebeian peasant, an insignificant yokel, I couldn't speak to her.

I was part of a charity group at my school who wanted to raise some money for overseas orphans.
We decided to have a record-breaking DJ show.

We advertised and got an article in the local newspaper.
As another marketing ploy, I volunteered to wear a sandwich board about the event.

I was looking for That Girl. She was with two girl friends, gracefully approaching me.

I danced a little, pirouetting and gestured with outstretched arms, inviting her to look at the information.
Still tongue-tied, I was a mime, a teenage Marcel Marceau impersonator, an adolescent embarrassment.

But our eyes met, and a warmth and closeness enveloped me.
She commented about the project, took the clipboard and pledged her name.

With another meaningful glance at me, she continued on. I was dazed. Stunned.

When I recall that meeting, I have two words: bells; intimacy.

When she talked to me I heard bells.
Just pure, ringing, brilliant-sounding bells.
They rang, and rang, crescendoing in my mind and eventually diminishing as she went on her way.

And I felt intimacy: not the sexual kind, but more holistic and meaningful and extraordinarily fundamental in my soul.

It transformed me. Defined me.
I knew, it was destined to be.
After the DJ event, on the pretext of ensuring she honoured her pledge, I spoke to her at last.
And I got her name: Annie Williams.

Destiny:
> *Love is our true destiny. We do not find the meaning of life by ourselves alone – we find it with another.*
> –Thomas Merton

— — — —- ~~~ — — — —

8:   *Lullabies*

Annie became my girlfriend and, after eight years, my wife.

We have three children: a girl and two boys.
They had the "Stephens' gene" – wakefulness.
From the age of two until six years old they didn't nap in the daytime but they still woke at night.

Annie and I didn't have a whole night's sleep for fourteen years!

I remember I was singing lullabies to the wakeful babes.

Before I went back to my welcome bed, I stood by the door humming the melody.

I had done this countless times, but one night, for each of them, tears welled up in my eyes.

I realised someday, somehow, the world would hurt my children.
And I would not be able to prevent it or protect them.
It gutted me, that I should be so impotent.

I recall that night and it still haunts me.
I can't speak about it though.
I would do anything for them but I can't protect them from living **their** lives.

But…I'm still here, and I can still listen.
And I can still sing lullabies – sort of.

Impotence:
> *Heart, be brave. If you cannot be brave,*
> *just go. Love's glory is not a small thing.*
> \- Jalal-U-Din Rumi

— — — —- ~~~ — — — —

9:   *The Whole Hole*

One time we went for Christmas at Lake Waikaremoana.[1]
The lake and the surrounding bush and hills is an amazing place – my favourite spot in the world.

Lake Waikaremoana was formed 2,200 years ago, when a massive landslip blocked a gorge.
The gorge gradually filled with water, creating a lake up to 248 metres deep.

---

[1] Waikaremoana - 'the lake with rippling waters' (Māori).

Well, that is the scientific, geological story.
I prefer the legend.

A rangatira named Māhu told his daughter Haumapuhia to go and fetch water.
Haumapuhia refused. She was transformed into a taniwha.[1]

The taniwha Haumapuhia longed to reach the sea.
Her attempts to force her way to the sea gouged out the land and formed Lake Waikaremoana.

We gazed out on 'rippling waters' on the lake.

Then we spied a DOC[2] sign that invited us to walk on the *Onepoto Caves Track, 40 minutes*.

The track zig-zagged up and down through monumental blocks of rocks.
Some were several metres deep giving the impression of caves.
There were many, many pseudo 'caves' on the track.

About twenty minutes in I spied a sink hole beside the path.

---

[1] In Māori mythology, taniwha are large supernatural beings that live in deep pools in rivers, lakes, dark caves, or in the sea.

[2] DOC = Department of Conservation, the government agency charged with conserving Aotearoa New Zealand's natural and historic heritage.

I examined the hole but the shadows drew closer and the depths were obscured by darkness.

I grabbed the cable and climbed down on the rough 'ladder' to see what was below.

I was almost returning but slipped on the 'ladder' and fell.
It was completely black but I sensed that I was falling.

Then I stopped.
It was about two and a half seconds before I landed.
I have "arrived" at my "destination".

My right leg was banged up and my ribs and my left arm were sore.
I thought: *My leg is sore. Very sore. And ribs. My head. And it is so silent. No birdsongs, no wind in the trees, no cicadas. Wait! Something…something…*

I focused my ears and I could make out a faint sound.

A plaintive cry. 'Daddy! Daddy! Where are you?'
My youngest son.

I yelled up to him, somewhere above me: 'I have fallen down the hole. Can you get help?'

I heard a muffled '…get help…' and he left, presumably (and actually) for his brother, sister and Annie to come back and rescue me.

Long story short, I was there for six hours.
Annie located a tramper, and he went out to raise the alarm.
A helicopter and Search and Rescue team arrived and they got me out of there.

[Just saying, that the abseiling rope they tied to me could have 'fixed' me so my three children were the only children I could have.]

For the six hours, I couldn't communicate with anyone sensibly.
Only one or two words.
Almost a "vow of silence."

This experience was thought provoking and illuminating. Life-changing.

I missed communicating to my whānau[1].
I could grunt and say 'Okay' but not much else.

For their part, I could only hear some snippets of information.

---

[1] whānau = [extended} family

Some encouragements. And updates.

So, I used my time reflecting on my life and what I have done with it.
Self-contemplation and meditation was forced on me.

But it was good to know what was important to me.
Whānau.

Love for whānau:
> *To 'listen' another's soul into a condition of disclosure and discovery may be almost the greatest service any human being ever performs for another.*
> *– Douglas V. Steere*

— — — —.. ~~~ — — — —

10:   *Different Strokes*

January 2015.
A Tuesday morning. Annie was fixing toast for breakfast.
I was just getting out of my bed.
But something was strange.
I stumbled down the stairs.
I wanted to say something to Annie but no words emerged.

I was collapsing.
My right side was paralysed, my limbs weren't working.
Things were foggy, fuzzy, incoherent.

I woke up in hospital.
Annie and the children were looking at me with a mixture of concern and relief.
I wanted to placate them. But my voice didn't work.

Apparently, I had suffered a stroke.
The doctors gave me the 'clot-busting' injection, so my limbs were free.
But my communication was gone.
Talking, reading writing… they were all gone.

I had aphasia.

The rudiments were there.
I remembered that I could speak, read and write.
Before my stroke,
But I couldn't remember **how** to do it.
Or **why I should**.

My whānau showed me that my aphasia was isolating me.
I had occupational therapy, speech therapy, curative eurythmy, and music therapy.
Still my speech was – suspect.

It's hard.
Depressing.
Frustrating.
I can't be what I was anymore.
Sometimes I think I have been diminished.

Now, so many years later, I can write, text, or email
what I want to say.
It takes me five times as long.

And I can read – but my concentration span is
severely curtailed.

Talking?
I'm still getting stuck on words.
They are on the tip of my brain but can't come out of
my mouth.

So, I am conversation-averse.
Discussion-discontinuoness.
Talking-shmalking

But a hug can convey much more than an oratorical
delivery.

My speaking is suspect but the people close to me,
understand me.
Most of the time.

Some other people try.
Some others give up.
Some shun me or avoid me.
Or they think I'm retarded.
Or drunk.

I think they are victims of their own insecurities.

And that's okay.

———— ——· ~~~ ——— —

11:   *Virtues:*

Have you seen what I was expressing in my
memories?

Most of my important lessons were talk-free.
That many of the virtues that I have were attained
when I didn't speak at all.

I cannot talk properly anymore. But that's okay.
Sometimes, lack of talking is a blessing.

Unspeakability rules!

Failure?

*Failure is only the opportunity to begin again,
this time more intelligently.*
> – Henry Ford

*By three methods we may learn wisdom:
First, by reflection, which is noblest;
Second, by imitation, which is easiest;
and third by experience, which is the bitterest.*
> — Confucius

6B: Unspeakability

Talking is overrated.

— — — —- ~~~ — — — —

1:   *A Place to Be*

I was obsessed by the shelves opposite the back door of our family home in Wilford Street, Lower Hutt[1].
No. Not obsessed. That is the wrong word.
Determined. That's it. Determined.

I crawled along the lino[2] from the kitchen and made for those shelves. My brother picked me up by my jersey and redirected me to the cosy kitchen. My brother, sister and Mum were having morning tea on the kitchen table: cocoa and Girl Guide biscuits with butter. They were discussing something – I didn't know what. I didn't understand. They were distracted so I spun myself round and headed back. To the shelves.

I think there were four of them.

They were triangular – painted timber boards closing off the angle of the room. I don't suppose I knew about right angles and Pythagoras or isosceles triangles and axes of symmetry, but the triangular shelf was somehow pleasing. Aesthetically.

---

[1] Lower Hutt – a city just north of Wellington, the capital city. Another example of boring colonial naming. Just north of Lower Hutt is, you guessed, Upper Hutt.

[2] 'lino' = linoleum, a floor covering which is made of cloth covered with a hard shiny substance.

They were painted a pale yellow. That was doubly pleasing. The lower shelf was only ten millimetres off the floor and the second shelf was about thirty centimetres above. I didn't know about millimetres, or centimetres, or measurements or mathematics, but I knew I could easily hoist myself in to the cupboard.

I wanted to hide in there. A wooden cave. A shelter from family bustle. I had two brothers and two sisters and they were always busy with bikes and dolls and bows and arrows and cops and robbers and dolls' prams and tea parties and cats and kittens…the business of family life and play things.

So I went for it, crawling into the space, turning myself around like a seal sunning myself on a rock, looking at the 'ocean' in the backyard.

I can't remember how long I was relaxing. I suspect not long. Maybe my brother returned to crane me back to the kitchen. Or Mum interposed. Or I was distracted by something else and refocused myself for another task. A determined effort, no doubt.

That's my earliest memory, crawling to the cupboards.

I know, later, that my Dad attached doors to make the shelves in to cupboards so my sister couldn't accommodate her many dolls in there. So it was before that. And I was crawling, not toddling, so I suspect it was before my first birthday. Nine or ten months old. I know I didn't argue my case with my brother. Or my mother.

I have no words to argue with. I didn't know "words".

Determination:

> *"Desire is the key to motivation, but it's determination and commitment to an unrelenting pursuit of your goal, a commitment to excellence, that will enable you to attain the success you seek."*
> – Mario Andretti

————————-· ~~~ ————

2:   Discovering

When I was three and half, my sister and I ambled along the pavement on our street, discovering.
She was five.

The gutter was always a treasure trove of strange and wonderful artefacts: stones and gravel, gooey mud, a delta of patterned rivers of silt and sand, a broken bracelet, bottle tops, autumn leaves, ants and beetles...   We were entranced. Time had no meaning as we sat down on our haunches and surveyed the world beneath our feet.

Then, an amazing sight: a hedgehog! I knew the creature from such stories as Beatrix Potter's "Mrs Tiggy-Winkle" and nursery rhymes. My sister and I studied the hedgehog carefully. It was quite tiny, about the size of an apple. I guess it was an infant. It crawled in slow motion along the gutter, its slender legs raised and wavered a bit before stepping onto the concrete as it moved its weight forward. It leaned to the left but the gutter kerb kept it steady, an obese circus clown or an inebriated vagrant. I reached to turn it over but my sister, thankfully, intercepted me. 'She has spines!' she warned. 'She will prick you!' *Good to know,* I thought.

We were so intent on our observation, that we didn't realise that a car was backing out of the driveway beside us. My sister stood up and looked at the car. She looked at the driver. I looked at my sister. *Any moment, she will alert the driver,* I thought. *Any moment.*

But she didn't. The car carefully reversed. I guess the driver was carefully missing **us**. I looked at the hedgehog. I looked at my sister. I looked at the hedgehog. Maybe the car would miss the creature? I vacillated – alternatively looking between my sister, the car and the hedgehog like a fearful spectator in a pistol duel.

When the car slowly reversed out of its driveway, the rear tyre delicately clipped the nose of the hedgehog. A little bit of blood gushed out. The car reversed onto the road, paused, changed gear and sped away. The hedgehog was motionless. I gazed at it, expecting its slow motion to be resumed.

Then I realised. It was dead. A slow motion execution.

It was a seminal moment in my life. I don't blame my sister, I really don't. I thought my elders [my sister] would step up. But she was relying on the driver. She expected that the driver would know and understand – but, of course, the driver had no idea about the life and death situation we were witnessing.

Since that time, I declared that I would not wait to speak out or act when I know something is not right, even if people senior to me are involved.

Courage:

> *"I learned that courage was not the absence of fear,*
> *but the triumph over it. The brave man is not he who*
> *does not feel afraid, but he who conquers that fear."*
> — Nelson Mandela.

— — — —· ~~~ — — —

3: The Fear of Cotton Wool

One day, when I was six, I was in the classroom in my primary school. A helicopter was passing over the school. All the kids got up from their seats and crowded to the window to see the 'whirly-bird' flying by. [It was 1965 and at that time, a chopper was a remarkable event.]

I can top that, I thought as I climbed on the chair and then the desk for a better view. In my excitement, I danced along the desktop and missed my footing. I plummeted backwards and whacked the back of my skull on the neighbouring desk. The panicked teacher took me to the nearby doctor's office in her car.

I was quite groggy – shock, I guess. I didn't hear or see the doctor's assessment or prognosis. When the nurse was tending the gash on the back of my head my mind cleared. I could feel the blood oozing out my head – a sticky mess.

The nurse faced me and grabbed cotton wool balls from the bowl in front of me. She tended the wound – I could feel her dabbing and sponging the cotton wool on the injury. Then she got another cotton wool ball. And another. And another.

I was terrified. I couldn't speak. Frozen. I thought she was packing the cotton wool balls into my skull. That my brains were leaking out and she was replacing them with cotton wool!

Later, I realised that the nurse had to have a handy rubbish bin behind me. When she dabbed my head, she chucked the bloodied cotton wool balls in the bin behind, and reached for another ball. I should have asked her, but fear made me silent.

I determined: never again.

Confront fear:

> *"Inaction creates terror, but action cures fear."*
> – Douglas Horton

———— —· ~~~ ————

4: *Cops and Robbers and Strawberry Punnets*

When I was eight, my mother decided that I could walk the two kilometres home from school by myself rather than be escorted by my siblings. My siblings and I were delighted – for different, independent reasons. For them: freedom from responsibility. Me: independence.

One day, after school, my mates and I played a game of cops and robbers. Juvenile – but what I can say! I was only eight.

Across from the schoolyard there was a concrete bridge above a stream that entered a culvert under the road. There was a drop of, maybe, three metres from the bridge's balustrade to the grass bordering the stream's trickle.

Six of us were the robbers. [I believe we didn't designate anyone to take the role of the cop. Too mundane. Robbers were more exciting!] We took turns dropping from the bridge to the ground and racing off to the path that returned to the road. Then we did it again, faster and faster, chasing each other like puppies. Or, apparently, eight-year old robbers. Not six robbers but a gang, a mob, a veritable horde of villains, jumping down to begin their dastardly deeds.

After four or five reiterations of our scampering robber rigmarole, I was climbing on the concrete balustrade. Well, struggling, I have to admit. I was not so trim as now. Some of the kids even called me 'pudgy'. I was quite out of breath and, seemingly, the bridge was taller and the balustrade was broader... One of the more choleric robbers – I think it was "Speedster" Laing – was behind me and he shouted 'Get over!' and pushed me over the railing. I fell. Well, plummeted really. Luckily my arm broke my fall.

Four of my mates crowded around me with comforting but fatuous comments like 'It's not so bad' or 'No blood!' or 'I had that last week'. "Speedster" Laing sped off, fearful of recriminations. The game summarily ended and I walked home, alone. Tearful, sore and sort of guilty, I crept along the two kilometre footpath until I reached our driveway.

My older brother was working on his vintage car in the garage. When he looked at my arm he was unequivocal: 'Hospital!'

Apparently I had a dislocated elbow and surgery was arranged. Much of the rest of the evening and night was a blur as the hospital arranged to operate and I was anaesthetised. About two or three o'clock in the morning I woke up in a hospital bed and vomited all over the sheet and blankets that covered me. I was confused and disorientated but a nurse heard me and she got me out of the bed into a chair and changed all the bedding. She tucked me in [much rougher because she didn't have my mother's gentle touch] and went to leave.

I had not said anything to the nurse – too bewildered – but I indicated to her by gestures that I could vomit again. "Okay," she said, fetching something from the set of drawers, "here. A container. If you're are sick again." And she officiously left the room.

I studied the container. It was a strawberry punnet. Clear plastic. And holes. Holes in the sides and the bottom of the punnet. Even as an eight-year old, I couldn't see how it could work. *Maybe it is a some sort a vomit colander for research purposes?* I thought. *Maybe the holes will close up? Maybe it was a medical magic item?* [Remember, Hogwarts didn't exist at this time!]

Five minutes later… **Bleeerrrrgggghhhhh!!!**

The holes in the strawberry punnet made a lovely Rorschach pattern on the bedding.
The nurse – now, the grumpy nurse – had to change the sheets and blankets again.

***Mistakes** [especially when they are someone else's]:*
> *"Pointing out the mistakes of others won't make you better. Strive to be a positive influence instead."*
> – Anon

– – – – –– ~~~ – – – –

5:   *Painter*

When I was thirteen years old, I got a job painting the Marshalls' fence over the Christmas holidays. The Marshall's were an old couple that had a flash house on a lifestyle-block before they called them lifestyle-blocks. My thirteen-year-old self thought they were both a hundred years old.

The property was situated at Tamahere, just south of Hamilton and about six kilometres from my house. The fence was post and four-rail timber construction that bordered the property on three sides – about 300 metres of fencing. I was tasked with painting it with Resene Lumbersider in a colour named Burnt Sienna.

They were generous to me: the summer was hot and they let me use their swimming pool any time; gave me cordial with ice for morning and afternoon tea; and roast lamb sandwiches for lunch. They didn't need to do that for me, and I hope I was grateful, or whatever 'grateful' sounds like from a thirteen year old. It took me three and half pampered weeks to complete the task.

For me, the roast lamb sandwich was a contentious subject. Not because I was vegetarian though – that came later. After Mrs Marshall served me up my cordial for morning tea, she fussed and bustled to get inside to put the roast in the oven every Wednesday and Saturday. It clearly agitated her. Roast lamb with potatoes, carrots, onions and the accompanying gravy.

As I said, it was a hot summer and it was often 27 or 30 degrees and her kitchen was stifling. I feared for her "centenarian" health. I wanted to say to her: 'Surely, you don't need to serve a roast luncheon every Wednesday and

Saturday to Mr Marshall with the summer sun beating down. Salad and sandwiches, cheese and crackers and cucumber would be perfect?'

But, I didn't. Despite my three-and-half-old resolution about people senior to me, I didn't think it was my place to interfere. They were not only adult, they were ancient and I realised that, after so many years, my adolescent opinion would be irrelevant to their way of "doing things". They were stuck in their routine.

But, for myself, I vowed to accept change.

Inflexibility:

> *"The only difference between a rut and a grave are the dimensions."*
> – Ellen Glasgow

Change:

> *"Progress is impossible without change, and those who cannot change their minds cannot change anything."*
> – George Bernard Shaw

———— ——·~~~ ————

6:   OCD [1]

Now, I am going to say something I have never told anyone. Never.

I used to bike from my place to the Marshalls and back every Monday to Saturday.

---

[1] OCD = Obsessive-compulsive disorder is a long-lasting disorder in which a person experiences uncontrollable and recurring thoughts (obsessions), engages in repetitive behaviours (compulsions), or both.

Every time I saw a squashed critter on the road, I had to pick it up and shift to the side of the highway.

Okay – I know what you are going to say. OCD. Well, maybe. But my thinking was: 'The tarmac or asphalt is impervious. The creature was squashed on the road so its bodily nutrients can't go anywhere. If I move the carcass onto the roadside grass verge or hedge its nutrients will go in to the earth, and the cycle of life will continue.' [I was always "green" at heart.]

I thought my task was reasonable, but actually it was more work than I anticipated. In my six kilometres to Tamahere and the six kilometres back home, I often had to pick up fifteen or twenty squashed critters. Each day. Birds – lots of birds – hedgehogs, possums, rabbits. Sometimes frogs. And some I couldn't clearly identify – I had to press some sticks into a makeshift shovel.

I don't think it was OCD because I didn't think that something bad would occur to me if I didn't pick them up. But I didn't want to be a waste. I just wanted to have that death, that animal sacrifice – admittedly unsuspecting – **matter**.

Even now, fifty years later, I still want it to matter.
[But I don't pick up squashed critters any more. Usually.]

Avoiding OCD:
"Whenever you see small problems starting to ruin a great day, say to yourself: This Too Shall Pass."
– Jocelyn Soriano

— — — —- ~~~ — — — —

7: *Sandwich Board Destiny*

When I was fifteen, I was enamoured by a girl who crossed my path almost everyday. Literally, on weekdays. I was going south to north across the crest of the hill to my school. She climbed the hill walking west and descended to the east to **her** school. She had long blonde hair, kissable lips, an athletic body, a confident, upright stance and a serene face that promised intelligence.

Sometimes I delayed my progress, loitering in the hedges and bushes on the footpath beside the neighbouring houses, until I was sure she was coming up the hill. I engineered several encounters, but she always got out of the way, avoiding the imminent collision, like a serene swan gliding from sedentary toad. She didn't look at me and I couldn't speak to her, adoring her from afar.

In the 1970s there was an adolescent ritual: Friday night in the city. The shops were closed on the weekend so they stayed open until late on Friday night. Youths gathered in the main street: the long-haired boys mooching about at the kerbside with studied poses; the girls would strut and prance past. The boys would wolf-whistle at the girls and made obvious and obscene gestures, thrusting their pelvis suggestively. The girls giggled and flirted with side-long glances, rolling hips and flipping their hair. [Now, in the 2020s, it seems so twee and hopelessly unsophisticated.]

Me? I was not so bold or brazen. And I was looking for That Girl – and suddenly, she was there, walking past with her girl friends, scanning the shoe and clothing shops. She was not caught up with coquetry like the other girls though. She was too fine for that. Her stance was regal, casually gracious, incuriously exalted. And still, like a plebeian peasant, an insignificant yokel, I couldn't speak to her.

I was part of a charity group at my school who wanted to raise some money for overseas orphans in the Pacific islands. We decided to have a record-breaking DJ show. The DJ was senior at the school and he was determined to perform a show for more than 72 hours in the front window of his father's shop in the main street. Apparently, if he succeeded, we could apply to have this event in the Guinness Book of Records.

We advertised and got an article in the local newspaper so people could call in and pledge some money. As another marketing ploy, I volunteered [God knows why?] to wear a sandwich board. For three Friday nights I walked up and down in the main street promoting the event. The sandwich board "bread" – front and back – outlined what we were planning to do. The filling – me – had a clipboard for people to pledge.

With bated [baited?] breath, I was looking for That Girl but I didn't see her. Until the third Friday. She was with two girl friends, gracefully approaching me. I guess the sandwich board blew my cover as a "cool dude" so I decided I could "ham it up". I danced a little, pirouetting and bowing as well as I could – after all I had a sandwich board attached to me – and gestured with outstretched arms, inviting her to look at the information. Still tongue-tied, I was a mime, a teenage Marcel Marceau impersonator, an adolescent embarrassment.

But our eyes met, and a warmth and closeness enveloped me. She commented about the project, took the clipboard and pledged her name, and gaily, with another meaningful glance at me, continued on.

I was dazed. Stunned.

When I recall that meeting, I have two words: bells; intimacy.

When she talked to me I heard bells. No tinny jangling bells. No 'wedding bells'. No Big Ben bells or alarm bells. Just pure, ringing, brilliant-sounding bells, like Tibetan Tingsha cymbals[1]. They rang, and rang, and rang, crescendoing in my mind and eventually diminishing as she went on her way.

And I felt intimacy: not the sexual kind, but more holistic and meaningful and extraordinarily fundamental in my soul.

It transformed me. Defined me.
I knew, it was destined to be.

After the DJ event, on the pretext of ensuring she honoured her pledge, I spoke to her at last.
And I got her name: Annie Williams.

[The DJ: he made it by the way – 72 hours – and the event was entered in the Guinness Book of Records, now surpassed!]

Destiny:
"Love is our true destiny. We do not find the meaning of life by ourselves alone – we find it with another."
– Thomas Merton

————·～～～ ————

---

[1] Tingsha are small cymbals used in prayer and rituals by Tibetan Buddhist practitioners. Two cymbals are joined together by a leather strap or chain. The cymbals are struck together producing a clear and high pitched, ringing tone.

8: *Lullabies*

Annie became my girlfriend and, after eight years, my wife.

We have three children: a girl, a boy five years younger and another boy three years younger than him. They had the "Stephens' gene" – wakefulness. From the age of two until six years old they didn't nap in the daytime but they still woke once or twice in the night. Annie and I didn't have a whole night's sleep for fourteen years!

I remember, when each of them was six months or so, I was on duty to sing lullabies and tuck the wakeful babes in. When they were settled, before I went back to my welcome bed, I stood by the door humming the melody of the lullabies in a staged decrescendo. I had done this countless times, but one night, for each of them, I gazed at the little infants and tears welled up in my eyes. A transcendent joy, but edged with a sense of mourning. They were so precious to me. I realised someday, somehow, the world would hurt my children and I would not be able to prevent it or protect them. It gutted me, that I should be so impotent. The emotion, the dichotomy of ecstatic joy and crushing guilt almost overwhelmed me.
One night. For each one.

Now that they are grown, I recall that night for the three of them and it still haunts me. I can't speak about it though. I broached the subject with Annie but the words didn't convey the horror of my helplessness, my impotent guilt. I would do anything for them that my morality will allow but I can't protect them from the vicissitudes and the fragilities of living **their** lives.

But...I'm still here, and I can still listen. And I can still sing lullabies – sort of.

Impotence:

"Heart, be brave. If you cannot be brave, just go. Love's glory is not a small thing."
   – Jalal-U-Din Rumi

————- ~~~ ————

9:   The Whole Hole

One time we went for Christmas at Onepoto[1], a hamlet at the south side of Lake Waikaremoana.[2] The lake and the surrounding bush and hills in the magical Urewera region is an amazing place – my favourite spot in the world.

Onepoto consisted of about thirty-five baches and houses, isolated by bush. Our friends were going elsewhere for Christmas and they told us we could have their bach[3] for a fortnight. It was a cosy cottage with four rooms – two bedrooms, a lounge/kitchen/dining room and a bathroom/toilet/shower/washing machine/freezer room and a deck outside the lounge.
Perfectly isolated, it seemed that we were the only people there and from our deck we could see the verdant and dense bush, glimpse the overweight kererū in the kōwhai branches, and hear the tūī and korimako singing and echoing their bell-like compositions.

---

[1] Onepoto = 'short beach' is the hamlet at the southern end of Lake Waikaremoana.

[2] Waikaremoana - 'the lake with rippling waters' (Māori).

[3] 'bach' (pronounced 'batch') in Aotearoa New Zealand is a holiday home. Te Waipounamu, the South Island, calls its holiday homes 'cribs'.

Lake Waikaremoana was formed 2,200 years ago, when a massive landslip blocked a gorge on the Waikaretāheke River. The gorge gradually filled with water, creating a lake up to 248 metres deep.
Well, that is the scientific, geological story.

I prefer the legend. A rangatira named Māhu told his daughter Haumapuhia to go and fetch water. Haumapuhia refused. Enraged, her father drowned her and threw her body into the waters, where she was transformed into a taniwha.[1] The taniwha Haumapuhia longed to reach the sea. She tried to go northward, but the Huiarau range prevented her; she tried to go east but failed again. Her attempts to force her way to the sea gouged out the land and formed Lake Waikaremoana. Her final effort south formed the outlet to the lake at Onepoto. Exhausted, it was here that Haumapuhia was overtaken by daylight. She remains to this day in the form of a rock.

We went to that rock. We gazed out on 'rippling waters' on the lake. Then we spied a DOC[2] sign that invited us to walk on the *Onepoto Caves Track, 40 minutes*. The track meandered and zig-zagged up and down through dense bush and monumental blocks of rocks. If you have a drawer of lego pieces and you tip them on the floor from a great height, they will stack up higgle-piggledy. These rocks were stacked up like those dropped lego pieces, massive blocks of stone that formed ledges and balconies and lean-tos. Some were several metres deep giving the impression of caves. There were many, many pseudo 'caves' on the track.

---

[1] In Māori mythology, taniwha are large supernatural beings that live in deep pools in rivers, lakes, dark caves, or in the sea.

[2] DOC = Department of Conservation, the government agency charged with conserving Aotearoa New Zealand's natural and historic heritage.

About twenty minutes in I spied a sink hole beside the path. It was like an uncovered man-hole in the street – completely circular and one metre in diameter. There was a broken cable tied around a nearby tree and some footprints down in the soil around the sink hole, like crude steps. I examined the hole but the shadows drew closer and the depths were obscured by darkness. Annie and the children were going on so I told my youngest son that I was 'just checking out the sink hole'. I grabbed the cable and climbed down on the rough 'ladder' to see what was below. Thank goodness my son tarried!

I was about two metres down, just below the level of the path, and I saw, about another metre below, that the sink hole was apparently closed. I was almost returning but slipped on the 'ladder' and fell. Hidden by a lump of soil there was an opening on the side of the hole and I popped through on the other side, like a champagne cork. It was completely black but I sensed that I was falling.

I can check it out: a physics problem. A body falling, acceleration ten metres per second per second...et cetera, et cetera...
Legend tells us that we can see that all of our life before we die. I didn't die, obviously, but I distinctly recall my thoughts on my journey to the "centre of the earth". It was not about my life, but what I got myself into. I thought: *Ah - I am falling. That was dumb – slipping. Somewhere I will reach the bottom. I don't want to damage my spine. That would not be good. A spine injury would not be good. I should turn over so my legs and arms will cushion the blow. Hopefully my head and my vital organs will be protected by my ribs.*

I turned over. Face first.

Then I stopped. It was about two and a half seconds before I landed. I have "arrived" at my "destination".

My right leg was banged up and my ribs and my left arm were sore. I looked around. Well – not 'looked'. The blackness was pervasive. I sensed non-ocular things: *Fresh, chill air. It seemed to be – well, earthy. It was like being in a – doh! A cave! Actually a cave, not a pseudo-cave. My leg is sore. Very sore. And ribs. Bugger. Sore as! Nothing else? That is a drip of water on my hand. My head. And it is so silent. No birdsongs, no wind in the trees, no cicadas. Wait! Something…something…*

I focused my ears and I could make out a faint sound.
A plaintive cry. 'Daddy! Daddy! Where are you?' My youngest son. I yelled up to him, somewhere above me: 'I have fallen down the hole. Can you get help?'

'Daddy! Daddy! Where are you? Where are you?' he reiterated.

Obviously my calling was muffled by the cave system. I redoubled my efforts and at last he heard: 'Fallen' and 'Help'. I heard a muffled '…get help…' and he left, presumably (and actually) for his brother, sister and Annie to come back and rescue me.

Gradually the blackness dissolved into shadowy greys. There was a faint glow above me. Daylight? I was about to limp in this direction when I realised, as I got used to the semi-darkness and my eyes adjusted, that it was not sunlight. It was glowworms[1]. I discovered that on a ledge about one metre wide and six metres long. The "champagne bottle neck" was twenty metres above me. Below me was a thirty, forty metre drop to rocks. The ledge's surface was soft soil that had washed out of the earth above – a relatively soft landing. [My right leg and ribs didn't agree!] If I had missed the ledge entirely – well – I would be dead.

Long story short, I was there for six hours. Annie located a tramper, and he went out to raise the alarm. The volunteer Fire Brigade from Tuai and the police from Wairoa[2] came but they didn't have the proper authority to rescue me from this situation. [Annie surreptitiously used her raincoat to cover the sign above the sinkhole that advised people to "Don't Go Into This Hole".] At last, a helicopter and Search and Rescue team arrived and a doctor from Hawke's Bay hospital and, with maximum difficulty, they got me out of there.
[Just saying, that the abseiling rope they tied to me when they hoisted me out of the hole could have 'fixed' me so my three children were the only children I could have.]

Some groups have a process of "reflective retreats" – religious groups, or yoga or wellness facilitators. My "cave incarceration" was a retreat. A forced and painful retreat. With the injury to my ribs, the effort to make myself heard was distressing. For the six hours, I couldn't communicate with anyone sensibly – only one or two words. Almost a "vow of silence." This experience was thought provoking and illuminating. Life-changing.

---

[1] glowworms = Arachnocampa luminosa, commonly known as New Zealand glowworm or simply glowworm, is a species of fungus gnat endemic to Aotearoa New Zealand. The larval stage and the imago produce a blue-green bioluminescence. The species is known to dwell in caves and on sheltered banks in native bush where humidity is high.

[2] Tuai and Wairoa are a village and town just south of the lake.

I missed my whānau[1]. I missed communicating to my whānau. I could grunt and say 'Okay' but not much else. For their part, I could only hear some snippets of information. Some encouragements. And updates.

So, I used my time reflecting on my life and what I have done with it. Expected, I guess, after my brush with mortality. Self-contemplation and meditation was forced on me – and it was good to know what was important to me. Whānau.

Love for whānau:

> *"To 'listen' another's soul into a condition of disclosure and discovery may be almost the greatest service any human being ever performs for another."*
> – Douglas V. Steere

————–·~~~ ————

10: *Different Strokes*

January 2015.

A Tuesday morning. Annie was fixing chai [real chai, Indian-style] and toast for breakfast. On the floor above, I was just getting out of my bed. But something was strange. My eyes didn't belong to me anymore. I was observing myself behind and above my body. I was listing to the right as if I was fighting a gale. I stumbled down the stairs.

I could see Annie and I wanted to say something about my strange feelings but no words emerged. She caught me, expecting an embrace but she realised that I was collapsing. My right side was paralysed, my limbs weren't working. Things were foggy, fuzzy, incoherent. I think I heard a phone,

---

[1] whānau = [extended] family (Māori)

and Annie was there, and some green uniformed people were lugging me down the steps to the front door. I was prone. Sirens. Bright fluorescent lights flashing like upside-down road markings. People studying at me. I felt like a frog, an insect, a specimen. Again I was absent from my body. The rest was blank.

I woke up in hospital. Annie and the children were looking at me with a mixture of concern and relief. I wanted to placate them. That I was okay. But my voice didn't work. Doctors and nurses and therapists and my family came into my bedside and I pieced the story together. Sort of.

Apparently, I had suffered a hemiparesis, a middle cerebral artery territory infarct. In a word, a stroke. We were handy to the hospital, so the doctors gave me the 'clot-busting' injection, so my limbs were free. But my communication was gone. Talking, reading writing… they were all gone.

I had aphasia.

For two or three months, I didn't realise the problem. The rudiments were there. I remembered that I could speak, read and write. Before. But I couldn't remember **how** to do it. Or **why I should**. In the colloquial sense, I was a "stunned mullet"[1] – an apt description. My whānau were more concerned than me.

Gradually, with a lot of help from my whānau, I realised that my aphasia was isolating me. I had occupational therapy, speech therapy, curative eurythmy, and music therapy. The

---

[1] An Australasian saying: dazed, stupefied, uncomprehending, unconscious. The phrase alludes to the goggle-eyed stare (and sometimes gaping mouth) of a fish (a mullet) that has been recently caught and made unconscious.

angelic therapists were compassionate but rigorous and I semi-recovered my reading and writing. [Obviously – I have not employed a ghost writer!] Still my speech was, well, suspect.

It's hard. Depressing. Frustrating.
I can't be what I was anymore. It has been taken out of my control. Sometimes I think I have been diminished. A half person. Some part of my persona has faded away like a sandcastle in the tide.

My stroke was in January 2015. Now, so many years later, I can write, text, or email what I want to say. It takes me five times as long, employing spell-checkers, dictionaries and thesaurus apps **all** the time, and I have to re-edit the prose three or four times – but I **can** write, text or email. And I can read – but my concentration span is severely curtailed.

Talking? I'm still getting stuck on words. Genders. Measurements. Phone numbers. They are on the tip of my brain but can't come out of my mouth. Often I get the beginning of a word but I can't sort the right end. My mental dictionary has found the correct page but can't determine which word is appropriate. And when I get it right, the topic or the subject has moved on for everyone else.

So, I am conversation-averse. Discussion-discontinuoness.
Talking-shmalking

A hug can convey much more than an oratorical delivery.
I can hug Annie, my children and partners, my grandchildren and they know what it means. And sure, my speaking is suspect but the people close to me, understand me. Most of the time. The real me.
Some other people try. Some others give up.

Some shun me or avoid me. Or they think I'm retarded. Or drunk.
I think they are victims of their own insecurities.

And that's okay.

11:   Virtues:

Most of my important lessons were talk-free. What I realise
now – now when aphasia has reordered and reinvented my
projected biography and all the things I wanted to do – that
many of the virtues I have sought to acquire in my life were
attained when I didn't speak at all.

Other senses were operating: sense of humour, sense of
balance, sense of justice and courage and compassion.

I cannot talk properly anymore. But that's okay.
Sometimes, lack of talking is a blessing.
Unspeakability rules!

Failure?

> *"Failure is only the opportunity to begin again, this
> time more intelligently."*
> – Henry Ford

> *"By three methods we may learn wisdom:*
> *First, by reflection, which is noblest;*
> *Second, by imitation, which is easiest;*
> *and third by experience, which is the bitterest."*
> — Confucius

— — — —- ~~~ — — — —

7A:

Sonder [1]
An invisible disability

An article for *Touchstone Magazine,*
June edition 2024
Author: Shami Fergusson

Sometimes, an article haunts you.
You think you are revealing something significant.
Something profound.
But this story revealed something about myself.

I discovered I have a disability.

The editor of *Touchstone Magazine* summoned me
to her office.

She trumpeted:
'A general interest article. A 'feel-good' story.
Someone who has a disability. But has overcome it.
Raised themselves up. Something uplifting.
You know what I mean… Go…go…go…'

Of course, I went to my trusted source. My mother!

---

[1] [Spoiler Alert: The meaning of 'Sonder' is the meaning of the whole story.
When you read the story, the meaning should be clear, but I have included
the meaning of 'Sonder' on the last page.]

'Hmmm. A cup of tea?,' she unhelpfully said to me
when I told her my problem.
I declined, impatient.

She sipped, contemplating the ceiling for a minute,
and said:
'Well…one of my friends…her husband had a
stroke. He is almost recovered, but his talking is
affected. Aphasia! Yes, aphasia.

'She said that it is a communication something.
Most people can't see it as a disability.
He recovered …physically… but his speech is…
well, suspect.'

I excused myself and went to the car. I typed
'*aphasia*' into my phone.

Dr Google displayed:
About 22,700,000 results (0.35 seconds).

I picked one at random from the first five and
discovered it was:

"a language disorder caused by damage in a specific
area of the brain that controls language expression

and comprehension. Aphasia leaves a person unable to communicate effectively with others."

Well done, Mum. This could be it.

— — — —. ~~~ — — — —

I typed all sorts questions about aphasia.
I typed 'aphasia near here' and Dr Google noted that there is an:

    Aphasia Group Meeting in our local
    Community Centre every Thursday.
    10:00-12:30
    Community Aphasia Advisor from AphasiaNZ[1].

Perfect. It was a Thursday.
It was twenty past twelve.
And the Community Centre was ten minutes away!

I went to the Community Centre.
I thought everyone had left, but suddenly I saw a young woman.
I opened the door.

---

[1] Aphasia New Zealand (AphasiaNZ) Charitable Trust is a national organisation and registered charity, providing support services, resources, education, and information for anyone in New Zealand living with or affected by aphasia. One of the services is CAA - Community Aphasia Advisor. Currently they have fifteen CAA in centres around Aotearoa New Zealand. [https://www.aphasia.org.nz/ - downloaded 15 April 2024]

'Can I help you?' she asked.
I spoke with more confidence than I felt: 'Kia ora.
My name is Shami and I write for *Touchstone Magazine*.
I want to write an article about aphasia.'

'Ah!' Her look was delighted and charming.
'Okay. I guess you have the right place.
I am Sue. Sue Lee. Come in, come in.'

She gestured to a chair and we sat down.
'I am the CAA for this area,' she explained.
'The Community Aphasia Advisor, for Aphasia New Zealand. What do you know about aphasia?'

'Well…I know it is a communication disorder.'

'Well…that's essentially true,' she laughed genially.

'There is a damage to the brain centres of language expression and comprehension.
It could be an accident, or disease that affects the brain.
But the main cause of aphasia is stroke.

'Do you know how many people in Aotearoa New Zealand suffer from stroke each year?'

'No, I don't' I admitted.

'About 9,500 strokes are experienced every year. That's one every 55 minutes.[1]
We estimate that twenty-five or thirty thousand people in Aotearoa New Zealand have aphasia.

'These are the people I work with.
Aphasia means that they can't speak clearly, or they miss words, or name them wrongly.
It is like a pathway from their brain and their mouth is … um… distracted.'

I nodded. 'So…how can you treat them? How can you give their speech back to them?'

'So…how does your group work?' I said.

———— —- ~~~ ————

Sue lead me through some processes that are helpful.

---

[1] Aotearoa New Zealand has a population of five million.
In UK, 100,000 people have strokes each year. There are 1.3 million stroke survivors in the UK.
In Canada, over 50,000 new strokes—that's one stroke every ten minutes. About 300,000 Canadians are living with the effects of stroke.
In the United States, about 795,000 people suffer a stroke each year. Someone has a stroke every forty seconds. There are over seven million stroke survivors live in United States and two-thirds of them are currently disabled. This includes two million people with aphasia.

Long story short, she outlined seven important points:

1: Intelligence remains the same

The brain is okay – however they may find it hard to talk, write, read, and understand what is being said.

2: Talking Stick – Patience

When a person has a turn to speak we don't interrupt them until they indicate that they want some help. Patience is the key.

3: S l o w e v e r y t h i n g d o w n

It promotes comprehension.

4: Use short sentences.

It promotes comprehension.

5: Noise makers

Often people with aphasia are sensitive to noisy distractions. TV, radio, too many people talking at the same time… These are hard for them.

6: 'Yes/No' questions

If we give them too much choice it is sometimes hard for them to figure out how to answer.

7: Communications options

Speaking can be overrated. Body language, sign language, drawing, writing, charades… are other means of communication.

I explained that I want to interview several of her members about their aphasic journey.

'Well, you can ask them and that is up to them,' she replied.
'We have the group on Thursdays.
I will introduce you and you can say what you need for the article. We'll see what happens?'

— — — —- ~~~ — — — —

Next Thursday I was at the door of Room 3 at quarter to ten.

Reuben, a volunteer, was setting out the tables and a circle of chairs.
Sue and I had a moment to sort out what we were going to do.

Then the door opened and a motley band of people came in.
I confess, I was not impressed.

Most seemed to septua-, octo-. or even nonagenarians.
Several of them had very visible disabilities – shuffling steps, limb paralysis and walking sticks.

Hannah and Norman were like twins.

Geoff came into the room singing: 'Goot maahning! Goot maahning! Goot maahning!'

Kiri, a Māori wahine, had a lip and chin tattoo[1] and a magnificent pounamu[2] pendant.

David shuffled along with the aid of a walker.

Peter, had a powered-wheelchair. He greeted the audience with muttered profanities.
Reuben assisted him, protecting the door frame from more damage.
With a cheerful smile he said: 'C'mon PePuk. Don't demolish the building!'

Anne, John, Ashmud, Mark… the same sorry story of diminishment.

The 'clients' nodded and waved to each other.

---

[1] Aotearoa/New Zealand women can have a moko kauae, a traditional Māori female chin and lip tattoo. It is considered a physical manifestation of their true identity.

[2] Pounamu is a hard, highly valued jade. It is also called greenstone. Pounamu is regarded as a taonga (treasure) by Māori, and most Aotearoa New Zealanders, many of whom have a strong spiritual connection to the stone.

But all I could hear were the tortuous attempts of the members to speak to each other.
It was shocking.

At this moment I almost reneged.
But Sue started the meeting and introduced me.
Too late.
I faced the elderly, mismatched and indecorous throng.

'I am Shami Fergusson and I'm a journalist for *Touchstone Magazine* and I want to write about aphasia and the journey you have suffered In your recovery, the trials and the tribulations – the way you have overcome or risen above the consequences of your condition…'

I glanced at Sue and saw she seemed to be was shaking her head.

Of course. I am prattling on…Remember…the seven points…
I stopped my tirade and looked around the circle.

'Sorry. Start again.'
S l o w   d o w n. Short sentences.
'I am Shami Fergusson.
I'm a journalist for *Touchstone Magazine*'.

'I want to write about aphasia.
And the journey you have … overcome.
The support you have had.

'Can I interview you for this story?
We could have a coffee and chat.
I could interview you here, at the community centre…'

'O-kaaay! O-kaaay! O-kaaay!'
Geoff, the singsong man, waved his hand at me.
'Cah-fé! Cah-fé! Cah-fé!'

It was a catalyst.
Hannah and Norman, the "twins", were the next to sign up.
The rest seemed to be happy for me to interview them.

So, I began.
As Sue had warned, it was difficult to pin them down.

What did I learn from these "elderly, mismatched and indecorous throng" of aphasic clients?

— — — —- ~~~ — — — —

Geoffrey Teadell (b. 1948 - 76 years)
At first, I had to translate Geoff's triplicating answers to meaningful phrases.
Geoff was very adept in writing things down.

Geoff gained his Law degree from Auckland University in 1978.
He practised law for forty years.

He was involved in the 1986 Homosexual Law Reform Bill.
He and his partner, Roger, met at university in 1974.

'It was not acceptable then. For most people.
We had a share of abuse: pooftahs, fairies, bum-chums etc...' he wrote.
'He was the love of my life.'
Tears rolled.

In 2013, they celebrated with a wedding.
'Old mar-ry coo-ple! Old mar-ry coo-ple! Old mar-ry coo-ple!' Geoff said, sad-gleefully.
They were each sixty-five years old.

Roger died the following year.

Apart from his work and campaigning, Geoff's passion was musical theatre.

I asked him what his favourite show was.

The answer was immediate. 'Chest do Sond-hm! Chest do Sond-hm! Chest do Sond-hm!'

[Translation: The musical *Chess* or anything by Stephen Sondheim.]

— — — —- ~~~ — — — —

Hannah Willowcott, née Pfeffe) (b. 1933 - 90 years)
Hannah produced a biography from the Holocaust Centre of New Zealand in Wellington[1].

In a nutshell: Hannah was born the last of three sisters in a well-to-do suburb in Lodz, Poland.
Her mother died giving birth to Hannah.
Hannah developed into a violin prodigy.
By August 1939 she was giving concerts with her sisters.

The following month, Germany invaded Poland.
Izrael wanted to protect his Jewish family so he sent his daughters with his cousin, Gyorgy and his wife, Marya.
Things didn't work out.

---

[1] Holocaust Centre of NZ [https://www.holocaustcentre.org.nz/] inspires and empowers action against antisemitism, discrimination, and apathy, by remembering, educating, and bearing witness to the Holocaust.

Gyorgy, Zelda and Tchiya were shot by SS guards on the way to the ship.

Marya and Hannah hid in ditches and barns, scared out of their wits.

They made it to the coast and eventually to England.

They got the news that Izrael was dead, killed in the Lodz Ghetto.

Marya had some contacts in England and she got work as a nanny for the Willowcotts.

When Marya explained Hannah's position, the family willingly took her in also.

In the family's country house Hannah discovered a violin in the sitting room.

That was that!

By 1953 she had a position in the London Symphony Orchestra.

Two years later, Hannah married Peter, the youngest Willowcott son.

Peter and Hannah Willowcott emigrated to New Zealand in 1963.

Hannah got a position in the first violins of the New Zealand Symphony Orchestra – Te Tira Pūoro o Aotearoa.

She and Peter never had children.
Peter died in 2007.
She had a stroke in 2011.

I asked her about her favourite music.
'Cham-merber mu-sick … Hay-dn ann Moz-ar-et.
Sch-uu-bertk… Marv-lel-lous.'
'German?' I cheekily questioned her.
She looked at me like I was a loon.
She said, unequivocally, 'Muu-sic con-querss…all.'

—————-~~~ ————

Kiri Pōhatu ONZM (b. 1948 - 76 years)
I met Kiri at her whare, beside her marae.
There were so many children in the house and she
had to shoo them out of the kitchen.
She left one teenager.

'My mok-ka…moko-pu-na[1]. E Aroha,' Kiri said.

'My name is Aroha,' said the girl, 'and Kiri is my
kuia[2] – my grandmother.
I can help you to understand her speech.'

---

[1] "mok-ka…moko-pu-na" is actually mokopuna – a grandchild.

[2] kuia = a Māori female elder.

In brief, Kiri had twelve children, thirty grandchildren, and twenty five great-grandchildren.

I asked about her childhood and her children.
With Aroha's help, she answered: 'I was the middle of eight children.
At primary school I was beaten by the teachers for using te reo Māori.
But it didn't stop me.

'We spoke Māori at home and English outside.
We went to the protest at Parliament in 1972.
When we presented Te Petihana o te Reo Māori, the Māori Language Petition.'

[Aroha interrupted. 'My kuia spoke at the protest. My mother said it was emotionally inspirational!'

'My children include three teachers, a doctor, three Kāritane[1] nurses, two mechanics and a builder who, between them, employ eighteen people.
My grandchildren include one government minister, three ministerial executives, a dentist, three doctors,

-----

[1] Kāritane Nurse is a type of nurse in New Zealand specialising in infant care, affiliated with the Plunket Society, an organisation founded by pioneering paediatrician and psychiatrist Sir Truby King.

two university lecturers, an All Black[1] and two Silver Ferns[2], a music teacher and composer, and a fashion designer.'

I asked about the magnificent pounamu pendant she wore around her neck.

Her eyes filled with tears.
'Taonga[3],' Aroha explained, taking her grandmother's hand.
'It has been in this whānau for generations. It is…'
Aroha searched for the word.
'It is more than a cherished heirloom. It is the … the soul of our whānau.'

Kiri rose and went out the back door with Aroha's help.
I followed.
Kiri clapped her hands, and said: 'Haere mai … koutou katoa![4]'

All the children, from twenty to three years old, came immediately to their kuia.

---

[1] All Blacks = The Aotearoa New Zealand national rugby union team, who represent New Zealand in men's international rugby union, which is considered our country's national sport.

[2] Silver Ferns = The Aotearoa New Zealand national netball team who represent the country in international netball tournaments.

[3] Taonga = a treasured possession in Māori culture, especially items of historical cultural significance.

[4] Haere mai …koutou katoa = Come here, everyone.

She looked at them all, each one.

She placed her hand on her pendant and said: 'Nau mai aku tamariki-mokopuna katoa! Kia tau mai ngā manaakitanga a te runga rawa!'[1]

For a moment, time seemed to stand still.

Then Kiri opened her hands.

Like a flock of birds released from their feeding ground the children went back to their activities.

Kiri looked at me, searchingly and with compassion.

'Whānau!' she said, meaningfully.

— — — —· ~~~ — — — —

Maybe, you can get my meaning? My disability.

No?

Okay. On we go.

In brief…

Norman Stanish, ONZM (b: 1930 - 94 years)

Norman was born in London.

He joined the British Merchant Navy in World War II in 1943, claiming he was eighteen.

---

[1] All my grandchildren are welcome! May the blessings of the almighty be upon you!

He was only thirteen.
He immigrated to New Zealand in 1948.
On the ship he met a nurse, Eileen, and they married.

Norman created a transport insurance company and was extremely successful.

Eileen died in 1998 after nearly fifty years of marriage.
Norman set up the NEWS Foundation: Norman & Eileen Water Sports Foundation.
The NEWS Foundation supported young people with water sports.
He said it was a gesture to his experiences as a teenager.

In 2005, Norman was awarded an ONZM.
He had a stroke nine years later in 2014.

David Kebson (Davit Kebabjian) (b. 1943 - 80 years)
His given name was Davit Kebabjian.
His grandparents were Armenian.
Their families emigrated to Australia as refugees when, between 1915 and 1923, the Turkish Ottoman regime waged a genocide of their race.

Davit's parents met and married in Australia and Davit was their only child.

When he was eighteen, Davit came to Wellington, New Zealand to create a new life.
He changed his name to 'David Kebson'.

He got a job in a menswear shop, became the manager and then bought the owners out.
By 1975, *Kebsons* was the premier menswear retailer in the city.

David (Davit) had a stroke ten years ago.
His speech is slow and oddly monotone and his mobility is challenged.

He said, philosophically:
'Dea-th … in-evit-a-ble.
Ch-ange … des-sir-a-ble.
Happ-i-ness … trans-form-a-tive.'

Anne Procter (b. 1952 - 72 years)
Anne was born in Eketāhuna, the ninth and last child of a sheep-farming couples.
Anne discovered a wanderlust.

She worked as a nanny, becoming the go-to child-minder and governess for the children of New Zealand Ambassadors.

She accompanied the ambassadors' families to embassies in Canada, Russia, Italy, Spain, Chile and Brazil.

'Danc-cies! I love…to,' she told me.
Gripping her walking stick she set her feet in a perfect third position and flicking her right foot out momentarily.
'Russ-ss-en ball-let…flam-men-co….
Oh…the Carn..i-vale!'
The joy on her face was marvellous to see.

John Winterfell (b. 1942 - 82 years)
John wrote the spy/action novels under the pen-name Jack Quince.
He produced nine novels, all best-sellers worldwide.
Three have been made into feature films.

He married four times and each time, his wife divorced him.
'But,' he says with a lascivious but fetching grin, 'man-ny luv-vers!'

Dr Ashmud Kantari (b. 1950 - 74 years)
Ashmud was born in Calcutta [now called Kolkata], India.
A psychiatrist, he has produced several ground breaking textbooks.

He was an expert in many high-level trials.
He was a consultant for many think-tanks and ministerial procedures.
He was awarded an MNZM in 2009.

Mark Rudfell (b. 1944 - 79 years)
Science teacher, senior master and eventually Headmaster at St Peter's College, Auckland.

He recalled the students he taught: ministers of parliament, supreme court judges, All Blacks, doctors.
His hobby was airborne: parachuting, hang-gliding, paragliding, base-jumping…

— — — —- ~~~ — — —

My disability? Surely you know now.
Still "No"?

The last interview confirmed my pedestrian and slow-witted perspective. On my disability.

Peter (Petro) Pavliuk: (b: 1943 - 80 years)
Reuben, Sue's helper, accompanied me with this interview.
Reuben had met Peter some months ago as a "volunteer" for the Aphasia Group.

He gave me a sort-of biography of Peter.

Actually Peter was Petro, a Ukrainian refugee and a great artist.
'A brilliant artist!' enthused Reuben.
'He is cantankerous, abrupt, angry and swears a lot but he is the real deal.'

Pavliuk kept calling me 'Sha-ame', even when I corrected him.
After the interview, Reuben told me that Pavliuk always referred to him as 'Rude Man'!
So, I was not the only one.

I spoke about his art.
'Art…differ-…differ-… F-Fuck…. differ-er-rest.
Diff-fe-rns. Per-spec…
Per-spec… Tive. I… I. Diff-fer-nt. Make. Shit. Um…'

He shook his head angrily.
Not at me, but at himself.
He clenched his hands and tried again.
'Make. A. Differ-en-ence.'

When I spoke to him about the others in the Aphasia Group, and the lives that they had led, he gave me a fierce look as if I were taunting him.

His glare intensified and he forcefully proclaimed: 'Son-duh. Sha-ame…son-duh.'

He showed me the image of one of his most recent art works.

Rather than animals and trees, the painting was all about people.

People whose arms and legs were woven and penetrating each other.

People with all sorts of shapes and animals and angels and devils and books and musical instruments and children and logos coming around and through and interlacing out of their bodies.

The colours were luminous, glorious.
All the people were climbing large cubes, like alphabet blocks for babies.

The blocks spelled S-O-N-D-E-R.

With a flourish Pavliuk trumpeted: 'Son-duh! Son-duh!'

Then he looked at me with a challenging stare and I understood his message implicitly: *That is what you need to know*.

When I got to my car, I googled on my phone:
`what is sonder`
The answer:
The realisation that each random passerby is living a life as vivid and complex as your own.

Pavliuk hit the proverbial nail on the head.
I got it.
All the pieces fell into place.

Sonder.

————-·~~~ ————

Pavliuk was right.
He named me 'Sha-ame'.

I was ashamed about my reaction to the Aphasia Group in that first meeting.

Remember what I said:
"All I could hear were the stuttering, tortuous attempts of the members to speak to each other. It was shocking… this elderly, mismatched and indecorous throng."

I was wrong.

When I interviewed them, I looked into their eyes and
saw their intelligence;
the experiences written into their every wrinkle;
the remembrances embossed into their body-language;
their memories of a life so varied.

Their life-experience was complex, intense, brilliant,
vivid, vibrant…
Their biographical histories were amazing.
Getting to know the stories of their lives was a revelation.
An epiphany.

Look at the people they have influenced and inspired?
Whānau, friends, acquaintances, clients … a whole
host of nameless people who have benefited from
their influence, activity, work.
Just by **being** what they are.

So, my disability.
Have I been able to really see others in a way that
honours who they are rather than as I expect or need
them to be?
No.

I was disabled. I had a lack of sonder.
Lack of empathy or compassion.
Lack of acknowledgement of the complexity of
another individual's life.

When I consider my first meeting of The Aphasia Group, I didn't just ignore them.
I was wantonly ignorant of the rich lives that they had – they have – led.
I was blatantly self-absorbed. Intellectually myopic.

And I see this lack in most of my peers, most of the people I know.
A lack of compassion for other people.
A lack of sonder.

Their disability was understandable, but they were overcoming the situation with humour, warmth and grace.
They were "getting on with it".
Their aphasia didn't stop them enjoying life.

My disability was unforgivably worse.

So…I determine that I will:
• Be curious about people you encounter.
• Practise compassion towards others.
• Develop your empathy skills.
• Challenge your thoughts about who they really are.

Can you do the same?

— — — —- ~~~ — — —

Sonder (adj):

What is "sonder"?

John Koenig coined this term in his *Dictionary of Obscure Sorrows*:

"The realisation that each random passerby is living a life as vivid and complex as your own."

No single word adequately captures **sonder**.

This term ties in many psychological concepts relevant to our well-being.

An awareness of others entails various abilities, but 'perspective-taking' is vital.

The skills behind this process involve empathy, compassion, and acknowledging the complexity of each individual's life.

It is "putting yourself in their shoes".

7B:

Sonder [1]
An invisible disability

An article for *Touchstone Magazine,*
June edition 2023
Author: Shami Fergusson

Sometimes, an article haunts you. You think you are revealing something significant about the people you are interviewing. Something profound. Earth-shattering.
But this story revealed something about myself that I have never suspected before. I discovered I have a disability. And, I suspect, a good number of people have this condition, this affliction, too.

As Maria sang in the *Sound Of Music*, "Let's start at the very beginning, A very good place to start…"

My boss, the editor of *Touchstone Magazine*, summoned me to her office. As usual, she was typing with one hand on her computer's keyboard, using the other to text on her phone, and still she trumpeted: 'A general interest article. A 'feel-good' story. Someone who has a disability. But has overcome it. Raised themselves up. Something uplifting. You know what I mean… Go…go…go…'

Her voice has a staccato effect like machine gun fire strafing we hostile journalists from her office bunker. I turned and ran out the door – she always makes me feel that I should run

---

[1] [Spoiler Alert: The meaning of 'Sonder' is the meaning of the whole story. When you read the story, the meaning should be clear, but I have included the meaning of 'Sonder' on the last page.]

everywhere – and she launched another salvo: 'Next month's issue!' as I dived for the trenches.

What to do? Of course, I went to my trusted source.
My CI[1]. Aka, my mother!

'Hmmm. A cup of tea?,' she unhelpfully said to me when I told her my problem. An infusion of chamomile, lemon verbena and raspberry leaf tea was on the table. I think she makes it up. I declined, impatient.

She sipped, contemplating the ceiling for a minute and said: 'Well…one of my friends…her husband had a stroke. He is almost recovered, but his talking is affected. She told me about it … something a dispatipia, or aspshastia. Um…um… it is on the tip of my tongue…um… Aphasia! Yes, aphasia. She said that it is a communication something. He can remember everything and his ideas…concepts…are fine, but he can't speak about them. It is so frustrating for him, and for **her,** but they are sorting it out. However, most people can't see it as a disability. He recovered …physically… He rides a bike, chops the wood, mows the lawn…but his speech is…well, suspect.'

She shrugged, carelessly, like a cat that was playing with a mouse. [By the way, the mouse is **me**.]
'Could be good? Anyway…', and proceeded to tell my about my cousin's fiancee's mother's brother-in-law who had won $200,000 in Lotto… And the dog next door who was pooping on her driveway… And when she could hopefully meet 'my paramour', as she called my invisible [and phantom] suitor…

---

[1] CI = Confidential Informant.

After dealing with the familiar half-hour mother/daughter maternal rigmarole, I excused myself and went to the car.

I typed '*aphasia*' into my phone.

Dr Google displayed:

About 22,700,000 results (0.35 seconds).

I picked one at random from the first five and discovered it was:
> "a language disorder caused by damage in a specific area of the brain that controls language expression and comprehension. Aphasia leaves a person unable to communicate effectively with others."

Well done, Mum. This could be it.

————.~~~ ————

I typed all sorts questions about aphasia: aphasia treatment, aphasia causes, celebrities with aphasia, types of aphasia, aphasia associations, etc...etc... and I got all sorts of information but my boss wanted to see a real person, not an interrogation of an internet search engine search results.

I had to see some**one** to interview.

I typed 'aphasia near here', not expecting any results, but Dr Google continued to oblige.

Apparently there is an:
> Aphasia Group Meeting in our local Community Centre every Thursday, 10:00-12:30, ran by a Community Aphasia Advisor from AphasiaNZ[1].

---

[1] Aphasia New Zealand (AphasiaNZ) Charitable Trust is a national organisation and registered charity, providing support services, resources, education, and information for anyone in New Zealand living with or affected by aphasia. One of the services is CAA - Community Aphasia Advisor. Currently they have fifteen CAA in centres around Aotearoa New Zealand. [https://www.aphasia.org.nz/ - downloaded 15 April 2024]

Perfect. It was a Thursday. It was twenty past twelve – and the Community Centre was ten minutes away!

The noticeboard in the foyer of the Community Centre announced that the Aphasia Group was meeting in Room 3. I went up the corridor and noticed the door for Room 3 had a glass panel. Apparently I was too late and I thought everyone had left, but suddenly I saw a young woman crossing the room to pack her bags. I opened the door and, surprised, she looked at me. 'Can I help you?' she asked.

I spoke with more confidence than I felt: 'Kia ora. My name is Shami and I write for *Touchstone Magazine.* I want to write an article about aphasia.'

'Ah!' Her look was delighted and charming. 'Okay. I guess you have the right place. Um…I am Sue. Sue Lee,' as she indicated her name tag. 'Come in, come in.'

She gestured to a chair and we sat down. 'I am the CAA for this area,' she explained. 'The Community Aphasia Advisor, for Aphasia New Zealand. What do you know about aphasia?'

'Well…I know it is a communication disorder that affects speaking…talking…um…well, communication?'

'Well…that's essentially true,' she laughed genially. 'There is a damage to the brain centres of language expression and comprehension. It could be an accident, or disease that affects the brain, but the main cause of aphasia is stroke. Do you know how many people in Aotearoa New Zealand suffer from stroke each year?'

'No, I don't' I admitted.

'About 9,500 strokes are experienced every year – that's one every 55 minutes.'[1] She gazed at me as I comprehended the statistic. I blinked. Apparently that was enough to continue.

'We estimate that thirty percent of the people who have a stroke would see some symptoms of aphasia. Some recover in the days following, but some have chronic aphasia. We estimate that twenty-five or thirty thousand people in Aotearoa New Zealand have aphasia. That's more than people with Parkinson's or multiple sclerosis.

'These are the people I work with. Aphasia means that they can't speak clearly, or they miss words, or name them wrongly. It is like a pathway from their brain and their mouth is … um… distracted. Some can't read or write clearly. Or their comprehension is affected.'

I nodded. 'So…how can you treat them? How can you give their speech back to them?'

'The neural pathways have to be…re-organised, reconstructed. The brain is a phenomenal organ – its plasticity is marvellous. I trained as a Speech Language Pathologist or Therapist, but basically it's practice, rest, practice, relaxation, practice and more practice.

---

[1] Aotearoa New Zealand has a population of five million.
In UK, 100,000 people have strokes each year. There are 1.3 million stroke survivors in the UK.
In Canada, over 50,000 new strokes—that's one stroke every ten minutes. About 300,000 Canadians are living with the effects of stroke.
In the United States, about 795,000 people suffer a stroke each year. Someone has a stroke every forty seconds. There are over seven million stroke survivors live in United States and two-thirds of them are currently disabled. This includes two million people with aphasia.

'Aphasia is…well…forever. People with aphasia can improve
– often immensely – but most will never recover the same
level of communication skills after their event. But we can
strive to reach that level.'

'So…how does your group work?' I said. 'How do you
"practise neural pathways reconstruction" in your meetings?'

— — — —· ~~~ — — — —

Sue lead me through some processes that are helpful.
Long story short, she outlined seven important points:

1: Intelligence remains the same
> The brain is okay – however they may find it hard to
> talk, write, read, and understand what is being said.

2: Talking Stick – Patience
> When a person has a turn to speak we don't interrupt
> them until they indicate that they want some help.
> Patience is the key.

3: S l o w   e v e r y t h i n g   d o w n
> It promotes comprehension.

4: Use short sentences.
> It promotes comprehension.

5: Noise makers
> Often people with aphasia are sensitive to noisy
> distractions. TV, radio, too many people talking at the
> same time… These are hard for them.

6: 'Yes/No' questions
> If we give them too much choice it is sometimes hard
> for them to figure out how to answer.

7: Communications options
> Speaking can be overrated. Body language, sign
> language, drawing, writing, charades…are other
> means of communication.

As a journalist – and a Virgo – I noted these processes and points religiously on my notebook. Then I explained that I want to interview several of her members about their aphasic journey.

'Well, you can ask them and that is up to them,' she replied. 'It will be hard to get their story down. Their speech is erratic, to say the least! But I welcome an article about aphasia because most people have no idea about this condition. People know "stroke" or "brain tumour" et cetera but they don't know the possible consequence of these things on a patient's speaking.

'So, we have the group on Thursdays. Can you come to the next meeting? I will introduce you and you can say what you need for the article and see what happens?'

For the next week, I committed the seven points to memory, practised them, and researched everything I could about aphasia.

————–- ~~~ ————

Next Thursday I was at the door of Room 3 at quarter to ten. Sue greeted me and introduced a volunteer helper, Reuben, who was setting out the tables and a circle of chairs.

Sue and I had a moment to sort out what we were going to do before the door opened and a motley band of people came in. I confess, I was not impressed. Most seemed to septua-, octo-. or even nonagenarians – grey-sparse-haired, bent or stooped.

The clothing and shoes were extremely varied and I suspected that the local op shop[1] was the source of much of their wardrobe. Several of them had very visible disabilities – shuffling steps, leg or arm paralysis, walkers and walking sticks.

Hannah and Norman were like twins – grey haired, clothed in bright colours that didn't match their physiognomy.[2]
Geoff came into the room with a flourish, singing: 'Goot maahning! Goot maahning! Goot maahning!', despite his obvious disability – a paralysed arm and leg.

Kiri, a Māori wahine came in dressed in a shapeless black. She had a lip and chin tattoo[3] and her green eyes matched the magnificent pounamu[4] pendant around her neck. David shuffled along with the aid of a walker, pausing every few steps. Anne, John, Ashmud, Mark… the same sorry story of obvious diminishment – halting steps, cowered stance, uncertain confidence.

Another grizzly individual, Peter, had a powered-wheelchair. He greeted the audience with muttered profanities and callously thumped the entrance with his foot rest – an insistent door knocker. Reuben magically assisted him, protecting the door frame from more damage.

---

[1] op shop = is a short form for 'opportunity shop', a thrift store, a retail establishment run by a charitable organisation to raise money.

[2] the face or countenance, especially when considered as an index to the character.

[3] Aotearoa/New Zealand women can have a moko kauae, a traditional Māori female chin and lip tattoo. It is considered a physical manifestation of their true identity.

[4] Pounamu is a hard, highly valued jade. It is also called greenstone. Pounamu is regarded as a taonga (treasure) by Māori, and most Aotearoa New Zealanders, many of whom have a strong spiritual connection to the stone.

With a cheerful smile he said: 'C'mon PePuk. Don't demolish the building ….yet!' as he wheeled him across the room to a position in the circle.

The 'clients' nodded and waved to each other, clearly delighted to see each other – even the taciturn and scowling Peter. But all I could hear were the stuttering, tortuous attempts of the members to speak to each other. It was shocking.
Human detritus, I thought uncharitably. *Dribs and drabs. Flotsam and jetsam. Adrift in the icy waters of old age...*

At this moment I almost reneged. Sidling to the door I was about to escape when Sue started the meeting and introduced me as the first item on the agenda. Too late.
I faced the elderly, mismatched and indecorous throng.

'I am Shami Fergusson and I'm a journalist for *Touchstone Magazine* and I want to write about aphasia and the journey you have suffered in your recovery, the trials and the tribulations – the way you have overcome or risen above the consequences of your condition, and the support you have had from your carers, families, the doctors and speech therapist and, of course, your meetings with Sue and the support you have from AphasiaNZ and...'

I glanced at Sue and saw she seemed to be was shaking her head.
Of course. I am prattling on...Remember...the seven points...
I stopped my tirade and looked around the circle.

'Sorry. Start again.'
S l o w   d o w n. Short sentences.

'I am Shami Fergusson.
I'm a journalist for *Touchstone Magazine*'.

I looked around the members and most were nodding.
I assumed that they were indicating that they know the magazine.

'I want to write about aphasia.
And the journey you have … overcome.
The support you have had.'
Again, the faces seemed to be open to the suggestion.

'Can I interview you for this story?
We could have a coffee and chat.
I could interview you here, at the community centre, or at a café or we could do it at your home.'
Hmmm…too many choices.
I looked around the group. There were puzzled faces.

I almost backed out of it – throw in the towel, apologise to Sue…but suddenly:
'O-kaaay! O-kaaay! O-kaaay!'
Geoff, the singsong man, waved his hand at me.
'Cah-fé! Cah-fé! Cah-fé!'

It was a catalyst.
Hannah and Norman, the "twins", were the next to sign up.
The rest seemed to be happy for me to interview them, a few at their home, some at the Community Centre after the meeting and some planned a lunch meeting at the local café – my treat apparently!

I studied Sue in this meeting particularly how she listened to her 'clients', questioning them when she was not clear about their garbled speech, getting them to mime, or draw, or write things down. And always with an attitude of phenomenal patience, patience, patience.

So, I began. As Sue had warned, it was difficult to pin them down. Some of the interviews were extended for several days and my boss gave a two-month extension to the article that you are now reading.

I used all the techniques that Sue gave me and others besides and met some others of their families and supporters.

What did I learn from these "elderly, mismatched and indecorous throng" of aphasiac clients?

— — — —·- ~~~ — — — —

Geoffrey Teadell (b. 1948 - 76 years)
At first, I had to translate Geoff's triplicating answers to meaningful phrases. His dominant right arm was paralysed after his stroke in 2018 but, thankfully, Geoff was very adept in writing things down with his left hand. That made all the difference with his story.

Geoff gained his Law degree from Auckland University in 1978. He practised law for forty years becoming a Senior Partner in his Wellington firm: Fulsom, Brighton and Teadell. He was instrumental in the determination of the 1986 Homosexual Law Reform Bill, the Human Rights Act of 1993, and the Civil Unions Act of 2005, campaigning vigorously despite personal vandalism, violence and death threats.

He and his partner, Roger, a civil engineer, met at university in 1974. 'It was not acceptable then. For most people. We had a share of abuse: pooftahs, fairies, bum-chums etc...'

he wrote. 'For a while we said we were room mates, but after the Human Rights Act, we stuck to our guns. Partners. He was the love of my life.' Tears rolled.

When, in 2013, New Zealand passed the Marriage Amendment Act allowing same-sex couples to marry, they celebrated with a wedding. 'Old mar-ry coo-ple! Old mar-ry coo-ple! Old mar-ry coo-ple!' Geoff said, sad-gleefully. They were each sixty-five years old. Roger died the following year.

Apart from his work and campaigning, Geoff's passion was musical theatre. Before I questioned him about that, he broke into a wicked grin and sang in ridiculous falsetto: 'Cli-ché! Cli-ché! Cli-ché!' Over his career he performed in the city's operatic society, singing lead roles or in the chorus of such shows as: *Annie, Jesus Christ Superstar, Oklahoma, Carousel, The King and I, Chess, Sound of Music, Les Miserables, Into the Woods, Sweeney Todd...*

I asked him what his favourite show was. The answer was immediate. 'Chest do Sond-hm! Chest do Sond-hm! Chest do Sond-hm!'
[Translation: The musical *Chess* or anything by Stephen Sondheim.]

———--·~~~————

Hannah Willowcott, née Pfeffe) (b. 1933 - 90 years)
Hannah produced a biography from the Holocaust Centre of New Zealand in Wellington[1]. After I read it, we had some lovely and poignant afternoons drinking tea and listening to

---

[1] Holocaust Centre of NZ [https://www.holocaustcentre.org.nz/] inspires and empowers action against antisemitism, discrimination, and apathy, by remembering, educating, and bearing witness to the Holocaust.

the musical recordings of orchestra and chamber works that she featured on.

In a nutshell: Hannah was born the last of three sisters in a well-to-do suburb in Lodz, Poland. Her mother died giving birth to Hannah. Her father, Izrael Pfeffe, was a manager of a big textile factory in the city. Raised by a governess and tutors, Hannah developed into a violin prodigy. By August 1939 she was giving concerts with her sisters – Zelda, on the piano and Tchiya, cello – to family and friends. She was just six.

The following month, Germany invaded Poland. Izrael wanted to protect his Jewish family so he sent his daughters with his cousin, Gyorgy and his wife, Marya, to a region west of Koszalin, a city beside the Baltic Sea, expecting them to be able to join a ship to Copenhagen, Amsterdam and then to England. He was planning to join them there.

Things didn't work out. Gyorgy, Zelda and Tchiya were shot by SS guards on the way to the ship. Marya and Hannah hid in ditches and barns, scared out of their wits. They made it to the coast and eventually to England but they got the news that Izrael was dead, killed in the Lodz Ghetto.

Marya had some contacts in England and she got work as a nanny for the Willowcotts. James Willowcott was a senior civil servant and his wife, Agnes, and two sons, William and Peter, went to the family's country home away, from the war in London. When Marya explained Hannah's position, the family willingly took her in also. In the country house Hannah discovered a violin in the sitting room and – well – that was that. Basically, the Willowcotts adopted Hannah, bringing her up as their daughter. By 1953 she had a position in the

London Symphony Orchestra, and two years later, Hannah married Peter, the youngest Willowcott son.

Peter, a soil scientist, and Hannah Willowcott emigrated to New Zealand in 1963. Hannah applied for and got a position in the first violins of the NZBC Symphony Orchestra [now named the New Zealand Symphony Orchestra – Te Tira Pūoro o Aotearoa]. She joined other orchestral colleagues for chamber music sessions and played in the symphony orchestra for thirty-seven years. 'Re-tired. Year 2000 – it waz…zeitpunkt. Time,' she said philosophically.

She and Peter never had children. Peter died in 2007. 'But ich… here,' she said with a shrug, 'home…here.' She had a stroke in 2011. Now, she is dedicating her life to music and remembering the victims of WWII and the Holocaust. She donated her violins as a prize for students at Te Kōkī, New Zealand School of Music in Wellington, and volunteered as an ambassador in the Holocaust Museum.

I asked her about her favourite music. Her answers were immediate. 'Some gut composers here … Lil-Iburnt…Whit-heed, Harr-is, Norr-is, Psa-thass, Farrrr… But – sym-momy… Mah-ler, Beet-hovink…and cham-merber… Hay-dn ann Moz-ar-et. Sch-uu-bertk… Marv-lel-lous.'
'German?' I cheekily questioned her.
She looked at me like I was a loon.
She said, unequivocally, 'Muu-sic con-querss…all.'

— — — —- ~~~ — — — —

Kiri Pōhatu ONZM (b. 1948 - 76 years)
I met Kiri at her whare, beside her marae. There were so many children in the house and she had to shoo them out of the kitchen, but she left one teenager.

'My mok-ka...moko-pu-na[1]. E Aroha,' Kiri said, with a generous caress of the girl's shoulders.
'My name is Aroha,' said the girl, 'and Kiri is my kuia[2] – my grandmother. I can help you to understand her speech.'

Aroha clearly adored her grandmother, and her translation made all the difference. Kiri interspersed so many Māori words in her stuttering conversation that Aroha's help was invaluable.

In brief, Kiri had twelve children, thirty grandchildren, and twenty five great-grandchildren. 'And another four great-grandchildren on the way!' said Aroha, obviously delighted.
'Your husband?' I questioned.
'Toru. Kua pau te hau!' Kiri chuckled. Aroha giggled and explained: 'She has been married three times, but she'd worn them all out!'

I asked about her childhood and her children. With Aroha's help, she answered: 'I was the middle of eight children. At primary school I was beaten by the teachers for using te reo Māori. But it didn't stop me. All of my dozen children were bilingual. We spoke Māori at home and English outside. We went to the protest at Parliament in 1972 – me, my second husband and five of our children – when we presented Te Petihana o te Reo Māori, the Māori Language Petition.'

[Aroha interrupted. 'My kuia spoke at the protest. My mother said it was emotionally inspirational! She galvanised everyone!']

---

[1] "mok-ka...moko-pu-na" is actually mokopuna – a grandchild.

[2] kuia = a Māori female elder.

'I have always been here – this my marae. But I wanted to make sure that my tamariki[1] would go into the world and make a difference. I think I did that. My children include three teachers, a doctor, three Kāritane[2] nurses, two mechanics and a builder who, between them, employ eighteen people. My grandchildren include one government minister, three ministerial executives, a dentist, three doctors, two university lecturers, an All Black[3] and two Silver Ferns[4], a music teacher and composer, and a fashion designer.

'And this one,' Kiri chucked Aroha's chin, 'who I think will be a SLP.' Aroha beamed. 'She means a Speech Language Pathologist.' She turned and eye-rolled her kuia. 'Maybe I will be an archaeologist? Or a rock star?'

I asked about the magnificent pounamu pendant she wore around her neck. Her eyes filled with tears. 'Taonga[5],' Aroha explained, taking her grandmother's hand. 'It has been in this whānau for generations. It is…' Aroha searched for the word. 'It is more than a cherished heirloom. It is the … the soul of our whānau.' Kiri nodded her understanding of what Aroha was saying, and turned to me again with an empathetic expression on her face. 'See. SLP!' she said.

---

[1] tamariki = children (Māori)

[2] Kāritane Nurse is a type of nurse in New Zealand specialising in infant care, affiliated with the Plunket Society, an organisation founded by pioneering paediatrician and psychiatrist Sir Truby King.

[3] All Blacks = The Aotearoa New Zealand national rugby union team, who represent New Zealand in men's international rugby union, which is considered our country's national sport.

[4] Silver Ferns = The Aotearoa New Zealand national netball team who represent the country in international netball tournaments.

[5] Taonga = a treasured possession in Māori culture, especially items of historical cultural significance.

Then, she rose and went out the back door with Aroha's help. I followed. Out in the back yard, some of the children were playing an uproarious ball game, others were quietly reading, and some were rapt in an intense card game.

Kiri clapped her hands, and said: 'Haere mai …koutou katoa![1]'

All the children, from twenty to three years old, came immediately to their kuia. Their respect of this old woman was spell-binding.

She looked at them all, each one, placed her hand on her pendant and said: 'Nau mai aku tamariki-mokopuna katoa! Kia tau mai ngā manaakitanga a te runga rawa!'[2]

For a moment, time seemed to stand still. Then Kiri opened her hands. Like a flock of birds released from their feeding ground the children went back to their activities.

Kiri looked at me, searchingly and with compassion. 'Whānau!' she said, meaningfully.

— — — —- ~~~ — — — —

Maybe, you can get my meaning? My disability.
No?
Okay. On we go.
In brief…

Norman Stanish, ONZM (b: 1930 - 94 years)
Norman was born in London. He joined the British Merchant Navy in World War II in 1943, claiming he was eighteen. He

---

[1] Haere mai …koutou katoa = Come here, everyone.

[2] All my grandchildren are welcome! May the blessings of the almighty be upon you.'

was only thirteen. In the two years that followed he and his fellows sailors were torpedoed three times. He survived the icy water **and** the war and joined the assisted immigration from UK to New Zealand in 1948. On the ship he met a nurse, Eileen, and they married. Norman created a transport insurance company and was extremely successful.

Eileen died in 1998 after nearly fifty years of marriage. Norman set up the NEWS Foundation: the Norman & Eileen Water Sports Foundation. The NEWS Foundation supported young people with water sports – swimmers, rowers, canoeists, yachting – to overseas experience, training and World, Commonwealth and Olympic Games competitions. He said it was a gesture to his experiences as a teenager. Norman said that his advertising logo is 'The Good NEWS!' In 2005, Norman was awarded an ONZM. He had a stroke nine years later in 2014.

David Kebson (Davit Kebabjian) (b. 1943 - 80 years)
David and Joanna invited me to their home for morning tea and between them they gave a brief biography. Actually, his given name was Davit Kebabjian. His grandparents were Armenian and with their families they emigrated to Australia as refugees when, between 1915 and 1923, the Turkish Ottoman regime waged a genocide of their race. Ninety percent of the Armenian people died in that conflict[1]. Davit's parents met and married in Australia and Davit was their only child. They never got over their grief over the deaths of their parents, relatives and compatriots and it became too much for Davit.

---

[1] [https://www.history.com/topics/world-war-i/armenian-genocide] and [https://www.armenian-genocide.org/genocide.html] – downloaded 16 April 2024

When he was eighteen, Davit came to Wellington, New Zealand to create a new life. He changed his name to 'David Kebson' – a much easier name for 1960 New Zealanders comprehend. He got a job in a menswear shop, became the manager and then bought the owners out. By 1975, *Kebsons* was the premier menswear retailer in the city. He married Joanna, a Kiwi, and they had five children: two daughters and three sons. Eventually he had branches in eight other New Zealand cities and two in Sydney, Australia.

David (Davit) had a stroke ten years ago. His speech is slow and oddly monotone and his mobility is challenged. 'But,' he related slowly, 'with Jo-ann-na, my chi-ldren and grand-chil-dren – I am qui-te con-ten-ted.'
He added, philosophically and with a serene, Buddha-like expression: 'Dea-th … in-evit-a-ble. Ch-ange … des-sir-a-ble. Happ-i-ness … trans-form-a-tive.'

Anne Procter (b. 1952 - 72 years)
Anne was born in Eketāhuna, the ninth and last child of a sheep-farming couples. Despite, or maybe **because** of her isolated back-country experience, Anne discovered a wanderlust. She escaped to the city and found work as a nanny, becoming the go-to child-minder and governess for the children of New Zealand Ambassadors. She accompanied the ambassadors' families to embassies in Canada, Russia, Italy, Spain, Chile and Brazil.

'Danc-cies! I love…to,' she told me, gripping her walking stick and, somehow, setting her feet in a perfect third position, and flicking her right foot out momentarily.
'Russ-ss-en ball-let…flam-men-co…. Oh…the Carn..i-vale!'
The joy on her face was marvellous to see.

John Winterfell (b. 1942 - 82 years)
John wrote the spy/action novels under the pen-name Jack Quince. He produced nine novels featuring the character CIA Agent Connor Solway, all best-sellers worldwide. Three have been made into feature films. He married four times and each time, his wife divorced him. 'But,' he says with a lascivious but fetching grin, 'man-ny luv-vers!'

Dr Ashmud Kantari (b. 1950 - 74 years)
Ashmud was born in Calcutta [now called Kolkata], India. A psychiatrist, he has produced several ground breaking textbooks used for university studies in twelve countries. He was an expert in many high-level trials and a consultant for many think-tanks and ministerial procedures. He was awarded an MNZM in 2009.

Mark Rudfell (b. 1944 - 79 years)
Science teacher, senior master and eventually Headmaster at St Peter's College, Epsom, Auckland. He recalled the students he taught: ministers of parliament, supreme court judges, All Blacks, doctors, architects... His hobby was airborne: parachuting, hang-gliding, paragliding, base-jumping...

— — — —- ~~~ — — —

My disability? Surely you know now.
Still "No"?

The last interview confirmed my pedestrian and slow-witted perspective. On my disability.

Peter (Petro) Pavliuk: (b: 1943 - 80 years)
Reuben, Sue's helper, accompanied me with this interview. Phew!

Reuben had met Peter some months ago as a "volunteer" for the Aphasia Group, and he gave me a sort-of biography of Peter. Actually Peter was Petro, a Ukrainian refugee and a great artist. 'A brilliant artist!' enthused Reuben. He showed many photos of Pavliuk's work on his tablet computer – murals, sculptures, paintings – mostly with an environmental conservation message. 'He is cantankerous, abrupt, angry and swears a lot but he is the real deal,' Reuben confided in me. 'When I met him at the beginning of the year he was very depressed, despondent, but I got him some help and he is now working again.'

Pavliuk was awarded an ONZM several years ago, 'for the arts and environmental activism in the community', but he turned it down with some 'fruity' language that the newspapers reported in an abbreviated and censorial form.

When I eventually interviewed him, he didn't say much at all – mostly one-or-two-word answers. I think he thought I was suspicious. Or worse. He said I was 'A men-dia-whoor dejour-na-lise,' – translated by Reuben, in a whisper, as 'a media whore journalist'.
He kept calling me 'Sha-ame', even when I corrected him. After the interview, Reuben told me that Pavliuk always referred to him as 'Rude Man'! So, I was not the only one.

I spoke to him about environmental issues and his activism. He fixed me with his glaring but intelligent eyes for thirty seconds, and then said brusquely, 'Shit. Nature…good. Men…suck.' Another thirty seconds, and he admitted: 'Mostly' with a lemony face.

I spoke about his art.

'Art…differ-…differ-… F-Fuck…. differ-er-rest. Diff-fe-rns. Per-spec… Per-spec… Tive. I… I. Diff-fer-nt. Make. Shit. Um…' He shook his head angrily. Not at me, but at himself. He clenched his hands and tried again.

'Make. A. Differ-en-ence.'

When I spoke to him about the others in the Aphasia Group, and the lives that they had led, he gave me a fierce look as if I were taunting him. His glare intensified and he forcefully proclaimed: 'Son-duh. Sha-ame…son-duh.' He struck the table and emphasised: 'Son. Duh!' and he pointed to Reuben's tablet, urging him to find something.

Reuben's face cleared and nodded enthusiastically. He fiddled with his tablet and showed me the image of one Pavliuk's most recent art works.

Rather than animals and trees, the painting was all about people. Abstract but identifiable people. People whose arms and legs were woven and penetrating each other. People with all sorts of shapes and animals and angels and devils and books and musical instruments and children and logos coming around and through and interlacing out of their bodies. The colours were luminous, glorious.

All the people were climbing, clambering, surmounting large cubes, like alphabet blocks for babies.

The blocks spelled S-O-N-D-E-R.

With a flourish Pavliuk pointed at the image on Reuben's tablet and triumphantly trumpeted: 'Son-duh! Son-duh!' Then he looked at me with a challenging stare and I understood his message implicitly: *That is what you need to know.*

When I got to my car, I googled on my phone:
what is sonder
The answer:
The realisation that each random passerby is living
a life as vivid and complex as your own.

Pavliuk hit the proverbial nail on the head. I got it.
All the pieces fell into place.

Sonder.

———--·~~~ ————

Pavliuk was right. He named me 'Sha-ame' and I was ashamed about my reaction to the Aphasia Group in that first meeting. Remember what I said:
"All I could hear were the stuttering, tortuous attempts of the members to speak to each other. It was shocking…this elderly, mismatched and indecorous throng."

I was wrong.

When I interviewed them, I looked into their eyes and saw their intelligence; the experiences written into their every wrinkle, weighing into their every movement and gesture; the remembrances embossed into their body-language; their memories of a life so varied – difficult, tortuous, heartrending but also joyful, resplendent, ecstatic.

Their life-experience was complex, intense, brilliant, vivid, vibrant… Their biographical histories were amazing. Getting to know the stories of their lives was a revelation. An epiphany.

Look at the people they have influenced and inspired? Whānau, friends, acquaintances, clients, colleagues and pupils and a whole host of nameless people who have benefited from their influence, activity, work. Just by **being** what they are, their **existence**, they have augmented other people's lives.

Okay, despite the communications difficulties and the attendant frustrations of the last few years, their lives were **rich**. I saw that they had **lived**! I was dwarfed by their achievements.

So, my disability.
Have I been able to really see others in a way that honours who they are rather than as I expect or need them to be? No.

I was disabled. I had a lack of sonder. Lack of empathy or compassion. Lack of acknowledgement of the complexity of another individual's life. When I consider my first meeting of The Aphasia Group, I didn't just ignore them. I was wantonly ignorant of the rich lives that they had – they have – led. I was blatantly self-absorbed. Intellectually myopic.
And I see this lack in most of my peers, most of the people I know.
A lack of compassion for other people.
A lack of sonder.

My editor wanted me to look up a community that has risen above their disability.

These people **had**.

Their disability – the lack of communication, and the frustrations and the anger – was understandable, but they were overcoming the situation with humour, warmth and grace. [In the case of Pavliuk, occasionally.] But they were "getting on with it". Their aphasia didn't stop them enjoying life.

My disability was unforgivably worse.

So…I determine that I will:
- Be curious about people you encounter.
- Practise compassion towards others.
- Develop your empathy skills.
- Challenge your thoughts about who they really are.

Can you do the same?

————- ~~~ ———

Sonder (adj):
What is "sonder"?
John Koenig coined this term in his *Dictionary of Obscure Sorrows:*
"The realisation that each random passerby is living a life as vivid and complex as your own."

No single word adequately captures **sonder**. This term ties in many psychological concepts relevant to our well-being. An awareness of others entails various abilities, but 'perspective-taking' is vital. The skills behind this process involve empathy, compassion, and acknowledging the complexity of each individual's life.
It is *"putting yourself in their shoes"*.

Poems

Thirteen Haiku [1]

Tympani thunder,
Rain splashes, spatters, sloshes…
My heart – wordless – speaks…

Birdsong radiates…[2]
Tūī laughs, huia sings:
One extinct. Like me.

Pīwakawaka
Chirping, darting, full of verve…
Remake me like you?

Horrible tūī
Clatter of words and meanings…
Toler'ble hui![3]

---

[1] A traditional Japanese haiku is a three-line poem. It is different in Japanese language, but the English version has seventeen syllables, written in a 5/7/5 syllable count. Often focusing on images from nature, haiku emphasises simplicity, intensity, and directness of expression.

[2] The vocal Tūī, the extinct Huia, and the darting Pīwakawaka (fantail) are Aotearoa New Zealand native birds.

[3] 'Hui' - Māori term for an assembly, gathering or meeting

Sounds echo boldly.
Nature speaks eloquently…
But not via me.

The waterfall speaks.
Clouds whisper their circumstance.
Prostrate words choke me.

A cloud adorned sky
Grey transmutes into azure
Time to move onward

Loud laughing people
Can pollute the sound-waves … but …
Better than weeping.

A hesitant word?
Speaking therapy practice.
Melioration.[1]

---

[1] melioration: (noun) a condition superior to an earlier condition.

Aphasia strikes.
Confused, frustrated, angry.
Seek reinvention.

Intelligence: fine.
Comprehension: A-okay.
Talking: Lost pathways?

Joyous dancing words:
Banter, viewpoint, jokes! A dream…
Wheelchair aphas'a.

Check: aphasia
Status: Complete frustration
Trust: Positive mood

Twelve Limericks [1]

Six limericks with the same first line:
'An aphasic had trouble with communication'

An aphasic had trouble with communication
His speech was littered with hesitations.
I can stand tall
And speak with a drawl.
They think I have a sacred revelation.

An aphasic had trouble with communication
So she practised with many obfuscations.[2]
Confused by her antics
They forget the semantics
And overlook her word mutilations.

An aphasic had trouble with communication
In his mind, it seemed an aberration.
It's a complete frustration
a mental emasculation.
It seems it is an oration castration.

---

[1] A limerick is a five-line poem that consists of a single stanza, an AABBA
rhyme scheme, and whose subject is a short, pithy tale or description.

[2] Obfuscation = to confuse or bewilder.

An aphasic had trouble with communication
So she practised with musical compositions.
Speech was better in song
And her talking was prolonged
But her rhythms were complex syncopations.

An aphasic had trouble with communication
So he decided to indulge with intoxication.
The alcohol he consumed
Didn't meet what he assumed
And the headaches were no compensation.

An aphasic had trouble with communication
So she practised with all sorts of quotations.
She stuttered and spluttered
With each quote she uttered.
'To be or no for being…um…be…then-when-so-um-
why-what-where-um-were…are…is the kes-tion.'

**Six limericks with the (almost) the same third line:
'She/He ********** aphasia'**

A woman was fit, active and did kung fu
But she suffered a brain injury: *I'm screwed!*
She was enslaved by aphasia
So she became a geisha
At least, being silent is a positive virtue.

When a lecturer was addressing his best-seller book
He faced a stroke with an uncertain outlook.
He conceded to aphasia
So he went to Malaysia
At least they would not question my gobbledegook.

A PPA[1] lass was reading Orwell's *1984*
Opined Ministry of Truth and Newspeak[2] was called for.
She was diminished by aphasia
So she mused: *That paraphernalia...*
Too many extraneous, highfalutin, ostentatious,
supercilious, extravagant, pretentious, presumptuous
words in English! Qu'elle adore!

----

[1] PPA: 'Primary progressive aphasia' is a gradual loss of language skills,
an underlying neurodegenerative disease.
[2] In George Orwell's *1984*, the Ministry of Truth sought to cull synonyms by
the destruction of language into 'newspeak' (rather than 'oldspeak'.)

A cinema celebrity – [can't mention his name] –
Had a stroke that silenced his voice; took his fame.
He succumbed to aphasia
And appeared at Bacchanalia[1],
Inebriated, they don't know my talking is the same!

A composer for strings, brass and drums
Had a debilitating stroke: *That's dumb!'*
She acquired fluent aphasia[2]
My spiels are semiquavers,
And my phrases are da capo ad nauseam[3]!

A heroic firefighter, said the newspaper's media hype
Had a brain injury when he was struck by a pipe.
He developed aphasia
But my rescues were braver.
They expect me to be the strong, silent type.

---

[1] Bacchanalia: Roman festival of Bacchus celebrated with dancing, song, alcohol and revelry.

[2] fluent aphasia = Wernicke's aphasia. The patient can speak in sentences that sound like normal speech, but some of the words are made-up words or have some sounds that are not correct.

[3] 'da capo' = musical term that means 'back to the beginning' and 'ad nauseam' = used to refer to the fact that something has been done or repeated so often that it has become annoying or tiresome.

Three Sonnets [1]

1:
Angry, furious, whole identity agitation,
My aphasia predicament leaves me depressed.
Frustration, frustration, frustration, frustration!
I can't voice the issues that should be addressed.

I am angry that I can't be the man I was before!
I am furious my persona has suffered so much
diminishment!
I am agitated that my communication has suffered
a tug-of-war,
Torn between my abject depression and my firm
commitment.

But, what kind of man would be deterred
By a challenge that could be a destiny turning point?
What kind of man could be prevented from being heard
By whatever means. That dialogue can be a viewpoint?

I will determine myself with a communication ascension
Drawing, charades, speech therapeutic reinvention!

---

[1] A sonnet is a poem of 14 lines that reflects upon a single issue or idea
with an ABAB CDCD EFEF GG rhyme scheme. Usually the 'mood' alters
with the nine line, and the last two lines offer a solution.

2:

Woken from a dreamless slumber, an enervation
I was confused, foggy, and somehow – broke.
A middle cerebral artery infarction.
In layman's term … I had a stroke.

I was paralysed – the whole right side.
The doctor's injection fixed that.
But my speech was absent, talking denied
I had aphasia and conversations fell flat.

It was odd to remember words but not to access them
Or words that emerged that I didn't intend
Or words that my mouth couldn't cope with'em
Or tip-of-the-tongue words: a pretence.

Give me time and space, my only plea
Just remember, word poor, I am – still – me.

3:

Like the fairy tales at my bedtime childhood:
The leafy roof impenetrable, the ground boggy,
Wandering the tangled pathways in the wood
Looking for witches or wolves or froggies.

That was my brain after my stroke.
Unnecessary talking. Disneedless conversations.
A few random words I managed with a croak,
Calm, unperturbed, despite bewildered hesitations,

Not comprehending my families concern.
Six months I languished lost in that forest.
The sunlight of recovery made me adjourn
My fairy tale muddle, my aphasic metaphorist.

'Speech therapies and practice', the family decreed.
(My loving whānau was there in my greatest need.)

An Aphasic Villanelle [1]

They said that my aphasia was a matter of degree
An issue for my personal communication
But this person before you? It's still me.

My speech, my talking, is suspect, unfree.
It leaves me depressed, angry and full of frustration
But, they said, that my aphasia was a matter of degree.

Stuttering and spluttering, hesitating and tongue-tied,
Wrong words, talking twisted – a matter of malformation
But this person before you? It's still me.

Uncertain, tentative, confused: you must agree.
Despondent, I feel a sense of self-castigation.
But, they said, that my aphasia was a matter of degree.

'How can I function in this world?' is my plea
Meaningful conversation, always an obscuration
But this person before you? It's still **me**.

I want to hide, be reclusive, just flee.
They thought I would improve, aphasia a flirtation,
They said that my aphasia was a matter of degree
But this person before you? It – is – **still** – **ME**!

---

[1] The villanelle was established as a French form in the 16th Century. It consists of 19 lines, organised into five stanzas of three lines each, and one closing stanza of four lines.
The repetition and rhyme scheme is A[1]BA[2] ABA[1] ABA[2] ABA[1] ABA[2] ABA[1]A[2].

Free verse

A wife's response[1] after her husband's stroke:

You looked at me with eyes that did not see
Annie Stephens

You looked at me with eyes that did not see
So quickly your self was hidden deep within
A grimace became your grin and from your lips no
sound came forth.
Is this your parting from this earthly realm we share
Or can love, man's skill and angels keep you here?
My dearest love of 40 years hence
How it gladdens me when your glance holds my eyes again
And your fingers clasp my own
No matter that no words are said
Your hum is blessed music to my ears.

---

[1] Annie Stephens – my wife – penned these poems in the days after my
2015 stroke. Ngā mihi nui ki a koe mo to nui aroha!

Midnight Sky

Annie Stephens

The midnight sky recedes with its secrets of sleep and
stars and moon
Its mystical workings tucked away from sight like a newly
made bed
With a clear blue cover pulled smoothly over
The barren hills glow golden as the sun reveals its
warmth
As a bald head tucked in the newly made bed of land
and sky with whispered secrets in between.

The Glorious Sun

Annie Stephens

The sun gloriously illuminates a new day
And people unfold and enter into the fresh new hope
light and warmth brings
Yet what does it bring you my love of many years
Held in a bubble that moves on its own path
Able to see and walk within its perimeters
Yet not embrace the day wholeheartedly with gusto,
espresso and eagerness as yesterday?

Onepoto Cave[1]

James Stephens

We skate, slip, slide and less than gracefully wander
over the surface of our lives.
How seldom do we note the depths – crevice, crevasse,
chasm
Paper over – but paper thin,
     a skin, a hide, a veneer.
I keep looking down the holes – wondering –
     at how they twist and open, or disappear into
murky distance.

All my life I've jumped, clambered or fallen down them –
Sometimes sliding – shallow, muddy.
Sometimes falling through coddling blackness
     air rushing past my ears – cold and quivering –
other senses blinded,
Wondering: where is bottom?
What is bottom?
When…?

---

[1] This poem is historical. I wrote this poem for my wife, Annie, after I fell in the cave at Waikaremoana Lake: see story 6: Unspeakability and the eighth account in this book. I have tweaked it, but the sentiments are still real and true – especially now I have aphasia.

Sometimes it **is** beautiful there –
       Warm wormlit in an earthly starscape –
       creviced constellations –
       galaxies in these gashes beneath the ground.

Sometimes uncomfortable – cold, wet, rocky – **hard**.
Sometimes it was a quick jaunt down easy steps –
Sometimes not so easy
Sometimes it **hurts** – and getting out is **hard**.

And you – you have been my rope, my lamp, my life-
line/lifelight
       else I should have been lost – lost.
Will the lamp still be lit? The line hold secure?
How often shall I fall and not extinguish or shred you?

You – more than I deserve. Do you too love my
subterranean self?

I can be comfortable here – in the dark, deep places
       but I can't live there.
I must live in the light –
       there my hope, my rescue is.

The Kumanu Group

Version A

1: The Kumanu[1] Group

2: Misheardliness – Liz

3: Aureateness – Thomas

4: Loquaciousness – Pa

5: PPA – Leslie

---

[1] Kumanu is a Māori word that means to cherish, support, nurse or care for someone.

1A: The Kumanu Group

Jane was nervous.

She looked at herself in the mirror.
Her unblemished face had a healthy tan and her eyes were dark brown with flecks of green.
With her non-distracting nose and generous lips married with an intelligent sense of humour, she was 'very attractive'.

Though, it didn't matter with this group, she considered.
These people are seeking more than 'attractiveness'.
They are seeking some sort of correlation about their experience with other people with aphasia.
They want to know how others deal with the frustrations.

And **that** made Jane nervous.

She went down the corridor waving to her colleague, Sue.
Jane and Sue were Community Aphasia Advisors for Aphasia New Zealand.
Jane had a new role: The Kumanu Group.

She opened the door to her room and surveyed the room.

Whew! she said to herself.
I got this. I got this. Breathe.

At two minutes to ten, her first 'clients' came in.
Jane greeted them individually and encouraged them to write their name on a name tag.
Checking her watch again, she was surprised to discover it was already five past ten.

Jane clapped her hands – gently.
'I think we should begin.
Can you take a seat in the circle? Sit. Sit.'
The people sorted themselves out in the circle of chairs.

'Mōrena[1],' Jane announced, with more conviction than she felt.
'Good morning. Kia ora[2]. Hello!

'I am Jane Forrest and I am a CAA – a Community Aphasia Advisor – for Aphasia New Zealand.
I think most of you have met Sue. She has been working with the people who **have** aphasia, your loved ones.

----

[1] Mōrena = Morning (Māori).

[2] Kia ora – a Māori greeting common in Aotearoa New Zealand. Literally it means "have life" or "be healthy".

'But this meeting is called The Kumanu Group.
Kumanu is a Māori word that means to cherish and support for someone.
The purpose of this group is to support the people who are caring with someone who has aphasia.
That's you. Okay?

'Most often we usually open the floor for anyone who wants to share about your experiences.
People with aphasia often have very different experiences.
It can be confronting, or frustrating or hilarious.

'Of course, the Kumanu Group should be a safe place.
So, I ask you that anonymity should be maintained.

— — — — —- ~~~ — — — — —

'So … Can you introduce yourselves, and the person who you care for? Shall I go first?

'So – I am Jane Forrester.
I was born in Palmerston North – the third child of five.
When I was fifteen my mother had a stroke.
She had aphasia.
It was, and still is, a puzzling disability.
My mother, basically, shut down.
Didn't communicate at all.

She died two years after her stroke with no improvement. I wanted to know more so I trained as a Speech Therapist.
I wanted to help people with aphasia and their loved ones.'

'So...' Jane looked to her right, gesturing with an outstretched hand, inviting ...

A blonde, curly-haired young woman looked nervously at Jane, and then around the group.
'I am Beatrix. Most call me Trixie.
And I care for mother who has aphasia. Liz.
She had several strokes over the last seven, eight years..'

Beatrix almost sighed with relief as she looked at the older woman to her right.

'Um...I am Patricia,' she said. 'My husband, Leslie... Les... has aphasia.
We are living in Waikanae, in the hills above the town.'

The person on Patricia's right acknowledged her with a faint nod.
He was tall and slim with dark skin.
His short black hair was carefully styled
His clothes were meticulously chic.

With a definite accent, he announced: 'My good name is Manisha Rajgopal. My partner, Thomas, has aphasia – a brain injury.
We live and work at Waikanae Beach.'

The next person on the right was the other male in the group.

He was a Māori tanē[1]: massively built, tall with strong shoulders and brawny arms.
He wore an impressive pounamu[2] pendant around his neck.
His upper body displayed traditional Tā Moko[3] with intricate designs stretching from behind his ears, across his robust neck, and adorning his shoulders and arms.

A beautiful moko, Jane thought, *but some people would see it at threatening.*
His face was beatific though, and he smiled as he gently spoke.

'Mōrena. I am Hohepa Tauhu.

---

[1] tanē = a male.

[2] pounamu = Aotearoa New Zealand jade (greenstone)

[3] Tā Moko is the traditional Māori art of tattooing intricate designs into the skin.

I live at a marae just out of Ōtaki[1].
'My koro, my grandfather, has aphasia.
He had a stroke, about six years ago. Kia ora.'

'Kia ora Hohepa,' said Jane.
'At the marae, you have extended whānau?' [2]

'All our whānau are involved but I am the main carer,'
Hohepa responded pleasantly.
'My koro raised me and I owe him everything.
Now, I care for him.'

Jane looked at the next person. 'And…?'

'Oh…um…Kia ora. My name is Sarah…Sarah
Gibson, and my husband has aphasia,' said Sarah
anxiously. 'Gary. Gary Gibson.
'He was born in the Hutt Valley and I was born in
Levin. Gary had a stroke. Three years ago.'

Jane smiled at Sarah encouragingly and then turned
to the next person.

'I care for my partner, Roberto,' the woman said,
with more of a trace than an accent.

---

[1] Marae = meeting place (Māori), usually including the wharenui (big
house) and the area and buildings around it.
[2] whānau = family (extended)

'Roberto had the stroke ago three years.
We born and lived for Quebec, but emigrated this New Zealand about six years ago.
My name is Amélie. Friends called my Ami.'

The last person was on Jane's left. She was young – early twenties.
Her long hair, bleached white with pink tips, was swept up into a loose bun.
Her top was a black T-shirt with a rock-band logo in jagged lightning fonts.
Her black jeans had jagged rents across them, fixed by safety pins.
On her feet she had unpolished crimson Doc Martin boots.

'Hi ya. Adrienne, Adrienne Foster,' she said with a very strong British accent.
'We arrive here 'bout five years since for 'ald country.
Ma and Pa had a car crash two-year ago and Ma, she gone ov'r.
Pa ha' a friggin' brain injury, innit.
So, Pa has de asp-ha-shia.' [1]

The group were perplexed but Jane rallied.

---

[1] Um…too hard! Get what you can from the context of what Adrienne says.

'Oh, I am so sorry about your Ma. Your mother,' Jane commiserated.
'And your Pa. You have other help? Any other relations or friends?'
'The Sallies[1] can help som'times,' Adja said. 'They's hel'ful, innit.'

'Good,' Jane carefully responded. 'That's good.'

Jane looked around at her 'clients', making sure that she remembered everyone's name.
Well…what a mix!

More confident now, she smiled encouragingly at all of them and said: 'Thank you. Kia ora.
So, we will open the floor to anyone who wants to share their experiences…
And remember…a safe place.'

Immediately, the curly blonde woman spoke up.

— — — —- ~~~ — — — —

---

[1] Sallies = The Salvation Army.

2A: Misheardliness – Liz

'Mōrena[1]. Beatrice…Trixie.
And my Mum – Elizabeth – Liz – has aphasia.
As I said, she has had several strokes over the last seven, eight years.'

'Um…she has improved but it is still hard to understand her.
It is confusing, and frustrating for me.

'When I pay attention, I can decipher what she means. The context is clear.
But if I don't know the context, miscommunication results.

'For example, we went to the zoo last month.
Mum and I and Rosalie, my daughter.
At the Zoo Café and mum flicked her hand.
You know what aphasiacs do – the stuttering words.
She said to Rosalie: "Um….um…hopt…full-it…fu-lly is… it…was not…a ce…cea-sse fire."

'Rosalie and I were puzzled.
She repeated: "Cease fire." '

---

[1] Mōrena = [good] morning

Beatrice gestured a "tah dah" with her hands.
'It was a "Tsetse fly".
The one that can give you sleeping sickness.
Context, I guess. Because we are at the zoo.'

Several of the group chuckled at the thought.

Beatrice went on. 'Rosalie wanted to go the toilet.
I didn't know where they are.
Mum was still finishing her coffee and she said to me "Monkey".
I nodded and raced off with Rosalie.
Then we went down to the monkey's enclosure.
We looked for Mum for half an hour.
We went down the path to the entrance and there she was!
I said to her: "I thought you were looking at the monkeys?"
She was clearly confused and indicated the tent.
"Mark-key? Mark-key!"
She meant the marquee.'

The Kumanu Group giggled among themselves, appreciating the confusion.

'But…she knows what's what though.
Sooner or later.

'For instance, I was going to the supermarket.
She wanted a brand of peanut butter.
She said: "Cloves" then shook her head.
"Comet?" Again the head shaking.
"Cosmic?" Again.
Then she changed tack and said:
"The goddess for horticulture! The Roman one!"
I had my phone and Googled it. It was Ceres.
The brand was Ceres Organic Peanut Butter.'

Some of the group burst out laughing.

'Sometimes, when I speak, she hears a different word entirely.
For example, we were sitting out on the patio and Mum went in to the kitchen for a homemade snack.
I saw a strange cat jumping on her neighbours fence.
It was a long-haired ginger cat with an amazing tail.
When Mum came out, I questioned her about the neighbour's cat.

'She said: "The…person this…this…there…has…no cat."
So I said; "I think it was feral."
She said: "That …it is… usually so."
I didn't understand, so I said: "What?"
She said: "They have… all that."
I **still** didn't understand.
She brushed her hand up the other sleeve.

"The hair…skin-thing."
I said: "The fur?" She nodded.
Then I understood.
"I think it was a *feral cat*. Wild. Feral."
"Oh" she said. "I …it was…um…tail is…was fur-ry." '

A burst of laughter from the group.

'She often confuses words.
She chooses a similar word but not the right one.
For example, I arrived when mum was clearing her bits-and-bob's cupboard.
She always gets articles out of the newspaper or magazines.
'She eventually said: "I should have a bag for the syphilis." '

Again, Beatrice dramatically made a gesture of helplessness.
'I said: "What?" "The syphilis" she said.
What on earth? I said to myself.
My perplexed look prompted her to have a charade session.

'She flattened her left hand and scissored her right hand with two fingers like she was punching holes.'
Beatrice demonstrated.

'Then she drew her right index finger on the flattened left hand with random paths.

'I went through a list. Lots of things. Rats or mice? Spiders? Ants? She fluttered her fingers on her right hand. Legs? Lots of legs?
Then she leapt across to some jewellery – some necklaces.
Then I got it. Silver. Silverfish. Insects, like slaters, that can eat holes in paper. She wanted a camphor bag to chase them out. Silverfish. Not syphilis.'

Jane heard hearty laughter from most of the group.
She looked around the circle.
Manisha, Hohepa, Amelie and Adrienne were laughing out loud.
Sarah's face was a study of confused puzzlement but she was grinning anyway.
But Patricia's face was stony.

The laughter dwindled. Beatrice sighed.
'What can you do? Miscommunication.
As I said, it is hard – it's frustrating – but at the same time, hilarious.'

— — — —- ~~~ — — — —

2A: The Kumanu Group

Jane responded: 'Thank you Beatrice – Trixie.
That's good that she has other strategies.
Charades or diversional thinking.
Clearly your mother is, well, "on to it", if you see what I mean.
I know it is frustrating for you but she is coping.'

'Frustrating but…good. Mostly,' Beatrice answered.
'I *know* she is improving, but it's good to speak about it in this forum. The Kumanu Group.
People who understand about aphasia.
It's an outlet for me.'

Beatrice looked around the group with a grateful expression.
'Thank you. All.'

'So…anyone else?' said Jane. 'Anyone else care to share?'

After a moment Manisha waggled his hand and spoke up.

— — — —- ~~~ — — — —

3A: Aureateness[1] – Thomas

'Hello – Manisha,' he confirmed to everyone.
'My partner, Thomas, have aphasia.
It was a brain injury, after rock climbing accident.'

Jane thought: *His accent was subtle. Some of the words were not quite right but he was a clear speaker.*

'I met with Thomas, when he was bubbly person.
He used talk to any topic.
After the accident he mostly struggles to say anything.
Any. Thing. At. All.

'He does not…um…stutter though, like Trixie's mother.
He just stopped speaking.
It seems the words stuck in his throat – like a block.

'Then he comes out with complex sentences.
Multi-syllable words. Clear. Precise.
But they are not the run-of-the-mill words.
It seems he has eaten a dictionary.
It's like living with Oscar Wilde. Or Shakespeare!'

---

[1] Aureateness - a person characterised by an ornate style of writing or speaking.

'That's amazing!' interrupted Beatrice.
'That's unusual, isn't it?'
She looks to Jane as the resident expert.

On the spot, Jane responded: 'Yes…but aphasia presents itself in various forms.
It is quite unusual but I guess Thomas's brain is working things out before he speaks.
Can you give us an example?'

Manisha thought for a moment.
'Well…for example, we were going to walk.
I said to him: "I like this path beside the sea.
It's peaceful. Tranquil."
He acknowledged by nodding.
We walk on.
After five minutes he said:
"Extremely amiable to perambulate with you." '

The fake-perplexed look on Manisha's face was comical.
Beatrice and Amélie giggled.
Hohepa chuckled and Adrienne laughed out loud.

'Oh my gawd!' she blurted out.
'Ha! Ha! Real talk? Oh my gawd!'

Manisha was pleased with this reaction and grinned.

'About this too. We had a cup of tea last week.
I brought the cup over to him but I spilled a little.
I got a cloth, wiped it up, put it back in the sink,
returned and sat down again.
Then he said to me:
"You should have reduced the capacity of the cup."

'Not "The mug is too full", but "You should have
reduced the capacity of the cup." '

'Or….we share the dinner duties.
One time I was making chickpeas and lentil red curry
in the slow cooker.
Thomas looked in the larder and glanced at me,
three, or four times.
At last he said: "You have depleted our resources!" '

Laughter erupted.

'And, when he tasted the meal, he eventually said:
"You have transformed our resources enchantedly!" '

More hearty laughter.

Jane spoke up. 'Manisha. Thanks for that.
It seems that Tom has almost sorted it out?
He seems to be recovering?'

'I guess,' he replied.
'But the thing is… We have no conversation.
And with other persons? It is impossible to have conversations with other persons.

'For example, we went to the park and there met three friends.
Jason, one of our friends, noticed some paradise ducks.
We admired their plumage.
Thomas didn't say anything – as usual.

'The discussion ranged through several topics.
Then John, another friend, pointed out a man and woman.
They were walking from their car to the noticeboard.
The body language was clear.
They were unhappy with each other.
John said: "Things are not right in Paradise."

'Another two or three topics were covered by the rest of us.
A couple of minutes later, we saw the man and woman again – obviously reconciled.
"Ah!" said John. "They have made up!"

'Thomas said: "If they are nodding, they will have sex."

'Startled looks were cast.

Then I realised.
He was thinking about the ducks.
I blurted out: "We were looking at the people, not the ducks."

'See what I mean.' Manisha looked around with a pleading look on his face.
'He can't…**can't** operate in a social situation.
I am patient, I think, but this situation has ruined our social life.'

'Have you talked about this with Tom?' suggested Jane.

'Yes…yes…But I don't know if he understands.'
I want to help…but sometimes I cry with frustration.'
Manisha broke into a wry smile.
'And when I cried, what do you think Thomas said.'
He struck a pose and in a posh voice, said: "What has instigated your pitiful tears?" '

Manisha held his hands wide, inviting everyone in to his feelings.
With a silly grin, said:
'It is like speaking with a slow-witted Shakespeare!'

The room broke into laughter.
They all knew what it is like to have a loved one with aphasia.

Manisha ducked his head smiling shyly, and sat down on his seat.

———— - ~~~ ————

3A: The Kumanu Group

'Thank you for sharing with us, Manisha,' Jane said.
'It is an unusual problem. Maybe we can all think about that for the next time we meet?'

Adrienne was gesticulating wildly with her right hand, her face a grimace of anticipation.
Jane took pity on her.
'Adrienne. You want to share?'

'Yeah! Yeah alright yeah,' Adrienne burst out.
She almost fell off her chair in her enthusiasm.

———— - ~~~ ————

4A: Loquaciousness[1] – Pa

'Hi y'awl,' Adrienne burst out.
'Trix - sounds da your ma is a hoot!
And Mansh – ye jolly-boy Tom is hilar'ous!
Shake-bloody-speare! Hah!'[2]

Adrienne's face lit up with unabated joy.

'For me. My Pa is compl'tely diff'rent, innit.
He is a gas-bag.
I can't understan' most of ari frickin' gobshite shit!
But-tah … plez call me Adja. Adja Foster.

'Pa done apha-si-a, from the acc'dent, the brain
injury. The car acc'dent. Ma karked it.
With Pa, most of his words are nonsensical.
He spills da vocals like a bluddy fauc't, innit.
I can't make heado'tail mostly, so that's dead sound.
He was da the ozzy ov three months.'

Jane looked at the rest of the group.
They were bewildered by the torrent of words.

---

[1] Loquacious - characterised by excessive talk; wordy.

[2] Too hard to translate it all here! Get what you can from the context or
what Jane requests in response.

Good lord! Jane thought to herself.
It is enough to deal with people with aphasia, but when the 'normal' people use jargon and…
Jane knew she must step in.

'Thanks Adrienne…Adja…but I think your jargon is escaping us.
Can you make them more clear. Um… for example: "dead sound" and "ozzy"? '

'Oh…sozz…um…sorry 'bout that,' Adja admonished herself. 'I get caught up.

' "dead sound" is…um… "okay", or "every'ing is alright" and um…"ozzy" is "hospital".
If I slow th' down, that could be better, innit?'

Adja looked about the group nodding her contrition.
Then she carried on.

'So…as I said, my Pa runs off all th'time.
He spills 'is words.'
Adja paused dramatically.
She chopped her hands like a cleaver.
'All. The. Time. Like a…a tap leaking wadder.
Sozz…Wa-ter.
She paused, and again beat the words again.
'No. Sense.'

'I can't understan' it.
Not sure if it's proppa, or he blaggin' me 'ead…'
Adja looked at the puzzled faces of the group.
'Sozz – sorry again!
Um…"blaggin" is…um…"did it delib'rately".

'Eee gee he says somethin' like,' and Adja dropped
her voice almost an octave:
' "Da wally wally looks it was wally ding to da jump
or wally yea, yea for da for la wally to wally…"
Adja shrugged her shoulders.
'He drives me nuts, innit.
He goes on and on and on and on.'

The group were bewildered.
The confusing jargon.
Her over-melodramatic, OTT[1] gestures.
And she spoke so fast!

Jane interrupted carefully.
'Thanks Adja. It's better if you slow down.'
Then, she looks Adja in the eye. 'I think I can help.'

'There are many forms of aphasia.
The most common ones are Broca's Aphasia and
Wernicke's Aphasia.'

---

[1] OTT = Over The Top – very exaggerated.

'I can spell it on the whiteboard…'
She took a marker from her table and crossed to the whiteboard.

She spelled out the name:
B-R-O-C-A-'-S A-P-H-A-S-I-A.
'And the other one is…'
W-E-R-N-I-C-K-E-'-S A-P-H-A-S-I-A.
Then Jane wrote "Non-fluent" with an arrow to Broca's Aphasia.
"Fluent" with an arrow to Wernicke's Aphasia.

'Most people have Broca's Aphasia.
Non-fluent aphasia.
For example, Thomas and Elizabeth have Broca's Aphasia.
They experience loss or mispronounced words.
But what they say is sensible. Eventually.'

'Their aphasia has a different response from your Pa's, Adja.
Your Pa, has Wernicke's Aphasia. Fluent Aphasia.
People with this type of aphasia speak fluently.
The words come out with no problem.
Your 'tap leaking water'!

'Often they use 'filler' words to fill the gap if they can't pronounce the word that they want to use.

I guess, your Pa is using 'wally' as his filler word?'

Adja was riveted.
Her mouth was open like a baby bird.
'Oh, yea! so…so…yea!
So…that's sensible to me!'
Adja stopped suddenly.

'Oh…I get that now. Hal-le-lu-jah!' she trumpeted.
' "Wally" 'is filler-word.
When 'e doesn't know what 'e wants to say.'

The pink-tipped head dropped to her chest again.
Puzzled, she looked up again at Jane.
'But what about the phrases that almost make sense?
He says: "Da secon' time proppa boss" all the time.
What's this 'bout?'

Again, several of the group had puzzled looks.
Adja spoke quickly: 'Sorry…"Da secon' time proppa
boss" is "the second time is great." "Amazing." '

'Often sensible phrases,' Jane confirmed, 'are
another filler phrase.
But it is more sensible. And that is a good thing!
If your father has moved to having a sensible phrase,
like "Da secon' time proppa boss", he is improving.'

Relief flooded Adja's face.
'Wow! That's dead sound – um… that's good.
Ta for your explaining. About Werneck Aph'sia.'

Something dawned on Adja's face.
Her face lit up again.

'Act'shally, Pa can say somethin' that I understand.'
Again, Anja spoke with a bass voice:
' "Eeyar. Da first time still de ozzy wuz Antwacky.
Youz hav jarg clobber.
Da first time ma kecks fallin' down.
And da doc dead divvy, la. Bevied up."

'That translates to "Here you are, first time in th'
hospital and it was so old-fashioned.
Th' clothes were fake an' my trousers kept fallin'
down. And th' doctor was so stupid an' drunk." '

Everyone giggled, laughed, guffawed out loud at this
account and Adja's idiosyncratic way of expressing it.

Everyone – besides Patricia.

She abruptly stood up.
Her seat clattered away to the wall behind.

'It's all a joke,' she sobbed.

'It's hilarious. That's what you all think.
A laughing matter...'

Abruptly, Patricia burst into tears.
She collapsed to her haunches, sobbing, hands over
her face.

— — — —· ~~~ — — — —

4A: The Kumanu Group

The mirth died on everyone's lips.
Everyone was aghast, even Jane.

Hohepa crossed the circle and gently took Patricia's
arms.
He raised her to her feet again.
He looked compassionately into her eyes.
He murmured 'That's okay. That's okay.
Ka taea e au ....Maaku koe e tiaki[1]
Shh. Kaua e tangi! Kia tau tō wairua![2] Shh. That's
okay.'

Patricia's sobbing eased. She dropped her head.
'That's okay. Kaua e tangi,' Hohepa insisted.

---

[1](Māori): I will take care of you

[2] (Māori): Don't cry! May your soul rest in peace!

'Whakamārie, whakamārie…' a mantra that calmed
the stricken woman.

Jane looked at Sue's list.
Ah! I should have known.
These stories are not helping…
She hurriedly looked at the group gauging what she
should do.

Most were getting over the shock of Patricia's violent
outburst and collapse.

Jane crossed the room to Hohepa and Patricia.
She indicated that they could sit down.
Hohepa looked at her with compassion and empathy.
Patricia welcomed his warm, teddy-bear comfort.

Jane took a big breath…
I am responsible. I am responsible.

'Are you okay?' she said to Patricia.
'Can you speak about your husband's aphasia?
Or should I do it…'

———— -~~~ ————

5A: PPA – Leslie

'I am okay,' Patricia explained.
'Thank you Hohepa. Thank you.
And the rest of you…
Sorry about that…outburst.
Jane can you explain about Leslie's condition.
The PPA…'

'Sure,' Jane agreed.
She looked at the group anxiously.

'Leslie, has PPA. Primary Progressive Aphasia.
It is a form of aphasia – a dementia of words.
The loss of words and meaning is progressive.
It doesn't recover.'

Jane lets the words sink in as she looked around the circle.

Adrienne spoke. 'So the words don't come back, innit?'
Her face was contorted with puzzlement and uncertainty.

'It's like Alzhe-mers?' Sarah said.
'The aphasia doesn't get better?'

'PPA is a rare type of aphasia,' Jane announced with more confidence than she felt.

'Frontotemporal dementia. This means that the brain is affected in the frontal and/or temporal lobes where the language centres are.
The symptoms get more severe as the dementia progresses.
Patients suffer word loss, and reading and writing skills are debilitated.'

She slowed down and breathed slowly.
Things were relatively calm now.
She looked directly at Patricia.
'Are you okay?' Jane asked.
'Do you want to go outside for some fresh air or…'

'Thanks Jane. Thanks…um…everyone.'
Patricia straightened up.
'I want to talk. About Leslie.
I apologise for my outburst. It was not fair to you – Trixie, Manisha, and Adja.
I know that some of the antics with aphasia are hilarious.
As they say: You have to laugh, otherwise you'd be crying all the time.'

Patricia's eyes filled with tears.

She shook her head and started again.

'It began with a few words,' Patricia spoke haltingly.
'Leslie, Les, was the chief librarian at Hamilton Public Library.
He could speak to anyone on any given topic.

'At first it was a loss of difficult words.
It was like your partner Manisha, Thomas.
Usually he was always saying grandiose words.
But, two or three years ago, he stopped doing that.
"Magnificent operatic aria" became "good song".
"Sumptuous and delicious kai" changed to "good food".
It was odd to me but I thought he was just tired.

'Then he forgot place names.
He said it was "A senior moment. Don't worry about it!"
But something was not right.

'I went to his office.
There were lots of yellow post-it notes all over the place.
On the drawers, on the computer, on the desk.
Beside the phone – a post-it note for **my** phone number.

'I insisted that we went to the doctor.
The diagnosis: Primary Progressive Aphasia.'

Patricia's head drooped.
She dabbed with the tissues hidden in her fist.
The circle waited in anticipation.

'Leslie retired early from the library.
They had a lovely farewell for him.
He was always a gifted speaker.
Now, he couldn't speak without writing it down.
He practised saying it to me, and I saw the humiliation.
The humiliation that he could not do what he had always done. Speak freely.

'He was very depressed.
"A librarian who lost his words!" he would often say.

'And last week...'
Patricia looked at the ceiling and her face contorted.
'He couldn't ... couldn't remember my name!'
She buried her head in her hands, sobbing.

Jane glanced around the circle.
They were all looking at Patricia.
They are all studying her, Jane thought.
No... Not studying, Witnessing. Empathising.

No-one spoke for a few minutes.

At last, Patricia raised her head again.
'Sorry. Sorry. I… I just… I would…. um…I thought I was getting… getting…'

'That's okay. It's fine,' Jane comforted.
'Take your time. It's a safe place, remember.'

Patricia looked up to Jane with appreciation.
Then she focused on the group.
Empathetic looks greeted her – from everyone.
Her eyes filled with tears again but from gratitude, not pain.

'Les is going to the Aphasia Group every Thursday.
It is marvellous what the Aphasia Group is doing.
Everytime Les comes out of their session beaming.
Often he can't tell me what happened, but it gave him some joy with others who have the same condition.'

'Have you some support?' Hohepa asked.
'Can you tell anyone about this PPA – whānau? Friends?'

'I guess the children?
But they are busy and overseas.
I have a younger sister. But we are not close.
I'm not sure if she will understand, or help...'

'Hav'yu told ya kids?' blurted out Adrienne.

She looked into Adrienne's eyes and saw Adja as a compassionate presence, genuinely wanting to help. She smiled cautiously.
'The children know that Les has retired.
But not about the PPA.'

'Well,' Adrienne responded. 'Better that you tell it. Deadly true!'

Jane confirmed:
'It is important to have some support.
And your children – your whānau. **And** your sister. They won't thank you for keeping this condition from them. You **have** to tell them.'

Patricia flinched.

Hmmm, Jane mused. *I think that Patricia is in denial herself.*

Jane changed tack.
'AphasiaNZ has a booklet about PPA. It is only a few pages long – not academic.
It came out last week,' Jane suggested, handing five brochures to Patricia.

'One for you, and one for your children and your sister. I suspect that they will contact you immediately. Maybe your children will get flights home. Sooner than later. Before Leslie can't talk anymore.'

Patricia's eyes welled up again, but she was not overcome.
Thankfully. I think it's getting through to her.

'Have you a good relationship with your doctor?' Jane ventured. 'Is he or she knowledgeable about PPA?

'I think so,' Patricia rallied. 'Dr. Sunwaro. She seems to know about it – the PPA. She suggested that Leslie should get his affairs in order – his finances, his will, his funeral wishes…'

Again, Patricia's eyes filled with tears.
She shook off her sadness, straightened her head and shoulders and carried on.

'We did that already. His affairs are in order.
It is only his words that are affected.
He can understand me, most of the time.
If I talk slowly and use simple sentences.'

Amélie suggested: 'I not sure if it could help, but Roberto joined a choir, a neurological choir.
The singing helps.
And music seemed to help with memory.'

'Ya, ya!' Adja excitedly called out.
'My Pa singing is deft betta than his talkin'.
And he mostly sings 'n tune.
It's nun' painful, I mean.'

Sarah spoke suddenly.
'I saw something … a documentary about Alzhemers, Al-zhe-imers?
They had a photo album that had all sorts of photos. I borrowed that idea and it was excellent for Gary. Seeing the pictures helped him with the words and he could talk about them.'

Hohepa nodded. 'Kia ora. We have something like that. For my koro[1], I set up a memory board in the wharenui.[2] It was helpful.
It gave him a feeling of oranga ngākau, reassurance.'

'Yes! Yes!' Manisha was excited.
'We could set up the image bank.
A database for things meaningful to him.

---

[1] koro = an elderly Maori man, especially a male relative or grandfather.
[2] wharenui = the main building on the marae.

We can print them out and make a book. There are several businesses that can do it.
I – and Thomas – could assist.
You and Leslie could come around.'

He looked at Hohepa and added:
'Maybe the four of us can come to the marae?'

Manisha jumped out of his chair excited about his plan.
'Yes! See what's what?
And…' he broke into a ecstatic grin, 'your koro, Thomas and Les could be…how you say it…the three amigos!'

'Ka pai! Kia ora ka pai!'
Hohepa enthusiastically responded.

Ten minutes had passed after Patricia's tearful almost-exit.

Now she was coddled and cared for.

She was overwhelmed by the care and concern of these one-hour-friends.

— — — —- ~~~ — — — —

5A: The Kumanu Group

Jane let the conversations go on.
She looked around the room.

Adja and Amélie were talking about the effectiveness of music therapy.
Amélie was encouraging Adja's 'Pa' to join the choir.

Sarah and Beatrix were comparing notes about their loved ones.

Manisha and Hohepa were flanking Patricia.
They were excited to share their ideas and plans with the online photo board.

Wow! This is wonderful! Jane thought.
I should have a photo! I didn't expect The Kumanu Group would work so quickly.

After a while, she stood up and called the group together.

'Thank you. Thanks for sharing your experiences. I hope it has been good for you all?

'I see some of you are swapping email addresses and phone numbers.

Just saying again, The Kumanu Group is a safe place. What we have discussed should be anonymous. Okay?

'We will meet again next month.
I will send an email to you all.
Maybe you can think about what else we can do to support our loved ones.

'But, the **most** important thing is – look after **yourselves**!
You are the reason that most of your aphasiac loved ones survive. Truly.'

She emphasised each word borrowing Adja's "hands-like-a-cleaver" gesture.
'Look. After. Your. Selves!'

After a moment, she relaxed her hands by her sides and grinned.

'Good luck! Haere tū atu, hoki tū mai[1]. Haere rā, haere rā, haere rā koutou.[2]'

---

[1] Māori idiom: "Go well and return in good health, have a safe trip."

[2] Māori: 'Haere rā' = farewell to someone who is leaving. 'Koutou' = 'three or more people.'

With an appreciative and congratulatory nod, the group eventually drifted out.

Jane sat down on a chair.

Whew! That was amazing!
I can't wait to tell Sue about it...

— — — —- ~~~ — — — —

The Kumanu Group

Version B

1: **The Kumanu[1] Group**

2: **Misheardliness – Liz**

3: **Aureateness – Thomas**

4: **Loquaciousness – Pa**

5: **PPA – Leslie**

---

[1] Kumanu is a Māori word that means to cherish, support, nurse or care for someone.

1B: The Kumanu Group

Jane was nervous.

She looked at herself in the mirror in the woman's bathroom at the Community Centre. Her black hair was fashionably streaked with blonde highlights. Her unblemished face had a healthy tan and her almond-shaped eyes were dark brown with flecks of green. *Courtesy of my Irish-Estonian-Spanish heritage.* Her left ear was pierced by seven studs with seven gem stones corresponding to her chakras. With her non-distracting nose and generous lips married with an athlete's body and an intelligent sense of humour, she acknowledged the popular opinion that she was 'very attractive'.

Though, it didn't matter with this group, she considered. Being nervous, she was quite prepared to have a silent conversation with herself in the mirror. *These people are seeking more than 'attractiveness'. They are seeking ... help. Comfort. Solace.*
No. Not that, Jane countered to her reflection. *They are seeking some sort of correlation about their experience with their loved one. With other people with the same problem. Aphasia. They want to know how others deal with the frustrations. The depression. The anger.*
And **that** made Jane nervous.

She looked again in the mirror, brushed her hair back into a ponytail, secured it with a red hair-tie, and set her face in a welcoming but no-nonsense smile.
I got this, she convinced herself. *I got this.*

Jane checked her watch. Ten to ten. She went down the corridor to her allocated room, waving to her colleague, Sue, in Room 3. *At least she knows what she is doing. But me? Whewww...*

Jane and Sue were Community Aphasia Advisors for Aphasia New Zealand. Sue had been a CAA for six years but Jane was a new arrival. Sue was looking after the people with aphasia in Room 3, but Jane had a new role: The Kumanu Group.

She opened the door to Room 5A and surveyed the room. She had already set out the chairs in a circle and laid a table with morning tea. On the left: tea bags – Indian, Earl Grey, Green Tea, Peppermint and Lemon & Ginger herbal teas; instant coffee and instant cappuccino sachets; sugar and milk and a kettle of boiling water; orange juice. On the right: biscuits – ginger-nuts, mallow puffs, chocolate digestives and several bunches of red grapes. In the middle, Jane had set out cups and saucers for the tea and coffee and glasses for the juice. *Whew!* she said to herself. *I got this. I got this. Breathe.*

At two minutes to ten, her first 'clients' came in. Jane greeted them individually and encouraged them to write their name on a name tag. She invited them to have some morning tea as she checked her resources and surreptitiously reviewed her notes. Checking her watch again, she was surprised to discover it was already five past ten. She faced the room. *Seven people – five women, two men. I think I know some from the notes that Sue sent me but...hmmm. Um...um...I should begin!*
Jane clapped her hands – gently.

'I think we should begin. Can you take a seat in the circle? You can take your morning tea with you. Not a problem. Sit. Sit.'
Jane again checked out the 'clients' as the people sorted themselves out in the circle of chairs.

'Mōrena[1],' Jane announced, with more conviction than she felt. 'Good morning. Kia ora[2]. Hello!
Tēnā koutou, ko Jane Forrest au, nō Paraparaumu au. Ko Estonian, French, Irish and Spanish te whakapaparanga mai. He Community Aphasia Advisor au i AphasiaNZ. Tēnā koutou katoa.[3]

'I am Jane Forrest and I am a CAA – a Community Aphasia Advisor – for Aphasia New Zealand. My heritage is Estonian, French, Irish and Spanish - quite a mix! I think most of you have met Sue – she is the CAA that has been working with the people who **have** aphasia, your loved ones. She is down in the other room, in Room 3, with them.

'But this meeting is called The Kumanu Group. It is a new venture from AphasiaNZ. Kumanu is a Māori word that means to cherish, support, nurse or care for someone. The purpose of this group is to support the people who are caring with someone who has aphasia. That's you. Okay?

'Most often…at these sorts of meetings…we usually open the floor for anyone who wants to share about your experiences of the person you are caring for. It can be

---

[1] Mōrena = Morning (Māori).

[2] Kia ora – a Māori greeting common in Aotearoa New Zealand. Literally it means "have life" or "be healthy".

[3] The pepeha (Māori) is a familiar template of phrases that define and describe connections and a biography. This is a non-Māori version of the pepeha, describing Jane's name, place, heritage, and role.

helpful to know, to share – how you deal with aphasia. Or not. You can share things that work for you, or ask other people how you can help with things that are not so good?'

Jane checked herself. *I'm gabbling. Talking too much? Are they okay? Um…now what should I say?*

'People with aphasia – um – their experiences can be so different. Their symptoms. Their behaviours. It can be confronting, or frustrating, or charming, or hurtful. Or hilarious. At AphasiaNZ we have heard it all!

'Of course, the Kumanu Group should be a safe place. So, I ask you that anonymity should be maintained. The things we discuss in here? The person concerned should be anonymous when we get out of this meeting. Okay?'

She looked around the circle of seats, smiling some encouragement, covering her nervousness with a friendly look on her face. *So,* thought Jane. *We'll see if anyone wants to share!*

—————- ~~~ ————

'So … Can you introduce yourselves, and the person who you care for? Around the circle. Shall I go first?

'So – I am Jane Forrester. I was born in Palmerston North – don't judge! The third child of five. The middle one. When I was fifteen my mother had a stroke. She was paralysed, in a wheelchair…and she had aphasia. It was, and still is, a puzzling disability. At that time most people, even in the health profession, didn't know much about aphasia. My mother, basically, shut down – didn't communicate at all. She died two years after her stroke with no improvement. I wanted to know more so I trained as a Speech Therapist in Wellington. Now, I'm a CAA for AphasiaNZ because…well, because I wanted to help people with aphasia and their loved ones.'

Jane paused. *Urgh! Too much information. Stop it now.*

'So…' Jane looked to her right, gesturing with an outstretched hand, inviting …

A blonde, curly-haired young woman looked nervously at Jane, and then around the group. She was in her thirties, pretty and trim but was obviously anxious.
'Oh…um…okay…um…I am Beatrix. Most call me Trixie. And I care for mother who has aphasia. Liz. She is called Liz. She had several strokes over the last seven, eight years. We are both living in Paraparaumu. I have two brothers but they are overseas, so…just me. I have a daughter too.'

Beatrix almost sighed with relief as she looked at the older woman to her right.

'Um…I am Patricia,' she said. 'Most people call me Patricia. My husband, Leslie…Les… has aphasia. We have three children but they are overseas – in England, Spain and America. We are living in Waikanae, in the hills above the town.'

Jane sneaked a look at Patricia. She had an elegant haircut – short, with delicately greying layers. Her clothes were stylish – a forest-merino poncho with a chunky, agate necklace over a gold top, black trousers and crimson red ankle boots. Patricia spoke confidently but there was something reserved about her manner. When she finished, she gestured with her hand to the person on her right. *Imperious. Haughty*, Jane thought, but she immediately chastised herself for her judgement.

The person on Patricia's right acknowledged her with a faint nod. He was tall and slim with dark skin. *An Indian heritage* Jane wondered. His short black hair was carefully styled betraying a weekly or fortnightly visit to a barber or hairstylist. His clothes were meticulously chic: a blue checked cotton shirt with patterned sleeves, then cuffs turned up; a turmeric-coloured silk/bamboo jersey loosely tied around his shoulders; olive green chinos and handcrafted tan shoes.
With a definite accent, he announced: 'My good name is Manisha Rajgopal. My partner, Thomas, has aphasia – a brain injury. I was born in the England. Thomas was the New Zealander, Auckland born. We met in London on his OE and I followed him out here. This place. We live and work at Waikanae Beach. IT consultants. We lived there for five years hence.'

Quaint expression!   'You work from home? Thomas too?' Jane questioned.
'Essentially, yes,' Manisha answered, with a wry smile.

The next person on the right was the other male in the group. He was a complete contrast to Manisha. He was a Māori tanē[1]: massively built, tall with strong shoulders and brawny arms. He had long black hair surmounted with a top-knot skewered by an intricately carved bone dart. He wore an impressive pounamu[2] pendant around his neck.

---

[1] tanē = a male.

[2] pounamu = Aotearoa New Zealand jade (greenstone)

He had a swandri[1] vest with its traditional red and black squares and black shorts. His upper body displayed traditional Tā Moko[2] with intricate designs stretching from behind his ears, across his robust neck, and adorning his shoulders and armsThe same moko design was on his legs below his shorts reaching to his sturdy hiking boots. *A beautiful moko*, Jane thought, *but some people would see it at threatening*. His face was beatific though, and he smiled as he gently spoke.

'Mōrena. Tēnā koutou, ko Hohepa, Hohepa Tahuhu au.' He looked at the others, each one for a moment, with a perceptive but kind gaze and a sensitive smile. He translated: 'I am Hohepa Tauhuhu. I live at a marae[3] just outside Ōtaki. My koro, my grandfather, has aphasia. From a stroke, about six years ago. Tēnā koutou katoa. Kia ora.'

'Kia ora Hohepa,' said Jane. 'At the marae, you have extended whānau?[4] Are you the only one caring for your koro or other people are involved?'

'Yes – my koro is one of the marae kaumātua[5]. All our whānau are involved – basically everyone in the marae is whānau – but I am the main carer,' Hohepa responded pleasantly. 'My koro – he basically raised me and I owe him

---

[1] 'swandri' is a trade name for a range of popular Aotearoa New Zealand outdoor clothing.

[2] Tā Moko is the traditional Māori art of tattooing intricate designs into the skin.

[3] Marae = meeting place (Māori), usually including the wharenui (big house) and the area and buildings around it.

[4] whānau = family (extended)

[5] kaumātua = a respected tribal elder.

everything. He put me through my degree as a registered nurse. Now, I care for him.'

'Ah. I see. Kia ora,' Jane nodded her understanding.
Then she looked at the next person. 'And…?'

'Oh…um…Kia ora. My name is Sarah…Sarah Gibson, and my husband has aphasia,' said Sarah anxiously. 'Gary. Gary Gibson. And – oh – um – we are in Paraparaumu. Live in Paraparaumu. Gary was born in the Hutt Valley. Me – um – I was born in Levin. Gary has two children but they are in the South Island with their mother. Um – Gary had a stroke. Three years ago.'

Jane glanced at her. She saw a brunette with a straight bob and a friendly but vacant visage. She was…well, portly. She had a shapeless black and white smock above khaki pants with black wedge-heeled boots. She was about thirty but, from Sue's notes, Jane knows that Gary was sixty-two. He had a stroke after his triple-bypass surgery and, given his height and weight information, Gary was likely to be portly too. Jane smiled at Sarah encouragingly and then turned to the next person.

This woman had straight ash-blonde hair down to below her shoulders which she lept in place with a yellow hairband. She had wide and pretty eyes framed by giant spectacles. About forty or forty-five years old, she was petite: red and white striped t-shirt above red pleated skirt and yellow strappy shoes. She rested her hands comfortably above her lap and her legs were folded like an aristocratic debutante. *She is quite….composed,* thought Jane.

'I care for my partner, Roberto,' the woman said, with more of a trace than an accent. *French*, Jane hazarded a guess. *Or*

Canadian? 'Roberto had the stroke ago three years. We born and lived for Quebec, but emigrated this New Zealand about six years ago. We are living out the town at Te Horo. My name is Amélie. Friends called my Ami.' She shrugged amicably gazed candidly around the circle at each person in turn.

I guess we should call her Ami then Jane decided. *I like her.*

The last person was on Jane's left. She was young – early twenties. Her long hair, bleached white with pink tips, was swept up into a loose bun with chopsticks anchoring the strands. She wore warpaint: purple eye shadow with kohl-black eyeliner, Amy Winehouse style, and violent crimson lipstick. Her top was a black T-shirt with a rock-band logo in jagged lightning fonts. Crude tattoos doodled across her arms. She had belted chains around her waist and her black jeans had jagged rents randomly across them, fixed by safety pins. On her feet she had unpolished crimson Doc Martin boots.

'Hi ya. Adrienne, Adrienne Foster,' she said with a very strong provincial British accent. 'Yo' can called me Adja, la. We arrive here 'bout five years since for 'ald country. Ma and Pa had a car crash two-year ago and Ma, she gone ov'r but Pa ha' a friggin' brain injury, innit. So, Pa has de asp-ha-shia. Phew…well…yea!'[1]

The group were perplexed but Jane rallied. 'Oh, I am so sorry about your Ma. Your mother,' Jane commiserated. 'And your Pa. You have other help? Any other relations or friends?'

---

[1] Um…too hard! Get what you can from the context of what Adrienne says.

'Yea. Som'times,' Adja said. 'The Sallies[1] can help som'times. Pa was tight with the Sallies an' they're sound. They's hel'ful, innit.'

'Good,' Jane carefully responded. 'That's good.'

Jane looked around at her 'clients', making sure that she remembered everyone's name. *Beatrice –Trixie. Patricia. Manisha. Hohepa. Sarah. Amélie – Ami. Adrienne – Adja. Well…what a mix!*

More confident now, she smiled encouragingly at all of them and said: 'Thank you. Kia ora. Tino pai. Very good, very good. So, we will open the floor to anyone who wants to share their experiences, problems, frustrations, or light moments…

'And remember…a safe place.

'So…anyone…?'

Immediately, the curly blonde woman spoke up.

———––- ~~~ ————–

---

[1] Sallies = The Salvation Army.

2B: Misheardliness – Liz

'Um…mōrena[1]. Beatrice…Trixie. And my Mum – Elizabeth – Liz – has aphasia. As I said, she has had several strokes over the last seven, eight years.'

'Um…she has improved, markedly, but it is still hard to understand her. It is confusing, and frustrating for me. And it is the same with my mother. She gets frustrated too. But sometimes it is hilarious.

'I visit her most days – she lives between my home to my workplace. Mostly, when I pay attention, I can decipher what she means because the…um…context is clear. But if I don't know the context, miscommunication results. Hers or mine!

'For example, we went to the zoo last month – Mum and I and Rosalie, my daughter. We were sitting down with a cup of coffee and a date scone at the Zoo Café and mum flicked her hand – I guess it was a fly. She said to Rosalie – and, you know what aphasiacs do – the stuttering, the mistooken words – she said: "Um….um…hopt…full-it…fu-lly…hopeful-ly is…it…is it…was not…a ce…cea-sse fire."

'Well. That what I heard her say. Rosalie and I were puzzled and…well, I will be more brief than Mum – you don't need the stuttering. So…she repeated: "Cease fire."

'We were no better off. Mum spelled it out to us – but her spelling is suspect too. She said: "T-S-C…no…E-T…um…S-E…um…F-R…no…L-Y!" '

---

[1] mōrena = [good] morning

Beatrice gestured a "tah dah" with her hands. 'It was a "Tsetse fly". The one that can give you sleeping sickness. "Tsetse fly", not "Cease Fire"! She was flicking a fly off the food and saying: 'Hopefully it was not a tsetse fly.' I should have known. Context, I guess. Because we are at the zoo.'

Several of the group chuckled at the thought.

Beatrice went on. 'Rosalie wanted to go the toilet and I didn't know where they are. Mum was still finishing her coffee and she said to me – apparently – "Monkey". I nodded and raced off with Rosalie to where I thought the toilets would be. After that, Rosalie and I went down to the monkey's enclosure. We looked for Mum for half an hour – the chimps, the spider monkeys, capuchins… They were so cute! But mum wasn't there!

'We looked everywhere for her, retraced the path to the café, went down the path to the entrance and there she was! Sitting on a seat beside an enormous tent that we saw when we came in. I said to her: "I thought you were looking at the monkeys?" She was clearly confused and indicated the tent. "Mark-key? Mark-key!" She meant the marquee.'

The Kumanu Group giggled among themselves, appreciating the confusion. Beatrice still wasn't finished.

'Sometimes it's my fault. Sort of. We went for a walk around the neighbourhood – my mum and I. Two men passed us walking their dogs. They were very similar, so I believe it was a father and son. You know about how dogs look like their owners? Both of the dogs were pug-nosed with white and brown fur and big double chins and the father and son owners had squashed noses, brown jerseys and bone-white trousers. And double chins!

'I said to mum: "Dogs and owners, huh? Father and son with their four chins?"
Mum interjected: "What…how…do you want…they worth?"'
Beatrice demonstrated a helpless gesture with her hands. 'What? I had no idea what she was talking about! Mum tried again: "Worth…how much? For-chun-ss?"
'Then I got it. I was saying 'Four chins' but Mum was hearing 'fortunes' – their wealth.'

Again, the Kumanu Group giggled and chuckled among themselves. Beatrice was warming up!

'But…she knows what's what though. If she knows a word and can't…um…retrieve it, she works around to it. Sooner or later.
'Um…for instance, I was going to the supermarket, helping her in the Covid-lockdown, and she wanted a brand of peanut butter – a particular brand. Again – without the stuttering – she said: "Cloves" then shook her head. "Comet?" Again the head shaking. "Cosmic?" Again. Well … that was five minutes worth! I wracked my brain about all the peanut butter brands. Then she changed tack and said, but stuttering: "The goddess for horticulture! The Roman one!" I had my phone and Googled it. See… here…'
Beatrice took out her phone and Googled 'goddess horticulture Roman'. She read the result:
'*In ancient Roman religion, Ceres was a goddess of agriculture, grain crops, fertility and motherly relationships.*'
'So…the brand was Ceres Organic Peanut Butter. I should have known.'

Some of the group burst out laughing.
Encouraged, Beatrice carried on.

'Sometimes, when I speak, she hears a different word entirely. Again, a similar word. For example, I was sitting down for a cup of coffee one morning before work. It was a lovely day – sunny with a warm, light breeze. We were sitting out on the patio and Mum went in to the kitchen for a homemade snack. She made them especially – her extra-special oat and date slice! Yum! Anyway, I saw a strange cat jumping on her neighbours fence – a long-haired ginger cat with an amazing tail. It raced off when it saw me. I guess it was spooked. When Mum came out, I questioned her about the neighbour's cat.

'She said: "The…person this…this…there…has…no cat." So I said; "I think it was feral." She said: "That …it is… usually so." I didn't understand, so I said: "What?" She said: "They have… all that." I **still** didn't understand. She brushed her hand up the other sleeve. "The hair…skin-thing." I said: "The fur?" She nodded. Then I understood. "I think it was a *feral cat*. Wild. Feral."
"Oh" she said. "I …it was…um…tail is…was fur-ry."

A burst of laughter from the group.

'She often confuses words. She chooses a similar word but not the right one. For example, I arrived when mum was clearing her bits-and-bob's cupboard. She always gets articles out of the newspaper or magazines and stores them away for a "historical resource"? Ten things you have to do when you visit the Coromandel Peninsula. Why Bees Dance. Photos of Prince William and Kate's babies. That sort of thing.

'I can't say the whole thing, we will be here for hours! She eventually said: "I should have a bag for the syphilis."

Again, Beatrice dramatically made a gesture of helplessness. 'I said: "What?" "The syphilis" she said. What on earth? I said to myself. My perplexed look prompted her to have a charade session.

'She flattened her left hand and scissored her right hand with two fingers like she was punching holes.' Beatrice demonstrated. 'Then she drew her right index finger on the flattened left hand with random paths, like drawing a map on a page.
'I went through a list. Lots of things. Rats or mice? Spiders? Ants? At each one Mum shook her head violently and reiterated the charade. She fluttered her fingers on her right hand. Legs? Lots of legs? Then she leapt across to some jewellery – some necklaces. Then I got it. Silver. Silverfish. Insects, like slaters, that can eat holes in paper – the magazine and newspaper articles she wanted to keep. She wanted a camphor bag to chase them out. Silverfish. Not syphilis.'

Jane heard hearty laughter from most of the group. She looked around the circle. Manisha, Hohepa, Amelie and Adrienne were laughing out loud. Sarah's face was a study of confused puzzlement but she was grinning anyway. But Patricia's face was stony. Jane thought, in a posh regal accent: *We are not amused,* and, again, immediately rebuked herself for such a judgemental attitude.

The laughter dwindled. Beatrice sighed.
'What can you do? Miscommunication. As I said, it is hard – it's frustrating – but at the same time, hilarious.'

———–- ~~~ ————

2B: The Kumanu Group

Jane responded: 'Thank you Beatrice – Trixie. That's good that she has other strategies. Charades or diversional thinking. And I like the "goddess" example, the Ceres peanut butter. Clearly your mother is, well, "on to it", if you see what I mean. I know it is frustrating for you but she is coping. And you? Is there someone else that can give you a break? Rosalie? How old is she?'

'Oh…she is only eight,' Beatrice answered. 'She is good with her grandma. Lots of body language and sharing things – knitting and crochet and cooking. Things that don't require much talking. For me, I am…um…good. Frustrating but… good. Mostly. I *know* she is improving, but it's good to speak about it in this forum. The Kumanu Group. People who understand about aphasia. It's an … outlet. For me.'

Beatrice looked around the group with a grateful expression. 'Thank you. All.'

'Kia ora Trixie,' Jane spoke for all. 'You're welcome.'

Things are going well, she thought, with more confidence.
'So…anyone else? Anyone else care to share?'
 Jane grinned at the group with her rhyming effort, and most grinned back.

After a moment Manisha waggled his hand and spoke up.

— — — —·~~~ — — — —

304

3B: Aureateness[1] – Thomas

'Hello – Manisha,' he confirmed to everyone. 'My partner, Thomas, have aphasia. He hasn't a stroke though. It was a brain injury, after rock climbing accident – about three, four years hence – so, aphasia developed.'

His accent was subtle and some of the words were not quite right but he was a deliberate speaker – carefully enunciating his words.
Maybe English was not his native tongue, thought Jane, *but I understand him better than most!*
She banished the thought as shameful, given her dual role as a Speech Therapist and a CAA.

She looked around the group. Most were attentive, but she saw a frown cross Sarah's face. *Hmmm. Maybe Sarah is not on board...* she thought to herself, but she ignored the judgement and concentrated on Manisha again.

'I met with Thomas, when he was bubbly, effervescent person. He used talk to any topic and he always have the sense of wicked humour. Now, after the accident, he mostly struggles to say anything. Any. Thing. At. All.

'He does not...um...stutter though, like Trixie's mother.'
Manisha looked inquiringly at Beatrice, shaking his head side to side. 'He just stopped speaking. It seems the words stuck in his throat – like a block. It is heartbreaking to see him struggle. On his speech.

---

[1] Aureateness - a person characterised by an ornate style of writing or speaking.

'Then, when you expect it least, he comes out with complex sentences. Multi-syllable words. Clear. Precise. But they are not the run-of-the-mill words. Not obvious words. It seems he has eaten a dictionary, or an encyclopaedia. It's like living with Oscar Wilde. Or Shakespeare!'

'That's amazing!' interrupted Beatrice. 'That's unusual, isn't it?'
She looks to Jane as the resident expert.

On the spot, Jane responded: 'Yes…but aphasia presents itself in various forms. It is quite unusual but I guess Thomas's brain is working things out before he speaks. Can you give us an example?'

Manisha thought for a moment. 'Well…for example, we were going to walk. There is a wet-lands pathway, from our house, just beside the estuary. The weather was fine – sunny. Few cotton wool clouds. Breezy. Lots of bird-life – oyster catchers, spoonbill, herons, pied stilts… I said to him: "I like this path beside the sea. It's peaceful. Tranquil." He acknowledged by nodding. Not speaking. We walk on. After five minutes he said: "Extremely amiable to perambulate with you." '

The fake-perplexed look on Manisha's face was comical and Beatrice and Amélie giggled, Hohepa chuckled and Adrienne laughed out loud. 'Oh my gawd!' she blurted out. 'Ha! Ha! Real talk? Oh my gawd!'

Manisha was pleased with this reaction and grinned, his head gently shaking. He continued on…

'About this too. We had a cup of tea last week. Thomas was sitting on the sofa and I brought the cup over to him but I spilled a little on the table. I got a cloth, wiped it up, put it back in the sink, returned and sat down again. **Then** he said to me: "You should have reduced the capacity of the cup." '

The laughing was more robust from his audience so Manisha joined in. He reiterated the punchline: 'Not "The mug is too full", but "You should have reduced the capacity of the cup."'

'Or….we share the dinner duties. One time I was making chickpeas and lentil red curry in the slow cooker. Thomas looked in the larder and glanced at me, three, or four times. At last he said: "You have depleted our resources!" '
More hearty laughter.
'And, when he tasted the meal, he eventually said: "You have transformed our resources enchantedly!" Just like Oscar Wilde!'
Laughter erupted.

Good. From everyone! Jane looked around. *No. Patricia is not laughing. Hmm…*

Jane spoke up. 'Manisha. Thanks for that. It seems that Tom has almost sorted it out? He seems to be recovering?'

'I guess,' he replied. 'But the thing is… We have no conversation. We used to having amazing conversations about **everything**. I'm frustrated because he doesn't discuss anything. His… process is too long – it's like I have to backtrack on my thoughts from two or three ideas earlier. And with other persons? It is impossible to have conversations with other persons.

'For example, we went to the park and there met three friends. For lunch. A picnic. We were sitting at the table enjoying wine, cheese, crackers. Jason, one of our friends, noticed paradise ducks, a male and female, on the grass – about thirty metres away. We admired their plumage – shining in the sunlight. Thomas didn't say anything – as usual.

'The discussion ranged through ducks, birds, the park, DOC organisation, the 1080 debate… Then John – another friend – pointed out a man and woman who were walking from their car to the noticeboard. The body language was indubitable – they were unhappy with each other. The man stalked ahead, hands clenched – the woman was about three metres behind, crossing her arms, angrily tossing her head. We friends made eye contact and John said: "Things are not right in Paradise."

'Another two or three topics were covered by the rest of us: marital problems, body language, celebrity couples, the last episode of the reality show, *Married at First Sight…* Anyway, a couple of minutes later, we saw the man and woman again, returning to their car, obviously reconciled. Hand in hand, the man kissed the woman on her temple. "Ah!" said John. "They have made up!"

'Thomas said: "If they are nodding, they will have sex."

'Startled and nonplussed looks were cast. Then I realised. He was thinking about the other conversation. The ducks. I blurted out: "We were looking at the people, not the ducks."

'See what I mean.' Manisha looked around with a pleading look on his face. 'The discussion has gone through three or four more topics but Thomas's thought processes were way, **way** behind. He can't…**can't** operate in a social situation. It is frustrating and I don't know what to do. I am patient, I think, but this situation has ruined our social life.'

Manisha looked at Jane imploringly.
On the spot...again. Um...

'Have you talked about this with Tom?' suggested Jane. 'Have you discussed it?'

'Yes...yes...But I don't know if he understands.'

'Do your friends know about this?' Beatrice suggested hesitantly. 'Maybe they could help, understand more of what's going on for Tom.' Manisha nodded doubtfully. Beatrice shrugged, saying 'I know, it's hard.'

Amélie interposed. 'Maybe he understands but he needs to have...prompts, or practice. You could direct the conversation to where Thomas has a practised response? At least he will be part of the discussion?'

Several of the group nodded vigorously.

'Possible, possible,' Manisha allowed, shaking his head again. 'Even then, I can't direct the conversation all the time. It doesn't work this way. But it is so...difficult. I want to help...but sometimes I cry with frustration.' Manisha broke into a wry smile. 'And when I cried, what do you think Thomas said. Eventually – about ten minutes later.' He struck a pose and in a posh voice, said: "What has instigated your pitiful tears?"

Manisha held his hands wide, inviting everyone in to his feelings and, with a silly grin, said: 'It is like speaking with a slow-witted Shakespeare!'

The room broke into laughter. They all knew what it is like to have a loved one with aphasia.

Manisha ducked his head smiling shyly, and sat down on his seat.

————-·~~~ ————-

3B: The Kumanu Group

'Thank you for sharing with us, Manisha,' Jane said. 'It is an unusual problem. Maybe we can all think about what solutions could work. For the next time we meet. Next month?'

Adrienne was gesticulating wildly with her right hand, her face a grimace of anticipation. Then she dropped her hand for a few seconds, covered her mouth with the same hand, then shot it up again. Down, up, down, up. It was like she wanted to answer the teacher's question but she recognised it was not the done thing in this group of adults.

Jane took pity on her.
'Adrienne. You want to share?'

'Yeah! Yeah alright yeah,' Adrienne burst out. She almost fell off her chair in her enthusiasm.

————-·~~~ ————-

4B: Loquaciousness[1] – Pa

'Hi y'awl,' Adrienne burst out. 'Trix - sounds da your ma is a hoot! And Mansh – ye jolly-boy Tom is hilar'ous! I know it's a problem for you – the conservating thing – but...Shake-bloody-speare! Hah!'[2]

Adrienne's face lit up with unabated joy.

Jane was stunned by the outburst.
That didn't go with Rocky Horror attire. It was like a punk character giggling about a bad knock-knock joke. But, don't judge a book by its cover, Jane mused.

Adrienne continued.

'For me. My Pa is compl'tely diff'rent, innit. He is a gobshite, a gas-bag an' I can't understan' most of ari frickin' gobshite shit! But-tah ... plez call me Adja. Adja Foster. And about da arl fella, my Pa? Pa done apha-si-a, from the acc'dent, the brain injury. The car acc'dent. Ma karked it. With Pa, most of his words are nonsensical. Sometimes I think he's a divvy. A nutter. He spills da vocals like a bluddy fauc't, innit. I can't make heado'tail mostly. Most I'm frickin' fumin'. He was da the ozzy ov three months. Then living wiv himself 'cos Ma died. So I come down. Moved away two, three years 'cross th' wadder. I used to be a stylist in town, and la queen has hired me agin for three days a week, so that's dead sound.'

---

[1] Loquacious - characterised by excessive talk; wordy.

[2] Too hard to translate it all here! Get what you can from the context or what Jane requests in response.

Jane looked at the rest of the group. They were bewildered by the torrent of words. Sarah's mouth had dropped open like a cartoon character. Beatrice and Manisha were obviously perplexed. Amélie smiled – bemused and amused. Hohepa was calm but a gentle smile played around his lips. Jane couldn't read Patricia's face. If she had to choose, it was abject distaste.

Good lord! Jane thought to herself. *It is enough to deal with people with aphasia, but when the 'normal' people have accents and colloquial jargon that confuses the communication issue…*
Jane knew she must step in.

'Thanks Adrienne…Adja…but I think some of your…idioms, your dialect or your…your jargon is escaping us. Can you choose your words more carefully. Or make them more clear. Um… for example: "ozzy"? And "stylist"? "Queen"?'

'Oh…sozz…um…sorry 'bout that,' Adja admonished herself. 'I get caught up. Um…"ozzy" is "hospital". My "stylist" job is a … um…ya know, a hair-sty'ist…um…hairdress'r. And the "queen" is my manager. Of the salon. The boss.'

Jane nodded and looked for confirmation of understanding from the others. 'And "dead sound"?' she asked again.

'Oh, "dead sound" is…um… "okay", or "every'ing is alright",' Adja apologised. 'Sorry…I get het up but…I go to me scouser talk…Used be'in Eng-land. If I slow th' down, that could be better, innit?'

Adja looked about the group nodding her contrition. Then she carried on.

'So…as I said, my Pa is a … a nutter. Pa runs off all th'time. He spills 'is words.'
Adja paused dramatically and she chopped her right hand down on her horizontal left hand like a cleaver: 'All. The. Time. Like a…a tap leaking wadder. Sozz…Wa-ter. And most itself makes nonsense.' She paused, and again beat the words again. 'No. Sense.'

'I can't understan' it. Not sure if it's proppa, or he blaggin' me 'ead…'
Adja looked at the puzzled faces of the group. 'Sozz – sorry again! Um…"blaggin" is…um…"did it delib'rately". But that's what he comes up wiv.

'Eee gee he says somethin' like,' and Adja dropped her voice almost an octave: ' "Da wally wally looks it was wally ding to da jump or wally yea, yea and for da secon' time proppa boss, da jump jump for da for la wally to wally…"

Adja shrugged her shoulders. 'I'm fumin'…um, sorry… He drives me nuts, innit. He goes on and on and on and on. Does he do blaggin' – does it delib'rately?'

Again, Adja fakes a deep voice and recites: "Da secon' time proppa boss, da wally wally to jump to wally da jump to bling for wally, da jump wally, da secon' time proppa boss da wally to bling for wally wally da secon' time proppa boss, da secon' time proppa boss to da secon' time proppa boss, da secon' time proppa boss…" and he goes on and on and on and frickin' on…'

The last paragraph was delivered with such speed as to be incomprehensible. The group were bewildered. Again.

The confusing jargon. Her over-melodramatic, OTT[1] gestures. And she spoke so fast!

Jane interrupted carefully. 'Thanks Adja. It's better if you slow down. S l o w. I t. D o w n!' Then, she looks Adja in the eye. 'I think I can help.'

Jane raised her right hand as if she were writing bullet points in the air. 'There are many forms of aphasia. The most common ones are Broca's Aphasia and Wernicke's Aphasia. You have heard about this?'

Manisha, Amélie and Hohepa nodded. Adja, Trixie and Sarah shook their heads in puzzlement. Pat shook her head but Jane was not sure if this was a negative judgement. *More like…frustration? Maybe I should…*
But Jane carried on with the others – a teaching moment?

'I can spell it on the whiteboard…'
She took a marker from her table and crossed to the whiteboard.
She spelled out the name on the left of the board: B-R-O-C-A-'-S A-P-H-A-S-I-A.
'And the other one is…' W-E-R-N-I-C-K-E-'-S A-P-H-A-S-I-A, on the right.Then Jane wrote "Non-fluent" with an arrow to Broca's Aphasia and "Fluent" with an arrow to Wernicke's Aphasia.

'Most people have Broca's Aphasia. Non-fluent aphasia. For example, Thomas…' Jane nodded to Manisha, 'and Elizabeth, Trixie's mum…' – again a nod to Beatrice – 'have Broca's Aphasia. They experience loss of words, or mispronounced words. Most people with the non-fluent

---

[1] OTT = Over The Top – very exaggerated.

version have stuttering speech, like Liz, or they forget words or sort them out later like Thomas. But, what they say is sensible. Basically.' Jane nodded to Manisha: 'Or eventually.'

Jane canvassed the room. Most of the clients nodded their heads in understanding of what Jane was saying. Adja had a puzzled but receptive face. Jane continued.

'Their aphasia has a different response from your Pa's, Adja. You have all meet the other CAA Sue?' Again the group nodded, but Jane addressed Adja directly. 'Sue told me that Mister Foster, your Pa, has Wernicke's Aphasia. Fluent Aphasia. Now, I have not met him, but what you are describing is what I would expect a Wernicke's Aphasia person to do.

'People with this type of aphasia speak fluently. The words come out with no problem … your 'tap leaking water'! But the sense of the words is not immediately apparent. Often they use 'filler' words to fill the gap if they can't pronounce the word that they want to use. I guess, your Pa is using 'wally' as his filler word?'

Adja was riveted. Her mouth was open like a baby bird. 'Oh, yea! so…so…yea! So…so…so…that's sensible to me!' So… so…so…' Adja nodded her head emphatically with every 'so'. Jane worried that Adja would do some damage to her neck, but she stopped suddenly.

'Oh…I get that now. Hal-le-lu-jah!' she trumpeted. ' "Wally" 'is filler-word. When 'e doesn't know what 'e wants to say… Ah – yep…yep…yep…'
The pink-tipped head dropped to her chest again and, puzzled, looked up again at Jane.

'But what about the ...the...um...phrases that almost make sense? Um..umm like, he says: "Da secon' time proppa boss" all the time. It not like "wally". What's this 'bout?'

Again, several of the group had puzzled looks on their faces. 'Translation?' Jane questioned Adja.
Adja spoke quickly: 'Sorry…"Da secon' time proppa boss" is…um… "the second time is great." Um…."amazing". '

'Often sensible phrases,' Jane confirmed, 'like "Da secon' time … proppa boss" is another repeated filler phrase. Again, it works when the speaker has not figured out what he wants to say. But it is more sensible. When your Pa uses this phrase, is it…um.. pertinent, or sensible to the conversation?'

'Um…' Adja mused. 'Yea. Yea – I guess so. I think so. Yea.'

'That's the way Wernicke's Aphasia works,' Jane said. 'And that is a good thing! The filler words like 'wally' are nonsense words and the person with Wernicke's Aphasia doesn't know they are making nonsense. If your father has moved to having a sensible phrase, like "Da secon' time proppa boss", he is improving.'

Adja thought for a few seconds. 'So…so…so …Times he do somethin' solid…um…sensible. Almost. He can say somethin' like: "Da secon' time proppa boss will ya look to da phone Adja?" Like, I am…dizzy 'cos usual…'

She looked around to the other people in the group and realised: 'Oh, sorry. I forgot. Um. Like I am su'prised that usually his words are nonsense and, out of the blue, somethin' is understan'able. Like, I scramble to do something – search for the phone 'cos somethin' made

sense...at last. Hal-le-lu-ja! But Pa says these things, like this few and far between.' Relief flooded Adja's face. 'Wow! That's dead sound – um... that's good. Ta for your explaining. About Werneck Aph'sia.'
Something dawned on Adja's face, and her face lit up again.

'Act'shally, Pa can say somethin' that I understand 'cos his... what do you say...his di'lect...is mine too. If I miss out th' filler-words, th' "wally" and things, 'e can say... Um...'
Again, Anja spoke with a bass voice:
' "Eeyar. Da first time still de ozzy wuz Antwacky. Youz hav jarg clobber. Da first time ma kecks fallin' down. And da doc dead divvy, la. Bevied up."
'That translates to...um... "Here you are, first time in th' hospital and it was so old-fashioned. Th' clothes were fake an' my trousers kept fallin' down. And th' doctor was so stupid an' drunk."'

Everyone giggled, laughed, guffawed out loud at this account of the situation and Adja's idiosyncratic way of expressing it.

Everyone – besides Patricia.

She abruptly stood up. Her seat clattered away to the wall behind.
'It's all a joke,' she sobbed. 'It's hilarious. That's what you all think. A laughing matter...'
Abruptly, Patricia burst into tears.
She collapsed to her haunches, sobbing, hands over her face.

— — — —- ~~~ — — — —

4B: The Kumanu Group

The mirth died on everyone's lips. Everyone was aghast, even Jane.

Hohepa crossed the circle and gently took Patricia's arms and raised her to her feet again. He moved his hands to her shoulders and looked compassionately into her eyes. He murmured 'That's okay. That's okay. Ka taea e au ....Maaku koe e tiaki[1] Shh. Kaua e tangi! Kia tau tō wairua![2] Shh. That's okay.'
Patricia's sobbing eased. She dropped her head.
'That's okay. Kaua e tangi,' Hohepa insisted. 'Whakamārie, whakamārie,' a mantra that calmed the stricken woman.

Jane looked at Sue's   list. She re-read the notes about Leslie, Patricia's husband.
Ah! I should have known. These stories are not helping…
She hurriedly looked at the group gauging what she should do.

Most were getting over the shock of Patricia's violent outburst and collapse. Adrienne was appalled and Sarah was bewildered. Amélie recovered somewhat and crossed to the side table, to get a glass of water for the forlorn Patricia. Manisha was clearly uncomfortable. Beatrice had her hand to her mouth as if she was holding in some sort of anguish that she couldn't express. She went over to Patricia and gave her some tissues, but retreated immediately.

---

[1] (Māori): I will take care of you.

[2] (Māori): Don't cry. May your soul rest in peace!

Jane crossed the room to Hohepa and Patricia.

Patricia glanced at Jane and nodded, tearfully, that she was recovered. Somewhat.

Jane indicated that they could sit down. Manisha retrieved Patricia's chair and changed seats with Hohepa so he could sit beside her. Hohepa looked at her with compassion and empathy. Patricia welcomed his warm, burly, teddy-bear comfort. Patricia sipped the water and dabbed her tearful eyes.

Jane went back to her chair and recomposed herself. *I am responsible. I am responsible.*

She took a big breath…

'Are you okay?' she said to Patricia. 'Can you speak about your husband's aphasia? Or should I do it…'

— — — —- ~~~ — — — —

5B: PPA – Leslie

'I am okay,' Patricia explained. 'Thank you Hohepa. Thank you. And the rest of you… Sorry about that…outburst.' She composed herself, looked at her lap, closed her eyes momentarily, then looked at Jane, intently. 'Um…Jane … can you explain about Leslie's…condition. The PPA…'

'Sure…' Jane agreed. She looked at the group anxiously, mustering the right words to convey this information. *I can do this,* she thought. *My responsibility…*

'Sue, my colleague, has confirmed that Patricia's husband, Leslie, has PPA. Primary Progressive Aphasia. It is a form of aphasia that …well…it's like a dementia of words. The loss of words and meaning is…progressive. It doesn't recover.'

Jane lets the words sink in as she looked around the circle.

Manisha, Beatrice and Amélie were shocked. Hohepa was still murmuring his mantra, his right arm around Patricia's shoulders and his left hand rubbing her left forearm soothingly. But there was concern on his face.

'So…so…so…'Adrienne spoke. 'So the words don't come back, innit?' Her face was contorted with puzzlement and uncertainty.

'Really…that's right?' Sarah said. Her face was confused. 'It's like Alzhe-mers? The aphasia doesn't get better?' She looked at Patricia, apprehension tempered with cautious compassion.

Jane was flustered. *What do I do now?* she panicked. But her training kicked in.
A survival mechanism. Some medical jargon would be in order. Bamboozle them with science!

'PPA is a rare type of aphasia,' she announced with more confidence than she felt. 'Usually it is a type of frontotemporal dementia. This means that the brain is affected in the frontal and/or temporal lobes where the language centres are. PPA is a type of aphasia that starts out with mild speech and language impairments. The nerve cells in the frontal and temporal lobes of the brain are atrophied. The symptoms get more severe as the dementia progresses.'

'There are three main subtypes of PPA. Agrammatic, logopenic and semantic variants of PPA, according to which areas of the brain has been affected. Patients suffer word loss, and reading and writing skills are debilitated. The second 'P' of PPA is 'Progressive'. PPA patients can't recover their speech.'

The apprehension in the circle was transferred from Patricia's plight to Jane academic statement.

Jane slowed down. She breathed slowly. Things were relatively calm now. Hohepa took his arm from around Patricia's shoulder. He clasped his hands together on his lap, touching his thumbs to his forefingers. *Ah,* thought Jane, *a yoga hand gesture. Consciousness raising. Or mindfulness. Whew – Hohepa is a treasure!*

Jane brought her own mindfulness to the situation in hand. She looked directly at Patricia. 'Are you okay?' she asked. 'Do you want to go outside for some fresh air or...' Jane cautiously gestured to the door.

'Thanks Jane. Thanks…um…everyone.' Patricia straightened up. 'I want to talk. About Leslie. I apologise for my outburst. It was not fair to you – Trixie, Manisha, and Adja. I know that some of the…antics with aphasia are hilarious. I suspect that your anecdotes are a coping mechanism too. As they say: You have to laugh, otherwise you'd be crying all the time.'

Patricia's eyes filled with tears, but she shook her head, dabbed a tissue at her eyes and started again.

'It began with a few words,' Patricia spoke haltingly. 'Leslie, Les, was the chief librarian at Hamilton Public Library. He was always erudite and academic. He could speak to anyone on any given topic: politics, history, art, music, literature, science and technological advancements, comparative religion and health systems. That's what attracted me to him. His erudition.'

As she spoke, Patricia became visibly more confident. She straightened her shoulders again and raised her chin. She faced the group, studying their faces.

'At first it was a loss of difficult words. It was like your partner Manisha, Thomas. Usually he was always saying grandiose words – it was a game to him. Um…for example, usually he would say about a song … "magnificent operatic aria". But, two or three years ago, he stopped doing that. "Magnificent operatic aria" became "good song". "Sumptuous and delicious kai" changed to "good food". "Our convenient transportation system" became "car". It was odd to me – I was used to his inflationary word choices, but at that time I was not concerned. I thought he was just tired.

'Then he forgot place names. He would get the first syllable or the first letter but the rest of the word was…gone. Even for the children. Lorraine is in London, Scott is in Los Angeles and Trent is in Barcelona. But Les couldn't remember where the children were living!

'He developed some clues or pointers. He associated the clues with our children so he could remember where they lived: BB – Big Ben – for London; La, La, Land – the film – for LA, Los Angeles; ER for Barcelona.

The rest of the circle, including Jane were puzzled.

'Aha! ER was an historical clue. ER is Elizabeth Rex – the Queen. And Freddie Mercury – front singer for Queen – sang at the opening event for the Barcelona Olympics in 1992. See...his mind was 'on to it', but his words were failing. He said it was "A senior moment. Don't worry about it!" But something was not right.

'I went to his office. There were lots of yellow post-it notes all over the computer and the drawers in his desk. I made a joke about it ... something like 'Autumn leaves are falling in your office' and he couldn't understand my joke. He was very brusque – not like him at all.

'I surreptitiously looked over the post-it notes. On the drawers: Correspondence; Projects; Personnel; Finances. On the computer: his password. On the desk: the name of his secretary and his phone extension. Beside the phone – a post-it note for **my** phone number.

'I left it for a while, but I told his secretary, Michael, to tell me what was going on at work. He reported some things over the next few weeks: Leslie couldn't remember the names of staff or their position. He could not understand what people were saying to him on the phone. Even me. He would say to the person: 'Could you relay that to my secretary?' and pass the extension on to Michael.

'I insisted that we went to the doctor, then an MRI, checked with a speech pathologist.
The diagnosis: Primary Progressive Aphasia.'

Patricia's head drooped. She dabbed with the tissues hidden in her fist. Then she shook her head, casting out the negative and doubting thoughts and carried on. The circle waited in anticipation.

'Leslie retired early from the library. They had a lovely farewell for him – lots of speeches, and gifts. I was there, at home, when he was preparing for the retirement party and I knew what it cost him. He was always a gifted speaker. Usually he could speak freely – extemporise. Now, he couldn't speak without writing it down – the whole thing, not bullet points. He laboured and laboured over his speech. He practised saying it to me, and I saw the humiliation. The humiliation that he could not do what he had always done – speak freely. He carried it off well. But when he got home, he said lots of the things he included in his speech didn't mean anything to him now.

'He was very depressed. "A librarian who lost his words!" he would often say.

'He reads the newspaper. "Journalists are wrong now. They make no sense," he would say to me. I read it later. It made perfect sense to me. Now, he has missing words all the time – too many for a clue or a pointer.

'And last week…' Patricia looked at the ceiling and her face contorted. 'He couldn't … couldn't remember my name!' She buried her head in her hands, sobbing. Hohepa put his arm around Patricia's shoulder again. Beatrix took Patrica's left hand in both of hers.

Patricia was struggling to compose herself. Jane glanced around the circle. They were all looking at Patricia. *They are all studying her,* Jane thought. *No... Not studying, Witnessing. Empathising.*

No-one spoke for a few minutes. At last, Patricia raised her head again. She gasped and rubbed her eyes from each side of her nose outwards, stretching the skin towards her ears, forcing her eyelids shut.
Telepathically Jane communed with Patricia.
Breathe in. Breathe out.
B r e a t h e   i n ...   B r e a t h e   o u t ...
B r e a t h e   i n n n   ...
B r e a t h e   o u u u t ...

Patricia inhaled. 'Sorry. Sorry. I... I just... I would.... um...I thought I was getting... getting...'

'That's okay. It's fine,' Jane comforted. 'Take your time. It's a safe place, remember.'
Patricia looked up to Jane with appreciation. Then she focused on the group. Empathetic looks greeted her – from everyone. Her eyes filled with tears again but from gratitude, not pain.

'Les is going to the Aphasia Group with Sue, your colleague, every Thursday. It is marvellous what the Aphasia Group is doing. Everytime Les comes out of their session beaming. Often he can't tell me what happened, but it gave him some joy with others who have the same... condition.'

Jane was almost sure that the last word that Patricia spoke was going to be "affliction".

Patricia continued: 'He has an appointment with Sue every fortnight. As you know, Sue is a speech-language pathologist and she is working with both of us on approaches to make communication easier. "Augmentative and alternative communication devices" she calls them, to me at least! iPads, and sketch books and key words.'

'Have you some support?' Hohepa asked. 'Can you tell anyone about this PPA – whānau? E hoa – friends?'

'I guess the children? But they are busy and overseas. Les has no-one else now. He was an only child and his parents died years ago. I have a sister – younger sister. She is in Tauranga. But we are not close. I'm not sure if she will understand, or help...'

'Hav'yu told ya kids?' blurted out Adrienne.

Taken aback by the blunt speech, Patricia's mouth looked grim and she was clearly on the back foot. She gazed at the girl – the punk hair, the tattoos, the piercings, the safety-pin sewing.
Then, she had a moment of insight. She looked into Adrienne's eyes and saw Adja as a compassionate presence, genuinely wanting to help.
She smiled cautiously.

'Um...the children know that Les has retired. But not about the PPA. We Skype or Zoom every so often but mostly I do the talking now. Les is there but he doesn't talk much anymore, and they didn't seem to mind...'

'Well,' Adrienne responded. 'Better that you tell it. Deadly true!'

Jane confirmed: 'It is important to have some support. And your children – your whānau. **And** your sister. They won't thank you for keeping this condition from them. Especially the children. Maybe they are busy and maybe Skype or Zoom is not a good place to talk. But you **have** to tell them.'

Patricia flinched.

Hmmm, Jane mused. *I think that Patricia is in denial herself. Careful. But...she has to know this is the only way out. Telling the kids would make it real for **her**.*

Jane changed tack. 'AphasiaNZ has a booklet about PPA. It is only a few pages long – not academic. Plain speech but informative.' She went to the table and rummaged through her bag and found some booklets, one of which she passed to Patricia. 'Have you seen this?' she asked.

'No. I haven't.' Patricia was busy flicking through the pages.

'It came out last week. I have more,' Jane suggested, handing another four brochures to Patricia. 'One for you, and one for your children and your sister. You could talk to them or text them and say you are sending information in the mail about something to do with Leslie. See what happens? I suspect that they will contact you immediately. Maybe your children will get flights home. Sooner than later. Before... before Leslie can't talk anymore.'

Patricia's eyes welled up again, but she was not overcome. *Thankfully. I think it's getting through to her. I guess – strike while the iron is hot...*

'Have you a good relationship with your doctor?' Jane ventured. 'Is he or she knowledgeable about PPA?

'I think so,' Patricia rallied. 'Dr. Sunwaro. She seems to know about it – the PPA. It was no surprise to her when she delivered the verdict.' Patricia's "courtroom" word choices made Sarah and Beatrix squirm, but she didn't notice it. 'She was quite matter of fact, explaining that Leslie's word sense would diminish until he could not say sensible sentences. She wants to see Leslie every six weeks. She suggested that Leslie should get his affairs in order – his finances, his will, his funeral wishes...'

Again, Patricia's eyes filled with tears, but she shook off her sadness, straightened her head and shoulders and carried on. 'We did that already. His affairs are in order before the....inevitable.'

'And Dr. Sunwaro doesn't think that the PPA is affecting other areas of Leslie's health?' Jane spoke cautiously. 'His comprehension? His short or long term memory?'

'No,' Patricia replied. 'At least, not at this stage. It is only his words that are affected. He can't remember the terms, his expressions, the place names that he used to say. He can understand me, most of the time, if I talk slowly and use simple sentences.'

'Hmm,' Jane looked intently into Patricia's eyes. 'That's why I urge you to speak to your children and your sister as soon as you can. Post the booklets. See what can happen.'

Then Amélie suggested: 'I not sure if it could help, but Roberto – after his stroke – had some music therapy. For him, singing is much better than talking. He joined a choir, a neurological choir – they have people with stroke, aphasia, Parkinson's, brain disease... The singing helps – the repetition of the words helps. And music seemed to help with memory. It could help Leslie too? The repetition, and the music, is...quite therapeutic.'

'Ya, ya!' Adja excitedly called out. 'My Pa singing is deft betta than his talkin'. That's true – dat the repetition is val'uble! And he mostly sings 'n tune. It's nun' painful, I mean.'

'Gary...um...Gary, when he lost his words,' Sarah spoke suddenly. 'I saw something ... a documentary about Alzhe-mers, Al-zhe-imers? They had a photo album that had all sorts of photos from this person's life and family and friends and places... I borrowed that idea and it was excellent for Gary. Seeing the pictures helped him with the words and he could talk about them. It could help?'

Hohepa nodded and spoke up. For a big man, his gentle tone was modest. 'Kia ora. We have something like that. My koro is kaumatua at the marae, so **everyone** is whānau[1]. After his stroke, after his aphasia, I set up a memory board in the wharenui[2] – lots of photos and newspaper reports or headlines and quotes about what koro has done for the marae. It was helpful. It gave him a feeling of oranga ngākau...um...reassurance. Comfort.'

'Yes! Yes!' Manisha was excited. 'We could set up the image bank – a database for things meaningful to him. Leslie is okay with computers? So, photos or images from your

---

[1] koro = an elderly Maori man, especially a male relative or grandfather. Kaumatua = a respected tribal elder. Marae = meeting place. Whānau = (extended) family.

[2] wharenui = the main building on the marae.

travels and hobbies. Holidays. The children, their houses or their work in LA, London, Barcelona. We can print them out and make a book. This is easy. There are several businesses that can do it. Online. I – and Thomas – could assist. In fact, you and Leslie could come around.' He looked at Hohepa and added: 'Maybe, we could come around, the four of us, to the marae?' Manisha jumped out of his chair excited about his plan. 'Meet you and your, um, koro isn't it? And see what's what? And…' he broke into a ecstatic grin, 'your koro, Thomas and Les could be…how you say it…the three amigos!'

'Ka pai! Kia ora ka pai!' Hohepa enthusiastically responded.

Patricia raised her knuckles to her mouth and nodded imperceptibly – a gesture of thankfulness and supplication. Only Jane noticed. *Good*, she thought. *Really good.*

Ten minutes had passed after Patricia's tearful almost-exit. Now she was coddled and cared for. The rest of the group supported her and the suggestions they had made were useful and apposite. She was overwhelmed by the care and concern of these one-hour-friends.

————- ~~~ ————

5B: The Kumanu Group

Jane let the conversations go on, but she had a twinge of caution. The support and the anecdotes were useful and a means to cope with a difficult situation, but The Kumanu Group is only two hours a month. The reality of a spouse or family member with aphasia, every day, was another thing.

She looked tentatively around the room.

Adja and Amélie were talking about the effectiveness of music therapy and Amélie was encouraging Adja's Pa to join the choir. Despite their different 'dialects' they were communicating well.

Sarah and Beatrix were comparing notes about their loved ones and how they coped creatively with the misunderstanding.

Manisha and Hohepa were flanking Patricia – the tall Indian man and the massive Māori tane towered over the diminutive Patricia. They were excited to share their ideas and plans with the online photo board and were formulating a plan to get Thomas and Leslie to visit the marae and meet with Hohepa's koro and the 'memory board'.

Wow! This is wonderful! Jane thought. *I should have a photo! I know it is the proper function of the Kumanu Group but it's…it's…taking off! I didn't expect it would work so quickly.*

Jane relaxed and let the conversations go on.

After a while, she stood up and called the group together.

'Thank you. Thanks for sharing your experiences. Thanks for your thoughts and ideas.

'I hope it has been good for you all?' She paused and the affirmative nodding from everyone in the circle was unanimous and vigorous.

'I see some of you are swapping email addresses and phone numbers. That's fine, but just saying again, The Kumanu Group is a safe place and the things we have discussed should be anonymous. Only the people in this room and the person you are looking after with aphasia. Okay?

'We will meet again next month. I will send an email to you all and maybe you can think about what else we can do to support our loved ones.

'But, the **most** important thing is – look after **yourselves**! You are the reason that most of your aphasiac loved ones survive. Truly.
'**Look. After. Your. Selves!**'
She emphasised each word borrowing Adja's "hands-like-a-cleaver" gesture, smacking her right hand on the left.

She looked intently at each of them. After a moment, she relaxed her hands by her sides and grinned.
'Good luck! Haere tū atu, hoki tū mai[1]. Haere rā, haere rā, haere rā koutou.[2]'

With a smattering of modest but heartfelt applause, the group stacked the chairs and tidied the morning tea dishes.

———————————————

[1] Māori idiom: "Go well and return in good health, have a safe trip."

[2] Māori: 'Haere rā' = farewell to someone who is leaving. 'Koutou' = 'three or more people.'

With an appreciative and congratulatory nod or a word, the group eventually drifted out.

Jane sat down on a chair.
Whew! That was amazing! I can't wait to tell Sue about it...

————· ~~~ ————

James Stephens

James is a New Zealander. He was a teacher, actor, musician and music director, a journalist and event manager – as well as a husband, father and grandfather. He was a voracious reader, a fluent writer and confident speaker.

In 2015, he suffered a hemiparesis, a middle cerebral artery territory infarct. In a word, a stroke.
He collapsed, paralysed on his right side, and couldn't speak or write. The hospital intervention was rapid and his limbs were free but his speech was absent. He had/has aphasia.

Aphasia is the loss of a previously held ability to articulate ideas or comprehend spoken or written language, resulting from damage to the brain caused by injury or disease – in this case, a stroke.

With expert therapists in speech, music and eurhythmy he has re-invented himself. He has a positive and optimistic outlook, electing to view his stroke as a 'stroke of luck'.
But his speech is still – suspect.

"My aphasia forced me to look at my life differently. My expected biography has changed. Now, I am an author – apparently."

email: james.stephens.dms@gmail.com
facebook: https://bit.ly/3bH6kZr

The Suspect Speaker Series - Reviews

The Suspect Speaker series is very unique and emotional, and the books are aphasia friendly! In each book author James Stephens presents a series of stories describing events with aphasia.

Most importantly, each story has three levels of reading to accommodate readers with aphasia: an easy level, an intermediate level, and a more advanced level.   A perfect way to tell his stories and reach all people with aphasia. Highly recommended for readers with aphasia and their supporters and care partners.

Darlene Williamson, MA, CCC-SLP,
President National Aphasia Association-USA)

You have captured so many aspects of aphasia – feelings and symptoms – and the different journeys and experiences that people have, in such a rich and compelling way and from different perspectives.

Professor Suzanne C Purdy,
The University of Auckland

His stories are both moving and funny. They are also encouraging and uplifting.

AphasiaNZ highly recommends Stephens's book to anyone with experience of aphasia.

AphasiaNZ

Very often, we hear what the protagonist is thinking, and wince at what happens when they try to get it out.

It's a helpful device, but it's also Stephens's truth, and the truth for thousands of other New Zealanders hit by strokes or tumours, injuries or primary progressive aphasia.

Catherine Woulfe
Books editor | Spinoff

Stephens's writing will serve to be an inspirational therapeutic tool for many others living with Aphasia and their whanau/families. Thank you for sharing insights into what it is truly like to live with this hidden disability.

Naomi Bondi, NZSLTA
NZ Speech Language Teachers Association

The stories draw the reader in to moments of real life with compassion, keen observation, and empathy.

I would highly recommend them to anyone looking for short stories that are straightforward to read and highly engaging, and to those with lived experience of communication difficulties and changes.

I would also highly recommend this book to those in health and social services who work with those with aphasia and other communication difficulties as these stories provide a fantastic insight into the experiences of someone with aphasia.

Robyn Gibson, NZSLTA
NZ Speech Language Teachers Association